CAROLINE

saw Justin's face come closer. Then, before she had time to react, she felt his lips touch hers. He kissed her lightly but lingeringly. Then he moved back. "Well . . .," he said. "That was precisely what I wanted to avoid."

"Why?" Caroline said.

"There are a million reasons. You must know some of them."

"That you're married?"

"For one. . . . *And* I don't want to lose my job. . . . *And* you're awfully young."

"I'm eighteen. I don't think that's as young as it used to be," Caroline said. "I think nowadays, well, people mature faster."

"True." He was gazing at her reflectively. Then he brushed her hair back off her forehead.

Her heart began to pound furiously.

Other Fawcett titles
by Norma Klein:

FRENCH POSTCARDS

IT'S OK IF YOU DON'T LOVE ME

THE QUEEN OF THE WHAT IFS

LOVE IS ONE OF THE CHOICES

Norma Klein

FAWCETT JUNIPER • NEW YORK

A Fawcett Juniper Book
Published by Ballantine Books
Copyright © 1978 by Norma Klein

ISBN 0-449-70198-0

This edition published by arrangement with The Dial Press

Manufactured in the United States of America

First Fawcett Crest Edition: November 1979
First Ballantine Books Edition: March 1983
Fourth Printing: December 1985

1

"How can he have mono? I thought that was something just college kids got," Caroline said. She was trying to share Maggie's umbrella, which was a big black one and should have been large enough for the two of them. But Maggie, who was several inches taller than Caroline, kept holding it too high, and rain slid down Caroline's neck.

"Anyone can get it," Maggie said. "It's a virus."

"Is it serious?"

"Not especially. . . . It just kind of konks you out for quite a while."

Maggie was the expert on all scientific and medical matters. Last year, when they both were in junior year of high school, Maggie won third prize in a nationwide science contest for a project which Caroline had never been able to understand. When they took biology together in sophomore year, it was Maggie who deftly and precisely dissected the frog while Caroline leaned limply against the table and tried not to look. During exam week, it was Maggie who tried, with infinite patience, to get Caroline to understand the geometry theorems she was memorizing. "I don't *want* to understand," Caroline would wail, ashamed of herself. "It's easier to just memorize." "No, it isn't," Maggie would say. "It just seems that way. Understanding's much easier."

They had reached West End Avenue. "I wonder what his apartment will look like," Caroline said.

"I saw it once," Maggie said.

"You did? How come?"

"I baby-sat for them."

"You never told me!"

"Yeah, well, it was just that once."

"What was it like?"

"Okay, nothing special. Not that fancy. I don't think they have much money."

"What do they have—a boy or a girl?"

"A boy—I forget his name."

"Was he cute?"

"He was okay." Maggie was utterly unenthusiastic about children. She baby-sat as rarely as possible. It amazed Caroline that this opportunity to get a glimpse into the private life of one of their most popular teachers—especially when the teacher, Justin Prager, considered Maggie his best student—was an event Maggie took so calmly. Partly, Caroline reflected, it must be that Maggie took everything about the school they went to, Whitman, more calmly. She had gone there since she was three, whereas Caroline, who had attended public school, had entered only in the ninth grade. Caroline still wasn't used to the fact that at Whitman most of the students called the teachers by their first names; she herself never could. Still stranger was the fact that there were no grades, only lengthy psychological comments not only on the students' academic work, but on their "behavioral adjustment." Even the mission they were on now—to bring Justin Prager a set of student papers to correct because he was still out for the third week with mononucleosis—was something Caroline could never have imagined happening at her former school.

"What's his wife like?" Caroline asked. They were both looking for number 270, which Maggie said she recalled was an old-looking apartment house with a blue awning.

"Vaguely neurotic-seeming. Kind of high-strung."

"Pretty?"

"I can't remember that well. . . . I think she might have had dark hair."

Maggie never seemed to notice what people looked like, which always surprised Caroline, whose favorite occupation was staring at people on buses, observing what they wore and how they spoke. If you asked Maggie to describe someone she'd met, she would usually say something vague like "I think he was about average height, sort of blondish." And if, afterward, Caroline said, "Maggie, how come you never said he was Black, or over six feet tall, or weighed nearly three hundred pounds?" Maggie would say, "Oh yeah, that's right, I forgot. Didn't I mention that?"

They found the right building and went up in the elevator. "I get the feeling he's very happily married," Caroline said somewhat wistfully as the ancient elevator began a slow ascent.

"Why?"

"Well, the way—I forget what it was exactly, but he's always making nice remarks about his wife. Remember when it was his anniversary? He just said something nice about marriage."

"I don't remember," Maggie said.

Caroline liked the idea of people having happy marriages. Her own parents had been divorced when she was one and a half and she rarely saw her own father more than once a year. Although he was American, he had lived in Paris and made documentary films there since the divorce. Unlike Maggie, she loved baby-sitting, precisely because it afforded her a glimpse into the private lives of other people. She loved homes where everything was a little chaotic and noisy, where the children tumbled around, yelling, where the parents hugged each other and said funny, intimate things without thinking about it. It was so unlike the quiet, organized, predictable life she led with her mother, a specialist in antiquities at the Parke-Bernet Galleries. Maggie, too, came from what their sociology teacher at Whitman would have called a "single-parent family." Her mother had died of cancer when she was nine and she lived in a rambling West Side apartment with her father, a plump, fifty-year-old Freudian psychoanalyst. But while Caroline was always intensely and painfully aware of not coming from a "regular" family, Maggie seemed either not to notice or to actually feel that being different was a kind of advantage.

Justin came to the door. He was dressed in pajamas and a wrinkled blue terry-cloth bathrobe. "Oh, hi kids, come on in," he said. They followed him inside. Caroline sneezed. "It's awfully nice of you to come out in this kind of weather."

"Shouldn't you be in bed?" Maggie said. "I thought you were supposed to be sick."

"Think I've just been pretending, huh?" Justin and Maggie had a kind of joking relationship which Caroline very much admired. She would never have had the temerity to joke that way with any person almost ten years older than herself, especially a teacher. "Don't I look sufficiently pale and wan?"

Maggie regarded him narrowly. "*Comme ci, comme ça*. . . . No, seriously, do you want to go lie down?"

He sighed. "In point of fact, I would. . . . Do you mind? I seem to lose all my energy around this time of day." They followed him down the hall into the bedroom. The bed was just a large mattress on the floor. A light was on nearby, and various piles of books and papers were stacked around it. "Excuse the confusion," Justin said. "I could excuse it on grounds of health, but in fact—"

"You're just a slob," Maggie continued for him. She plunked the papers down on the bed.

"How's it going?" Justin said. "Is the substitute okay?"

"He's dumb," Maggie said.

"You mean unfamiliar with the material, or what?"

"Just, kind of . . . I don't know. He's okay if he's reciting from his notes, but if you ask him a question, he gets all panicked."

"Some of your questions—"

"No, no," Maggie said. "I haven't been giving him a hard time."

"I'll bet." He got back under the covers and leaned against a pile of pillows.

Caroline, unable to think of anything to say, was gazing at the bookshelves. They always said you could tell something significant about people by what books they had. Justin, catching her doing this, said, "What is this, the Gestapo?"

She blushed. "Oh, I'm sorry."

"My wife was a Russian major in college—that's why we have all those strange-looking tomes in dark-red leather bindings."

Caroline looked up and saw the volumes he was referring to. "Is she Russian?" she asked politely.

"Not by birth. Her father was born there."

Caroline now recalled that Justin's father-in-law was a famous scientist who had won the Nobel prize. She remembered the announcement of his winning it had been made during one of their biology classes and everyone had started congratulating Justin, even though, as he pointed out, he hadn't done anything himself to merit it.

"My grandfather was born there," Maggie said. She was sitting cross-legged on the floor, leafing through a book. As usual, Maggie was in Oshkosh overalls and a turtleneck. She claimed only overalls were comfortable and had big enough pockets for all the loose junk she liked to carry around.

"Well, a lot of Jews of that generation came from somewhere in Eastern Europe," Justin said.

"Did *your* father?" Caroline said, feeling slightly more at ease.

"Poland," he said. "Same difference."

Caroline wasn't Jewish herself, although almost everyone in the school was, and she was utterly unable to tell who was and who wasn't the way Maggie, who was, could at a glance. Now she wondered if, apart from Justin's name, perhaps she should have been able to tell. He had eyes and hair almost as dark as Maggie's, but then lots of non-Jews had dark coloring. With his snub nose he looked young for his age, so much so that, he had told them, he was still sometimes asked to show his driver's license at bars to prove he was over eighteen.

Maggie was looking at him critically. "You're really sick, huh?"

Justin looked at Caroline. "Why is this girl so suspicious? You know I love my work. Why would I want to spend three weeks lying in bed when I could be plying my trade like an honest man? . . . No, actually, it's a drag. For a week it's okay; then you really want to get going again."

"When does the doctor say you can come back to school?" Caroline asked.

"I hope by Monday. . . . He says play it by ear—I might try going in for half a day the first week."

Caroline wondered why they just had a mattress on the floor and not a real bed. Maggie had said she thought they weren't that well off, but even not-well-off people—Caroline considered herself and her mother to be in that category—could afford a bed. And Justin didn't seem like a hippyish type especially.

"We used to have a regular bed," Justin said, although she hadn't said a word, "and then we gave it away thinking we'd get a new one, but this is really comfortable."

"It doesn't *look* comfortable," Maggie said.

"Well, maybe not for a hedonist like you, Margaret."

Maggie gave him a dirty glance. She got up. In her sneakered feet Maggie was five feet ten, taller than most of the boys in the class. She had lousy posture, but it was more out of absentmindedness than being ashamed of her height. "I think Maggie's lucky," Caroline's mother often said. "Tall women can wear clothes so beautifully." But since Maggie never wore anything but jeans or overalls, it was hard to test this theory on her. "Okay, Prager, we'll pass the word on that you're legitimate. We'll say you could barely crawl out of bed."

"Thanks a lot, kid."

"Only for you would we do this, you understand."

"I appreciate that. . . . Listen, I'm sorry I didn't offer you anything to drink."

"We're not big drinkers," Maggie said.

"I never would have suspected that. . . . No, seriously, if you want to grab a glass of milk or some cookies on the way out—"

"Milk and cookies!" Maggie said. "What are we, in kindergarten?"

Actually, Caroline wouldn't have minded milk and cookies, but she gathered Maggie felt it was beneath their dignity, so she said nothing.

As they were near the door, Justin suddenly called out, "Hey!"

"Hey what?" Maggie said.

"You wouldn't, either of you, be free to baby-sit tonight?"

"Aha," Maggie said. "I knew it. . . . Going out on the town the minute our backs are turned."

"Margaret, did anyone ever tell you you have an incredibly suspicious soul for one so young? The fact is, Ariella has tickets for a concert tonight and we need someone to be with Noah and put him to bed since I go to sleep earlier than he does these days."

"I'm busy," Maggie said.

Caroline hesitated a second. "I can do it," she said.

"Would you? That's terrific. . . . I really appreciate it. Is seven-thirty okay?"

"Sure," Caroline said.

"Noah's easy to handle. He's six—you won't have

any problems. You'll just have to read him a couple of stories."

"Oh, that's okay. . . . I do a lot of baby-sitting," Caroline said.

Outside in the hall Caroline noticed a large Chagall lithograph that she hadn't seen on the way in.

"I saw that in a show with my mother," she said, stopping to gaze at it.

"Do you still go to art shows with her a lot?" Maggie said.

"Yes, or just on my own, if she's busy. . . . You should come with me. There's a retrospective at the Guggenheim on Klee that—"

"Sure, maybe," Maggie said in a way that made Caroline feel she wouldn't come. "Hey, the elevator's here."

"Wait just one sec—I want to just look at this a little longer. God, look at the way he does that old man's face! Isn't that incredible."

Maggie looked, obviously trying to share Caroline's feeling. "You mean because it looks so real?"

"No, I don't think it does exactly. . . . But it has such a fine looseness."

"A fine looseness?" Maggie said, kidding.

Caroline blushed. "It's just beautiful," she said, continuing to look as the elevator door closed. She knew it would stay in her mind the rest of the day.

It had stopped raining.

"Ariella is a pretty name," Caroline said, "isn't it?"

"Yeah, it's kind of nice. . . . It's a little bit fancy, though."

"What are you doing tonight?" Caroline put down the hood of her yellow slicker.

"Nothing, why?"

"You said you were busy when he asked if you could baby-sit."

"Oh, I just said that. Baby-sitting's a drag."

12

"But some kids are really nice," Caroline said.

"Very few," Maggie said. "Very few of the ones *I've* met. . . . I think I'm going to have my tubes tied when I'm twenty."

Caroline was horrified, though she was used to Maggie's extremist statements. "What if you changed your mind?"

"I can adopt."

"I think I'd like to know what it's like," Caroline said. "Being pregnant."

"Not me—I *know* what it's like. You get huge and ugly and your stomach sticks out a foot."

"I don't mean how you *look*. . . . I mean how you *feel*."

"You feel tired all the time, you throw up every morning—it somehow never sounded so great."

Caroline was unconvinced. "But I don't know, I should think it would be a terrific feeling."

"So, go ahead. Who's stopping you?"

"I don't mean *now*. I mean eventually."

His wife came to the door. Caroline had been wondering what someone named Ariella would look like. She had decided she ought to have white skin and blue eyes and golden hair and be very tall and slim. She would wear a dress of some flowing greenish material like silk that swirled around her as she moved. Instead, Ariella Prager was small, shorter than Caroline, and dark-haired. Her hair was curly and a little untidy-looking and she had big hazel eyes, almost comically round. She did have white skin, which seemed unusual in someone with such dark hair. Maggie, who had the same color hair and eyes, had skin of such a deep olive that people were always mistaking her for Italian or Puerto Rican.

"Hi," Ariella said. "Are you Maggie?"

13

"No, I'm Caroline," Caroline said. "Maggie's my friend."

"Oh, right, gee, I'm sorry, I remember, Maggie's the tall one. Well, listen, it's terrific of you to do this. I won't be back late. I know you have school tomorrow."

"Oh, that's okay," Caroline said. She moved into the front hall and took off her coat. Since Ariella didn't take it, Caroline folded it and put it on a long bench.

"Justin's been absolutely comatose since this thing hit him," Ariella went on. "He just goes to bed right after supper. It's weird. . . . Noah! Come meet Caroline. He can read, but he likes it if you read to him."

"I always liked that too," Caroline said. She looked at Noah, who was already in his pajamas. He looked a little small for his age. He strongly resembled Ariella, with the same mass of curly dark hair and big eyes.

"You can read me *Through the Looking Glass*," he said. "We're on Chapter Six."

"He *says* he understands it," Ariella said. "I don't see how. I always thought it was more for grown-ups."

"I do understand it," Noah said.

"Okay, so that's about it," Ariella said, looking around as though trying to make sure she hadn't forgotten anything. "He should be in bed at eight thirty. . . . Oh, and if Justin should wander out at some point, don't faint. I mean, he looks kind of like the wild man of Borneo."

"We saw him this afternoon," Caroline said, "when we came to drop the papers off."

"Oh?" Ariella looked surprised, as though Justin hadn't mentioned it. She gave Noah a hug. "Sleep tight, sweetheart."

"Say sweet dreams," he said as she started out the door.

"Sweet dreams," she called.

After she had left, he explained to Caroline, "If she doesn't say it, I might not have good dreams."

14

Caroline nodded. She rememberd having felt that way if her mother didn't come in to kiss her good night. "Would you like to read now?" she asked.

"Okay." He brought the book and sat down on the couch next to her. Caroline had a special fondness for little boys. Of the children for whom she baby-sat, those she developed a real closeness with were usually boys between the ages of five and ten. Once they began emerging into adolescence, they became strange and somewhat alien to her.

While she read, he listened quietly, occasionally asking the meaning of a word. He didn't smile at parts Caroline thought were funny, and she felt, as Ariella had said, that he must be missing a lot of it, but he seemed interested and kept his eyes glued to the page.

When they were finished, Caroline said, "Shall I read one more chapter?"

"No, I'm only supposed to have one a night," he said, seeming very conscious of not wanting to break any rules. "Now I have to brush my teeth."

"Would you like a bedtime snack?" she asked.

"It can't be chocolate," he said.

"How about ice cream?"

"We don't have any."

"Well, you tell me what you want."

They went into the kitchen and he selected a doughnut. While he was eating it, Caroline picked up a pencil and a scrap of paper that was lying on the table and began sketching. Noah looked at what she was doing. "Who's that?" he said.

"The Red Queen," Caroline said, continuing to draw.

"But she doesn't look like that in the book!"

"I know." She erased part of the head. "This is how I always imagined her, though."

"I sometimes imagine things different from in books,"

he said. "I wish I could draw faces like that. Do the other queen," he said as Caroline stopped.

"I'll do it when you're asleep," she promised. "Now it's time for bed."

"Will you leave it for me?"

"In the book. . . . Sleep tight," she said after she tucked him under the covers. "Sweet dreams."

"You too," he said politely.

She went back to the kitchen and kept on sketching, for nearly half an hour. The time passed quickly as she tried different faces on the two queens, not satisfied with the second attempt. The first one she'd done quickly while Noah was watching pleased her most, but even there something was not quite right. The hair? She tried a new hairdo and finally felt the result was what she'd had in her mind when she'd started. After putting the scraps of paper in the book, she went back to the living room.

Caroline always felt there was something slightly eerie about the silence in a house after the children were asleep, especially if she was alone. Now the fact that she wasn't really, that Justin was inside asleep, didn't make it any less eerie. On the other hand, she looked forward to this time so she could browse—she sometimes thought "snoop" was a better word—around the house. She loved looking at other people's houses: the kinds of ashtrays they had, the way they kept their plants, the magazines they subscribed to. She began looking at the bookshelf in the living room. It seemed to contain mostly modern novels, although there was a group of science books in the two rows toward the top. She took a novel which she had thought of reading out of the shelf. As she was leafing through it, a small slip of white paper folded in two fell to the ground. Picking it up, she saw written on one side, "Darling, forgive me." She turned it over, but there was nothing on the other side. Guiltily she replaced it and the book.

At the very bottom of the bookshelf was a large album marked "Photos." Caroline loved looking at family albums. Her mother had taken or preserved very few photos of her during her childhood, and it sometimes gave her the feeling that her childhood, of which she remembered very little, had never actually existed. She thought of one photo of herself, her father, and her father's girl friend which had been taken when she was about ten and visiting him in Paris. Both her father and his girl friend were dark haired and looked, she thought, intense and interesting. Her father was dressed casually, as always, in some kind of turtleneck and slacks and sandals, and Danielle was in a long, gray dress, chic in a casual way, the way most Frenchwomen looked to Caroline. She herself was in a tweed coat selected by her mother and brown oxfords with neatly turned down white socks. Her hair, which was blonder then, was cut straight to her shoulders, and she was staring straight out at the camera with a grim expression. It always struck her that it could be the photo of some middle-class child who had been kidnaped by a pair of bohemian misfits, the contrast between her and the two of them was so extreme.

She sat down on the couch and began looking through the Prager family album. There were photos of Justin when he was younger.

He was shown in some setting which was countrylike, sailing, sitting next to a man who probably was his father. He looked more athletic and lighthearted than she thought of him from class. Then there was a series of Justin and Ariella getting married. They weren't the kind of stiff, professional shots she didn't like, but more candid ones. It looked like they had been married in a church or synagogue—the photo of them kissing after the ceremony was a little dim, as though there hadn't been enough light. Then there was a whole series of the two of them on a lawn drinking what must have been champagne with some other people. Justin looked thin and his face had a tense, awkward expression, as though he were not quite at ease. Ariella, who was wearing a white dress to her knees, not to her ankles, looked like a Spanish princess with smoldering eyes and flushed cheeks. Although she didn't look like what Caroline had imagined someone named "Ariella" to look like, she did look beautiful and somewhat exotic. Then there was a group of Ariella in the hospital holding a baby. Caroline looked at those photos a long time. Ariella was lying back on the pillow, her hair longer and loose to her shoulders, a pink rose tucked behind her ear. On her face was a dreamy, radiant expression as she smiled—glowed would have been a more accurate term—at whoever held the camera. You see, Caroline said to Maggie in her mind, *that's* what it's like. It was only after having stared for a long time that she noticed that underneath the photo it said: "Ariella and Vera." Who was Vera?

Just then the door opened and Justin came into the living room. Caroline tried guiltily to conceal the photo album, which was just about impossible since it was open on her lap.

"Hi," he said. "How's it going?"

"Okay." She remembered what his wife had said about his looking like the wild man of Borneo, and it was true—he looked paler and more unshaven than he had that afternoon. She felt awkward, with him in his pajamas and robe and her dressed. Somehow that afternoon, with Maggie along, it hadn't bothered her so much. Now it seemed to imply an intimacy between them, whereas they had actually barely exchanged more than a few sentences outside class.

"What time is it, anyway?" he asked.

"Ten."

He yawned. "Oh God, I don't know. I just can't get into a regular sleeping schedule. If I could make it through the afternoon maybe I'd sleep at night, but I always take a nap and then I"m up at some crazy hour like one or two. . . . Would you like some tea?"

"Sure." She jumped up, trying to shove the album under a pillow, but casually.

But Justin reached down and picked it up, idly leafing through it. "Those are nice," he said, "aren't they?"

"I'm sorry," she stammered, "only I—I like family albums."

"They're great," he affirmed, not seeming mad. He remained standing, looking at some photos, then abruptly closed the album.

In the kitchen they sat at the table waiting for the water to boil.

"That was our daughter Vera whose photo you were looking at," Justin said suddenly.

Caroline nodded. She felt nervous both at his unexpected appearance and at being caught looking at his family pictures.

"She lives in a home. . . . She had some brain damage at birth," he said.

"I'm sorry," Caroline said.

Justin was silent a moment. "She's lovely, isn't she? Did you see the later pictures?"

"No. Did you—um—has she always lived in a home?"

"No, we tried it the other way until Noah was born, but it didn't work. It was too hard on Ariella. It was tremendously depressing, and then when Noah came, the doctor said he thought it wouldn't be fair to him—they were just a year and a half apart anyway. So we . . . And it seems to have worked out. We go to see her once a month." He looked pained. "I don't actually know if it— She doesn't seem to recognize us, and it's kind of a grueling thing, going there."

"But you wouldn't want to just not go?"

"I suppose not. . . . Well, actually, *I* might, but

19

Ariella feels we have to. I just don't know. It takes so much out of both of us."

"Does Noah go too?"

"No, but he knows about her." He sighed. The kettle was whistling and he poured some water into two large brown mugs.

"Noah's very nice."

His face lit up. "Yes, he's terrific, isn't he? I do think being an only child isn't so ideal, but . . ."

"I guess, well, I'm an only child so I'm used to it."

"Why was that?"

"Well, my parents got divorced when I was one and a half," she said.

"Hmm." He looked thoughtful. "It must be lonely then, at times."

"Yes, I guess, well I'm used to it," she insisted. "I mean, I don't know what it would have been like otherwise." She remembered how, when she was younger and had a large number of imaginary playmates, her teacher had told her mother it was because she was an only child. "Well, what exactly does she expect me to do about it?" her mother had asked.

"I come from a family of four," he said. "All boys. We used to fight a lot, but, well, we were friends. At least I feel friendly to them now."

Sipping her tea, Caroline realized that at some point since they had entered the kitchen, her nervousness had disappeared. He talked to her so openly, about such personal things! It was almost as though they were the same age. "Does your wife do anything?" she asked. "I mean, does she work?"

"She has a masters in Slavic languages. She was going for her doctorate when all that business started . . . and now she's thinking of teaching again. It's just hard now. Teaching jobs aren't so easy to come by."

Caroline nodded. "I've thought of teaching, but . . .

20

what I guess I'd really like to do is illustrate children's books."

He smiled. "I've seen you doodle in class."

She blushed. "I shouldn't."

"Actually, I saved one of them—I had the impression it was of me."

Caroline was startled. She couldn't remember. She did sometimes draw pictures of people in the class or teachers. Justin disappeared into the other room and a few moments later handed her a piece of paper with her own drawing. It showed Justin dressed as a jester, one foot up on the chair as he habitually stood in class. "I'm sorry," she said.

"No, it's amazingly good. I think you really caught something. Ariella liked it too. . . . Do you mind if I keep it?"

"No," she said, terribly flattered that he would want to.

"I think you'd be a good illustrator," he said.

"Well." Her cheeks were still blazing; she touched her hands to them. "I don't know if I'm good enough." Although there were infinite things she admired about Maggie, one of the things Caroline admired most was not so much her brilliance at science, but her sureness that what she wanted in life she would get or die trying. "Sometimes I wish I was like Maggie," she admitted.

Justin smiled. "Yeah, Maggie's great. . . . She's a fantastic girl. When I was that age, I didn't know if I was going to turn left or right. I think if I'd met a girl like Maggie then, I'd have been terrified."

Caroline's admiration of Maggie abruptly sharpened into envy. It wasn't fair. She wanted Justin to think *she* was a fantastic girl! *She* wanted to be terrifying!

"Not everyone has the capacity to be a world beater," Justin said gently.

Caroline grimaced, almost in pain. "No, but I think to make it in anything it's more than just talent."

21

"And you're not sure you have the 'more'?"

"Yes, I guess." Partly it was because her mother kept worrying about it so much that she worried herself. Her mother said she had intended to be an artist and had given it up to get married. Her work at Parke-Bernet was a way of earning a living, but she always spoke of it wistfully, as a compromise. She painted a little, on weekends and vacations, but spoke with contempt of "Sunday painters." "You have to want to conquer the world," her mother would say, "and settle for nothing less. Otherwise you'll fall by the wayside."

"Caroline, I'm afraid I'm going to have to turn in again," Justin said.

Although she knew he was sick and probably tired, Caroline felt rebuffed. Maybe if she had said more interesting things, he would have wanted to stay up. "I hope you feel better," she said, trying to conceal how she felt.

"Thank you."

After he had disappeared into the bedroom, the hurt feeling, instead of diminishing, grew so strong it was like a pain in her stomach. It didn't seem fair for him to have come out, talked so openly and warmly, and then just vanished like that. Without stopping to think, she went and rapped lightly on the bedroom door.

"Yes?"

Caroline opened the door softly. "Um, I was wondering, if anyone calls for you, shall I say you've gone to sleep?"

"Yes, would you?" He was under the covers; she could see him only hazily.

"Would you—like anything? I mean, some juice," she went on, not wanting to leave.

"No, that's okay, the tea was fine. . . . I hope I haven't kept you from your homework."

"Oh, no," she said. "I wasn't doing anything." Suddenly the thought flashed through her mind: What if she

22

were to take all her clothes off and get into bed with him? What would he say? What would he think? Horrified at this unexpected image, she retreated from the room.

Shortly afterward Ariella came back.

"Was everything okay?" she said.

Caroline said everything had been fine. She decided not to mention Justin's having gotten up. "It is kind of amazing, Noah's wanting to read *Through the Looking Glass* at six," she said, wanting somehow to ingratiate herself with Ariella.

"Listen, I hate mothers who do this, but he is *incredibly* bright. He taught himself to read at four. Just taught himself! I have no idea how. . . . He has a fantastic mind for words. When he was a baby he used to sit with this book, pointing at different birds and saying, 'Egret, swallow, parrot.' I remember I took him for a nursery school interview and they must have asked him what different animals were and he came out saying, 'I *think* it was an egret. . . .' All they wanted was for him to know 'bird.' "

Caroline put on her coat. "Would you like me to babysit again sometime?" she asked, trying not to seem overly eager.

"Sure, that's a good idea," Ariella said. "We used to have this girl in our building, but she's into the dating thing now. . . . Do you date?"

"Not so much," Caroline said.

"It's not that I care if they bring a guy, but, you know, there are limits. This isn't a rent-a-bed place."

Caroline swallowed nervously. "I don't have a boyfriend," she said.

"Look, have one!" Ariella said. "I have nothing against boyfriends. I mean, I know kids these days do everything earlier, and Lord, who am I to say that's a bad thing? No, it's just there's a time and a place for everything and Noah does sometimes wake up in the middle of the evening."

She talked very fast and intensely, the words spilling out, and Caroline just stood there, nodding. She took the money Ariella handed her and put it into her wallet. "Good night," she called as she went out the door, and almost inadvertently added "Sweet dreams" before she could stop herself.

At home her mother was already asleep; her bedroom door was closed. Her mother went to bed every night at ten. Sometimes on weekend nights she would sit up watching TV, but she always claimed she was only really happy with ten hours of sleep. Caroline often wondered how her mother and father had gotten along even for the brief time they had been married. Her father, whenever she visited him, was the exact opposite, sleeping till noon, staying up till three or four. And Danielle seemed to keep the same hours.

Her mother always called Danielle, whom she had never met, her father's "common-law wife." She said that was the term that was used for a woman if she had been living with a man for over seven years and they were still not married. Caroline always felt that "common-law wife" sounded dreary and unpleasant, whereas "mistress," which her mother never used, sounded more exotic and cheerful. Her father said he preferred just "friend," since that could be used equally for men or women, but Caroline thought that was misleading since a friend could be just a friend and nothing more. Maggie said that "wife," even just regular "wife" and not the common-law kind, had a derogatory connotation. That was one of the things she had against being married. Caroline wasn't sure she would mind so much being someone's wife, though she was reluctant to admit this to Maggie.

Maggie was always saying what she would do if she were the dictator of a totalitarian society. One of her laws would be that people couldn't get married before they were twenty-five or have children before they were thirty.

To get married a couple would have to live together for at least one year. Then they would have to wait another two years, before they'd be allowed to have a child. Caroline agreed about people waiting till they were older and even the living together part. It was only by living with someone that you found out things like whether he left his dirty underwear on the floor or if he rolled the toothpaste tube up from the bottom—things that were, according to the magazine articles she read, just as important to conjugal adjustment as sex. But she didn't see why, if you really did love someone, getting married would be so bad. "There's no reason it *should* be," Maggie would say. "It just usually *is*."

Caroline acknowledged that, never having seen a marriage close up, she probably tended to idealize it, to fill in the blanks with rose-colored pictures. But until these were actually proved wrong, she decided to let herself continue.

2

Looking out at the audience from her stiff-backed chair on the stage of the school auditorium, Maggie could see Caroline sitting in the front row. Caroline always sat in the front row when Maggie was debating, and she always looked nervous. Though she had no mother, Maggie sometimes thought Caroline was as good—or bad—as one in that she got more nervous when Maggie appeared in public than Maggie did. She desperately wanted Maggie to do well.

Maggie was not in the best of moods. She knew she was not doing especially well in this particular debate. It made her mad rather than upset, mad at herself as well as mad at her opponent from the other school, a boy with bright-red hair named Todd Lamport. The topic was: Should there be special facilities such as lounges for gay students in high schools? The topics of these weekly debates were preselected, but the visiting school had the option of choosing which side it wanted to defend. Maggie's debating teacher said it was good practice to deliberately defend the side you didn't believe in—it made you more aware of the complexities of any given issue. To her surprise Maggie had come to find that she argued best when she was defending the side she *didn't* believe in. When she believed in something, she got emotional, her voice shook, she was usually so carried away she felt like physically annihilating her opponent. She hated this in herself because it seemed to fit so precisely into the classic stereotype of the semihysterical woman, more capable of feeling than of rational exchange. Yet today it was happening all over again. She did believe, vehemently, in special privileges for gay students, yet she knew that in the twenty-five minutes that had already passed she had not done their cause much good.

According to Todd Lamport, students, being teen-agers, were at a point in their lives when their sexual identities were hanging in the balance. It was one thing, he said, to not discriminate *against* gay students. But to actively encourage them might turn some into homosexuals due to group pressure.

"But what about becoming heterosexual due to group pressure?" Maggie asked in rebuttal. "How is that any better?"

"I think most people are probably happier as heterosexuals," Todd Lamport said in a calm, even voice and he produced from his pocket a clipping describing a study in which both heterosexual and homosexual students were asked about how happy they were. It seemed the homosexual students all felt quite miserable.

"But that's because of society!" Maggie said. "They're unhappy because they're discriminated against!" Damn him! Not only was he winning the debate and causing her to lose her always-precarious cool, but he had thought to bring in clippings—this was the third time he had pro-duced one from his pocket in the half hour allotted for each debate. Often Maggie brought in clippings, but this time she had forgotten. "Anyway," she said as an after-thought, reckless as she saw by the big clock at the back of the auditorium that only one minute was left, "why is being *happy* so important? Why should *that* be someone's main goal in life?"

"What do *you* think it should be?" he asked.

Maggie got flustered. "Well, I think—I think if some-one *wants* to be happy, fine. But if they'd rather work for the betterment of society, I mean if they don't feel their own personal happiness is the only thing that matters—that's to their credit."

"I wonder if people can make a really good contribution to society if they aren't happy," he said somewhat reflectively.

"Of course they can!" Maggie said. "No one who made a contribution to society was *ever* happy!"

The moderator smiled. "Well, I think this has been very interesting, but I'm afraid our time is running out." After each debate the judges voted on who they thought had made the best arguments. At the end, after a pause to describe the next week's topic, the winner was announced.

Todd Lamport came over to shake Maggie's hand. She looked up at him balefully. Maggie was a poor loser. But, trying to muster all of her good graces, she drew her mouth up in a polite smile.

"I thought some of your arguments were really very good," he said. "Basically I agree with you, but our debating teacher likes us to take the opposing side once in a while just to—"

"Yeah, ours does too," Maggie said. She refused to hate him any less for agreeing with her.

"Have you done this often?"

"For two years," she admitted. Somehow that only made her loss even more humiliating.

"I just started this year," he said. "It still makes me nervous. Sometimes I get this strange humming in my ears so I can't even hear my own voice."

Maggie was amazed that he would admit something like that to a complete stranger. "Does it go away eventually?"

"Pretty much. . . . It comes and goes, sort of like an echo. Actually, that's partly why I decided to try debating, to see if I could get over it."

Caroline came up on the stage. She looked mistrustfully at Todd Lamport, angry at him for having defeated Maggie. "I thought you were wonderful," she said to Maggie.

Maggie sighed. "I had all these points I wanted to make, but I forgot them."

"I always do that too," Todd Lamport said amiably. "That's why I carry those clippings with me."

"Maggie *usually* carries clippings," Caroline said quickly. "Only this time she didn't."

When they left the studio, Caroline said, "I just don't see why he won. You said much better things, Mag."

"But I didn't say them right," Maggie said. Caroline's admiration, dependable though it was, always made her feel better.

She was surprised when, that evening, Todd Lamport called and asked if she wanted to go to a movie on Saturday night. Without thinking, she said yes. She was surprised, because boys her own age rarely liked her or wanted to take her out. Although it was hard for her to admit it, her pride was wounded by it; she blamed her height. The other exceptionally bright girl in their class, five feet tall, was always saying that being small was a great advantage. "It means no one is intimidated by me," she said. "It gives me freedom." Sometimes it seemed to Maggie that everyone of the male sex under the age of twenty-five was intimidated by her. Her father kept promising that in college it would be different, that older men would accept her more easily. Publicly Maggie always claimed she didn't care, but inwardly she had mixed feelings.

If you were pretty and not intimidating, look at what happened to you! Most often you ended up marrying young and having babies and throwing aside everything you'd spent your life striving for. Sometimes Maggie worried about this for Caroline. True, she seemed almost oblivious of her appearance, even when men made remarks on the subway or when they walked down the street. Certainly she lacked the air of breezy self-confidence that was supposed to accompany beauty. Yet wherever they went, saleswomen exclaimed over Caroline's long eyelashes; her skin never seemed to break out no matter how much candy she ate; her hair, unlike Maggie's shaggy mop, hung smooth and honey blond to her shoulders, neatly parted on the side. Even when she spoke, it was usually in a low, hesitant voice that was quite musical in its softness. Yes, Carrie might well be in danger, Maggie thought. She felt relieved; at least she didn't have *that* to worry about.

On Saturday evenings Maggie's father usually went to the theater or a movie with his woman friend, Nina Bolonkin. A Russian refugee, Nina was divorced and slightly younger than Maggie's father. She was plump, with dark hair parted in the middle; she wore flowered print dresses, had tiny feet and had once, many years earlier, studied ballet with the Bolshoi. At parties, when she was high on vodka, she liked to recite Pushkin and Lermontov in the original. Maggie understood Russian, but couldn't speak it very well. She loved the flowing, melodious sound of it and the way Nina looked when she "declaimed" her pieces about how youth had fled, where, no one knew, and other typically Slavic sentiments. Maggie's father, Raymond Tarachow, and Nina had been "going together" for years. According to him, they had begun seeing each other even before Maggie's mother's death. Maggie's mother had been ill for five years before she died, and Maggie's father claimed she had understood that it was necessary for him to have a "friend." She had even, he said, encouraged it. Partly, Maggie accepted this as reasonable and practical. Partly, even eight years after her mother's death, she got very mad just thinking about it. She had always hated books where people on their deathbeds said they hoped their partners would remarry and be happy because they had made *them* so happy. Maggie felt that on *her* deathbed she would never dream of making such a soupy, phonily altruistic remark. She would naturally want the person to be absolutely miserable for the rest of his life and, if the dead could look down on the living, she would be highly indignant if she found that her wishes had not been obeyed.

The house was empty save for Maggie when Todd Lamport rang the front doorbell at eight o'clock on Saturday. He looked around the front hall. "Where do those come from?" he said of a row of African masks on one wall.

"Oh, my father collects them," Maggie said. "He's a psychiatrist. There're more of them in his office."

Even when her mother had been alive, Maggie's father had always used the living room as his office. That way when he woke up late, he could dress hastily, grab a giant mug of black coffee, and be in his office in five minutes. The office was a large gloomy room that received little direct sunlight. The windows were almost concealed by a number of large junglelike plants. Against one wall was the dark-green analytic couch and, directly behind it, the black vinyl reclining chair in which her father sat (or reclined). A soundproof foot-thick white wall faced the couch. On it row upon row of dark African masks hung almost to the ceiling.

"Is he the kind where people lie on the couch?" Todd asked.

Maggie nodded. "He's the kind where they tell their dreams—an analyst."

"It must be interesting," he said, looking around.

"It's expensive," Maggie said. Then, afraid he would think they were rich, she added, "He has lots of patients that come free, or, if they're artists, they just pay with paintings and stuff like that."

"Have you ever gone?"

After her mother's death Maggie had gone to a woman analyst for about two years. Mainly she remembered that they had played chess a lot and that she used to get mad because she couldn't tell if the doctor was deliberately allowing her to win or just wasn't a very good player. "I went once," she said laconically. She hated mentioning her mother to anyone, so she just added brusquely, "I was sort of young."

Todd went over and lay down on the couch. "It seems comfortable," he said.

"It's not supposed to be *too* comfortable," Maggie explained, "or they'd fall asleep." She remembered going with her father when he had picked this couch after his old one had finally given way. He had wanted a super-long couch, in case he ever acquired any super-long patients. After lying down on couch after couch to make sure he found one that was the right degree of softness and comfortableness, he had selected the green velvet.

"Do they take their shoes off?"

She shrugged. "I guess they can. . . . I mean, they don't have to. But probably most of them do."

"My father went to a psychiatrist once," Todd said, still lying there. "He said it helped him a lot."

Maggie felt better. Usually when people heard her father was a psychiatrist, they brought up stories of all the people they knew who had been wrecked by analysis or whom it hadn't helped at all, or who had wasted tons of money and time. "Which kind did he go to? A Freudian?"

"I think so. . . . The regular kind, I mean, with a couch."

On the subject of Freudianism Maggie and her father had had an infinite number of pitched battles which were always shelved when it became apparent that neither of them would give an inch. Maggie insisted that penis envy was an absolute myth, that she herself had had no such envy as a child or ever and that no one she knew had ever suffered from it. Like the Tooth Fairy and Santa Claus, it was something psychoanalysts obviously just wanted to believe in and so convinced themselves evidence for it existed in the outside world.

Todd gazed at the ceiling, looking pensive. Maggie went over and sat down in the black reclining chair. "I should think it would be interesting to be a psychoanalyst," he said.

"Would you want to be one?" Maggie said.

"No, I guess not," he admitted.

"What *are* you going to be?"

"When I grow up?"

"Yeah."

"You mean what would I *like* to be or what am I *going* to be?"

"Either."

"Well, I guess I'd *like* to be an artist . . . but I'll probably be an architect. I'm just not sure."

"If you want to be an artist, you *should* be one!" Maggie said indignantly. One reason she knew she would make a lousy analyst was that she didn't see how her father could restrain himself from telling people exactly what he thought they should do with their lives. He had said it wasn't a moral issue—it just didn't work to tell people; they had to find out for themselves.

"Sure, but it's not exactly the easiest way to make a living," he said.

"So?"

"So . . . you have to eat."

"Why?"

He turned around to look at her. "What do you mean, why?"

"Are you some kind of materialist?"

"Well, no, not exactly. . . . Do you think you have to be a materialist in order to want to eat?"

"Listen, is painting what you most love to do in the world?" Maggie said intensely.

"It's one of the things," he admitted.

"So do it! Then you've got to do it!" Maggie cried. "Otherwise you're going to be stuck in some dull, meaningless office job slogging away for the rest of your life!"

"I don't know . . . that sounds sort of extreme. I mean, I like architecture. I don't think it would be dull and meaningless necessarily."

"But you'd be doing awful things like designing banks and supermarkets," Maggie said. "It wouldn't be creative. . . . Anyway, they say there's no work for architects either. That's what *The New York Times* says."

"I thought *I* was supposed to be the materialist," he countered.

"I just want to know one thing," Maggie said. "Are you a good painter?"

He hesitated. "I think I'm quite good."

Maggie hated words like "quite." "You can't say quite! That's a dodge. You're either good or not good."

"How come you see the world in such black-and-white terms?" he said, not angrily, more as though curious. "That seems odd for a psychiatrist's daughter."

"I don't," Maggie said. People were always telling her that. "I just see things clearly"

"Even your own life?"

"Yes."

"You're lucky, then."

She sat in silence for a moment. Sometimes it seemed to her that she wanted desperately to see things clearly, yet often did not, and that seemed unfortunate. What she was sure she would attain someday was true, effortless clarity. It seemed to her it was *because* her father was a psychoanalyst that she wanted this. It was from hearing for so many years about wasted, blighted lives, about people immersed in one tragedy after another, people sinking into quicksands of despair or inertia. Maggie's father often emerged from his study shaking his head and saying lugubriously, "Poor wretch, poor wretch." Even though

34

Maggie knew he meant this in a kindly way, she hated the idea of anyone being able to call *her* a "poor wretch." She didn't ever want to be one of those people who called her father at eleven at night because they wanted to kill themselves or because their husbands had just left them. She didn't *ever* want to be one of those people she met in the elevator or saw in the waiting room nervously leafing through old copies of *The New Yorker* or *M.D.*, at whom she was supposed to smile reassuringly but not condescendingly.

Todd sat up. "Why does he put these masks here? I should think it would be sort of scary to look at them while you lie here."

"Maybe that's why—to bring out childhood fears and stuff. But I think it's really just that he likes them."

They took a bus down to Times Square and walked along, looking at the various movies that were playing. Almost every other one seemed to be a pornographic movie of some kind.

"Did you ever see one of these?" Todd asked.

Maggie shook her head. Actually she had once won an interschool debate where the topic had been: Are pornographic movies degrading to women? She had argued that they were not, a viewpoint in which she did not believe at all. At the time she had deliberately refrained from actually seeing any such movies because she was sure they really *would* be degrading to women and she didn't want to weaken her argument.

"Would you like to? I mean, we don't have to. I guess I've just always been sort of curious about them."

Maggie hesitated. "Okay, sure," she said. To be afraid to see one was obviously cowardly, and the one in front of which they found themselves at that moment had gotten good reviews. It was supposed to be a spoof or witty or some such thing.

To her complete dismay, even horror, Maggie found

the movie an incredible turn-on. And she thought it probably *was* degrading to women, which seemed to make it even worse. She sat there, glaring at the screen, trying as hard as she could to distance herself from it, hoping that nothing about her expression or her movements revealed even the vaguest inkling of what she felt. Todd sat quietly watching the movie. He didn't try to hold her hand or even to sling his arm over the back of her shoulder. Partly she was relieved. If he had tried to hold her hand, he might have discovered her hands were terribly sweaty, although he wouldn't necessarily know they weren't always that way.

After the movie was over, they went and had a glass of coconut champagne at a hot-dog-and-orange-juice place. "So, what did you think of it?" Todd asked.

"It was, uh, okay," Maggie said, swallowing hard.

"I didn't think it was at all sexy though," he said, "did you?"

"Well, no . . ." she said.

"I wonder why they pick such ugly women. They all looked like big blobs of silicone."

Maggie stared at him. She decided he must have had an inordinate amount of sexual experience if he could dismiss women like those in the movie as "big blobs of silicone." Actually, she had thought the men weren't so bad.

"I just think that if you can't get involved with the characters as people, it's hard to care about their sex lives," he said.

"Sure," Maggie lied. "You're right." She told him how she had once debated the topic: Are pornographic movies degrading to women? and won. She didn't say which side she had defended.

"Well, they certainly are degrading to women," he said. "But to men too, really." He mentioned that his sister, a lawyer, was involved in a case involving the civil rights of an actor who had appeared in such a film.

"Is she your only brother or sister?" Maggie asked.

He nodded. "She's ten years older than I am. She's married. Everyone thinks Mom and Dad had me as an accident, but they say they waited that long on purpose so Lindsay could be a built-in baby-sitter. Of course, Lindsay wasn't too delighted about that."

"What does your sister think about these movies?" she asked.

"She thinks they're horrible. . . . But she still thinks it isn't fair to jail someone for acting in one."

They went back to Maggie's apartment house.

"Umm, would you like to come in?" Maggie said.

"Okay."

They went into her room rather than back into the living room. Maggie always had a sense of the ghosts of former patients hovering around in the living room. She felt more at east in her own room, messy though it was. Todd sat on the floor and leaned against her bed. Maggie wasn't sure what she wanted to have happen next. She wanted Todd to kiss her, but she was afraid that if he did, he would detect her overly horny mood, a residue of the movie. Up close he had beautiful greenish eyes and soft curly-looking auburn hair, attributes she had noticed but not specifically reacted to up to this moment.

Tentatively he put his hand on her hair. At the same moment they both leaned forward and kissed. When they broke apart, five minutes later, Maggie felt alarmed. Until then she had always worried that probably she was undersexed because so few men appealed to her physically. Now she suddenly felt that with even a modicum of encouragement she would have thrown off all her clothing and done anything he suggested. She was immensely relieved when he stood up and said, "I guess I should be getting home." He was breathing slightly too fast.

Maggie leaped to her feet. "The door is this way," she

said. People always got lost in the large, winding, eight-room apartment and frequently ended up in the closet.

"Maybe we could see some other movie next time," Todd said, clearing his throat.

"I think it was good that we did see it," Maggie said. "I mean, I think you should know, one should know, what they're like."

"That's what I thought," he said. He leaned over and kissed her lightly on the lips. "I'll call you, then," he said.

On Monday, when they were at Caroline's house studying after school, Maggie told Caroline she had seen a pornographic movie.

Caroline was doing a charcoal sketch of Maggie. She had that dreamy, intent look on her face that Maggie was used to when Caroline was immersed in drawing. "Was it awful?" Caroline wanted to know.

"Sort of," Maggie said cautiously.

"I think it might spoil sex for me," Caroline said.

"Why should it spoil it?"

"Well, by making it seem sort of crude."

"Maybe it's like that."

"Not with someone you love."

"I think I'm going to hate sex," Maggie said gloomily.

"Why?" Caroline was startled.

"Just the idea of it, of someone climbing on you, like a horse!"

"Well, there are other ways too," Caroline said.

"But that's the basic one," Maggie said. "Then you try the other ones."

"I know what you mean," Caroline said. "The feeling of being squashed."

"Exactly."

The whole topic of sex was one Maggie felt confused about. Her father was always saying that sublimation of sexual energies had led to most of civilization's great achievements. So on the one hand Maggie sometimes had a fantasy of living with her father when she grew up, of being a Henry James-like daughter (only brilliant and with a career), sexless in a *directed* way; but that fantasy seemed to leave something to be desired. On the whole she preferred her other fantasy. Instead of sexlessness she would have affairs the way men were supposed to and the way women were supposed to be learning to—carelessly, trying various types of men, being blithe and experienced, never letting emotion wreck things in any way.

"I just can't tell," Caroline said, looking down at her drawing and then up at Maggie.

"What about?"

"In some ways I like this the best of the lot . . . at least the eyes. This time I got the eyes the way I wanted."

"Can I see?"

Caroline brought the drawing over. "The hair isn't bad either," she said.

"Do I really look like this?" Maggie said. She was a little taken aback by the glaring, intense, wiry-haired person who stared back at her.

"I guess I wanted to capture something about you," Caroline said. "I didn't want it to look literally like you. . . . Well, I think it's good, anyway."

"I didn't mean I didn't like it," Maggie said.

"No, you don't have to like it," Caroline said. About her drawing she had a firmness that was absent in her opinions about most other things. "I might put it in my portfolio for Parsons. I don't want to put in too many realistic things, but—"

"What does your mother do about sex?" Maggie asked.

"What?" Caroline looked startled.

"Carrie, come on, put the drawing down one second."

Caroline obeyed. Maggie felt she had her undivided attention, at least for the moment. "We don't really talk about it," Caroline admitted.

"Doesn't she ever have any boyfriends?"

"Not really. . . . I mean, there's this man, Malcolm, who works where she does. He does the African things and they go around, you know, evaluating people's estates and stuff. But it's more like he's a friend. It doesn't seem that romantic."

"Maybe they're having a rip-roaring affair," Maggie suggested hopefully.

Caroline wrinkled her nose. "No, I don't think they're the type. He's shorter than she is and, well, sort of bald."

"Still—" Maggie seemed reluctant to relinquish the fantasy. "You never can tell."

Maggie had always been intrigued by Caroline's mother and by their household. Even though it was small and they didn't have much money, there was a colorful brightness about it which made it a pleasant place in which to be. Maggie liked neatness and brightness, even though the apartment she shared with her father would never have shown it. Caroline's mother collected paintings by young artists—there was a big one of orange and white flowers that dominated the living room and a series of clowns that lined the entry hall. One wall of the kitchen was purple, and the orange pots and yellow potholders made it look like a painting itself. Even small things like a stand with various-sized umbrellas or a calendar with bold black-and-white numbers over a desk in the bedroom seemed designed to give you something to look at and ponder in simple everyday objects. I don't spend enough time looking, Maggie always concluded when she came home from Caroline's apartment.

She was intrigued, too, by Caroline's delicate, small-boned mother, next to whom Maggie always felt especially oafish and large. Caroline's mother always wore dresses—Maggie had never seen her in slacks—in small flowerlike prints. She wore shoes that matched her pocketbooks. Something about Caroline's relationship with her mother aroused Maggie's envy. She liked the way they called each other by pet names—Caroline called her mother "Moth" and her mother called her "Caro." On Saturday afternoons they went to see musicals together and afterward had ice-cream sodas at Rumpelmayer's. For Caroline's birthday her mother always got her tasteful gifts like volumes of Edna St. Vincent Millay's poetry or slips or leather jewelry boxes that played tunes when you opened them. Even the discreetness, the fact that they had lived alone together for so many years and still did not discuss so many things, seemed almost magically non-Jewish to Maggie, a kind of behavior that seemed light years removed from her own relationship with her father.

Maggie confessed to Caroline that she had felt attracted to Todd Lamport. "Though I might have just been horny because of the movie," she added.

"I hate the word 'horny,'" Caroline protested.

"Car, you seem to have all these romantic hang-ups about sex. . . . That might not be good."

"Look, you say you don't like it when people say 'shrink' for psychiatrist. Well, that's the way I feel about 'horny.'"

"Okay. . . . Did you think he was good-looking?"

"Who?"

"Todd Lamport!"

"Oh . . . well, not fantastically. I guess I didn't notice much."

"He has beautiful eyes," Maggie said dreamily.

"So do you," Caroline said.

"Yeah, I guess." Maggie hated it when people said, as they often did, that she had beautiful eyes. It seemed to her that if someone was really pretty, like Caroline, people said just that. But if you were somehow odd or un-usual-looking, they tried hard to find an acceptable fea-ture like your eyes or your hair to focus upon.

Just then the front door opened. It was Caroline's

mother, home from work. She looked into Caroline's room. "Hi, Maggie," she said.

"Hi," Maggie said, getting up. "I guess I better get home."

Caroline's mother looked very neat, as always, her light hair drawn into a bun. Maggie wondered if she ever let it loose. She thought it would look pretty that way.

"Call me about the chemistry," Caroline said.

"I will," Maggie promised.

At home, still thinking about Todd Lamport, Maggie opened her bottom bureau drawer to look at her diaphragm in its small brown plastic box. It had never been used. When she had turned sixteen, Maggie's father had sent her to his friend Dr. Friedman to get fitted for a diaphragm. He said that although he had nothing against abortion, there was no excuse, in this day and age, for a woman to get pregnant without intending to, and he knew Maggie wasn't the type to do so foolishly, out of rebellion. "Why a diaphragm?" Maggie had asked. "Well, once you're having consistent sexual activity," he had said, "the pill or an IUD might make sense, but not now." Maggie couldn't remember if he had said "consistent sexual activity" or "constant sexual activity." In any case, the message was clear. Still, she sometimes wondered how it would work. Would she at some point go to Dr. Friedman and say, "I am now engaging in constant sexual activity. Put me on the pill?" "Constant" or even "consistent" sounded as though you were doing nothing else.

Maggie liked the fact that her father was forthright and open with her about topics like contraception, but she sometimes felt his attitude was almost too cut and dried.

The year she and Caroline had first become friends, they had discussed the possibility of Maggie's father marrying Caroline's mother. They had both seen on TV a Hayley Mills film, *The Parent Trap*, where a pair of twins had reconciled their divorced parents. Caroline's father seemed perfectly happy with his girl friend and Maggie's mother wasn't living, so how terrific it would be not only to get the two parents together, but to be real sisters. Caroline's mother had found Maggie's father interesting, but slightly alien. She said, never suspecting that any "fix up" was being planned, that he smoked too much—three packs a day—which she objected to on health as well as on ecological grounds, and that he really needed to lose weight, since men had as much obligation as women to keep themselves "fit." Further, she had always thought psychoanalysis was a little spurious. She really didn't see why, if people put their minds to it, they couldn't solve their own problems.

When Maggie had pressed her father for his opinion of Caroline's mother, he had said she seemed like a perfectly pleasant person, although a little "flat." According to him, there were "round" people and "flat" people. "Flat" people had narrowed their options about life down to a minimum and led serious straightforward lives, but they often went into severe depressions in later life. Maggie decided not to pass this information on to Caroline. Her father always spoke as though he were the ultimate authority; he had the force of so many years of analytic practice to draw on. Whenever Maggie saw Caroline's mother after that she worried a little that maybe her father was right and Caroline's mother really *should* go out and live a little.

"A young man called for you," Maggie's father announced at dinner.

"What was his name?"

"He didn't leave his name," Maggie's father said. "He said he'd call back." In a very different way from Caroline's mother, he respected Maggie's privacy and never probed into her personal life unless she offered information herself.

Maggie told him how she and Todd had seen a pornographic movie together.

"But they're for men," Maggie's father protested. "Why should you see one?"

"To see what they're like," Maggie said. "Anyway, why *should* they be just for men? I don't see why they don't make pornographic movies for women."

"Women wouldn't be interested," Maggie's father said in his offhand, emphatic way.

"How do you know?"

"They just wouldn't be. . . . It's like those centerfolds of men in magazines like *Playgirl*. Women don't enjoy staring at men's nude bodies."

"Don't you think men's bodies can be beautiful?" Maggie wanted to know, wanting to tell him how she'd felt during the movie, but embarrassed.

"Only to homosexuals," Maggie's father said.

"But, Daddy, that's so prejudiced!" Maggie cried. "That's just conditioning anyway. Women have been conditioned not to like to look at photos or movies of nude men, so they don't."

"Sweetheart, you blame *everything* on conditioning. There are also certain basic human traits."

"You don't *know*!" Maggie said. "You'll never know if they're basic unless you change the conditioning."

"Look, I have a patient," he said. He always had a patient to draw on to suit every occasion, a fact which often annoyed Maggie, who had no similar trump card. "A woman whose husband is doing a book on pornographic movies, drags her to all of them. This poor woman has sat through maybe two hundred porn films, hating every minute of it, trying to ape her husband's views. Finally she admitted she had never felt a twinge of sexual feeling while watching any of the films! Whereas her husband comes home all hot under the collar."

"But Daddy, that's just *one* couple!" Maggie protested.

"It's typical. . . . Look, sweetheart, men have no breasts. They have nothing to compare visually with breasts."

"Penises?" Maggie suggested.

"Penises are all very well," he said. "Look, let's take another example: Why is art history filled with countless paintings of nude women? Why were artists drawn to that theme? Because there is something intrinsically beautiful in a nude female body, like in a . . . flower."

"But those artists were all men!" Maggie said.

"So?"

"So, men artists like to draw nude women and women artists like to draw nude men."

"Mags, I've seen plenty of shows by women artists and very few of them draw male nudes."

"Some do," Maggie insisted.

"They just do it to prove a point."

"They don't!" Maggie said. "They do it because they *want* to!"

As usual, there was no way to end the argument except for them both to stop talking.

Maggie's father moved into his office, where, as he did almost every night, he turned the hi-fi on full blast and lay back in his reclining chair to read the stock market page. He had been a radical in college, but he enjoyed playing the stock market and claimed to have made several spectacular deals in the sixties by "selling short," a concept Maggie, despite repeated explanations, refused to understand. She thought the stock market was stupid and materialistic; she couldn't understand how her father could be interested in it.

She went to her room and waited for Todd to call again.

3

Caroline had been baby-sitting for the Pragers for two months. She wasn't sure how she would have classified them as a family. They were definitely not the unhappy kind who yelled at each other even in front of strangers, but neither were they the happy-go-lucky, hugging kind. At most she had to say that she liked all of them as separate people, but that they never quite came together and jelled as a family to her.

This evening, a Saturday, was unusual. When she arrived, slightly late, Justin was sitting on the living-room couch dressed in a suit and a tie. Ariella emerged a moment after Justin let Caroline in. She was dressed in an orange bathrobe and was barefoot.

"Darling, what's going on?" Justin said. "It's almost eight."

"Oh, fuck, I don't feel like going," Ariella said.

Caroline was always surprised to hear adults using four-letter words; she thought of them as having been especially designed for teen-agers.

"You were the one who got the tickets," he pointed out.

"I know. . . . Look, do I have to go?"

"You don't *have* to, no," he said, "only I wish you'd let me know an hour ago so I could have called someone."

"Take Caroline," Ariella said, as though Caroline weren't there.

"Do you want to go?" Justin asked Caroline.

"To what?" she said.

"It's a revival of *Who's Afraid of Virginia Woolf?*" Ariella said. "It's supposed to be terrific."

Caroline hesitated. "Well, I'm not . . . I don't think

I'm dressed right." She pointed at the jeans and sweater she was wearing. In fact, she always took great care in dressing when she came to baby-sit for the Pragers, changing out of her school clothes into a pretty blouse or a new sweater. But if she had thought she was going to the theater, she would have worn something more elegant, a new pair of pants or a skirt.

"Oh, that doesn't matter," Ariella said. "People go any old way to the theater. You look fine. Listen, that's a perfect solution. You'll like it, Caroline. Did you ever see it?"

Caroline shook her head.

"I've seen it twice, the original production and the movie. . . . Go on, get going," she said. "You're going to be late."

Caroline put on her coat, which she had just taken off. They drove to the theater district in the Pragers' small car, which Justin parked on Ninth Avenue. "It's not too cold," he said. "You can walk three blocks, can't you?"

"Sure," Caroline said. She still felt awkward. She had fantasized this precise situation so often that now that it was happening she felt peculiar. Besides, in her fantasy, it had been different—not only had she been beautifully dressed, but she had been with Justin because he had arranged it and wanted it. She had not simply been tossed at him like an old shoe by his wife. "Take Caroline!" She had said it so flatly, as though Caroline could not possibly represent any kind of threat. Wanting to make up for this, to be dazzling and charming, she found herself even more tongue-tied than usual.

"You don't usually wear suits, do you?" she said finally, just to break the silence.

He smiled, as though snapping out of a daze. "No, I hate them. Ariella finally convinced me I should have one at least, so I had this one made."

"It's nice," she said politely.

"I guess I just feel better in sweaters and slacks."

47

The theater was completely full. Their seats were in the third row of the orchestra. "Ariella likes to see really well," Justin explained. "She'd have brought binoculars, even with seats like these."

"My mother's like that about ballet," Caroline said.

The play seemed long to Caroline. Her consciousness of Justin's physical presence created a kind of static through which the actors' voices only occasionally penetrated. Once, in the middle of the act, she dropped her *Playbill*. They both reached for it simultaneously and his hand momentarily touched hers. For the rest of the act she kept, without wanting to, going back over that moment, feeling his touch.

In the intermission they met a couple Justin knew. "Caroline, this is Theodora and Frank Goren," he said. To them he explained, "Caroline's our baby-sitter. Ariella just didn't feel up to it somehow."

Caroline thought she saw the Gorens exchange glances, as though wondering if Caroline were someone Justin was seeing, as though he had made up that she was the baby-sitter. She felt excited and flattered at the possibility of that mistake, but at the same time conscious again that she didn't look the role. Theodora Goren was in a long brown velvet skirt and a white blouse with lace at the collar.

"How do you find it, Caroline?" she asked.

"I think it's, uh, good," Caroline stammered.

Theodora turned to Justin. "Somehow this time around it strikes me completely differently. . . . They seem to have such a terrific marriage, so much in common."

"She's too pretty for the part," Frank Goren said.

"I know!" Theodora said. "Him too, though. . . . I mean, you feel they could just wipe that other couple out of existence sexually. And I think you shouldn't feel that way."

Caroline thought that was odd. She gathered they

48

meant the older woman who played Martha was too pretty, whereas to Caroline she looked overweight and at least in her fifties. "I think he's nice," she said.

Three pairs of eyes instantly focused on her. "Who?" Theodora said.

"The man who— Her husband, I forget his name," Caroline said. "I mean, the man in the play, not the person who plays him."

"He really strikes you as nice?" Theodora said, as though this were an unusual observation.

"Well, yes," Caroline said. "Compared to her."

"I don't know," Theodora said. "I just don't know. I think there's an awful lot of hostility underneath that niceness. I think he *uses* his niceness."

"You've seen it too many times," her husband said.

"I know!" She smiled. "You just can't react freshly when you've seen it so often. It must be a very different experience for you, Caroline."

Caroline was relieved when they returned to their seats. She hoped somehow they would not meet the Gorens at the next intermission, but they did.

"So, how's Ariella doing?" Frank Goren asked Justin. "Did she get a job?"

Justin shook his head. "No, it's a total dead end. She just keeps sending out her resume and getting the same 'don't call us, we'll call you' type of answer."

"That's such a crime," Theodora said. "Ariella would make such a marvelous teacher!"

"Has she thought of going back for her doctorate?" Frank Goren said.

"Yes, but—well, it's such a grind," Justin said. "And then, what good would it do? People with doctorates are being turned down."

Theodora sighed. "There ought to be *something* one can do. . . . Is she terribly depressed by it all?"

Justin hesitated. "A bit."

After the play the Gorens apologized that they couldn't take Justin and Caroline out for a drink. They said they had to go back to Englewood. Caroline felt immensely relieved.

"Would you like to go out for a drink or coffee?" Justin asked.

"Okay," Caroline said. Although she felt nervous at the prospect, she was excited at the idea of their being alone together.

They went to a small hotel with round tables. Justin ordered a drink and Caroline ordered coffee. He asked how she had liked the play.

"Well, uh . . . I did," Caroline said cautiously. "Only I like to identify with someone and there was no one . . . I mean the older woman, Martha, was so mean and the younger one was sort of silly."

"Yes, I know what you mean," Justin said.

She was always so afraid he would regard what she said as foolish that she felt herself relax at his quiet, serious response.

"I don't see why people that got along so badly would still be married," she said. "I mean, they didn't seem to love each other at all."

He smiled.

She hoped that hadn't sounded naive. "Did *you* think they loved each other?" she said.

"Well, I think they had a kind of tie. When people live together as long as they had, maybe it's not love in a romantic sense, but it can be just as deep a connection in another way."

"I would think they would want to marry other people."

"Maybe they don't think it would be any different," Justin said. "Or they may not have that many options. People that age get into ruts and it's hard to make any move. It's easier to stay with something you know about, even if it isn't perfect."

Caroline wondered fleetingly if he was talking about his own marriage. "She was so mean to him, though!" she said. "I didn't really understand why."

He thought a moment. "Well, I see it almost in a women's lib way. It's odd because the play was written before the women's movement as such had even started. But I see Martha as a woman who's been trapped. She hasn't been able to have children, but she hasn't been brought up to look to work or a career as a means of satisfaction. So she's looked to her husband, who's not especially interested in making it, and she's disappointed in him. It's the old thing of a woman wanting to live vicariously through a man . . . which I think often does lead to disaster."

Caroline frowned. "Do you think she'd have been happier with children?"

"Maybe. . . . In her case I felt even more that she needed some outside work. She came across to me as a brilliant woman, a little like Hedda Gabler. Have you ever seen that?"

"We read it in school," Caroline said. "Do you, um, think all women should have outside work?"

"I think it helps—otherwise too many expectations go into marriage which most marriages can't sustain."

Caroline thought again of the difference between herself and Maggie. She stirred the spoon slowly and sadly around in her coffee.

"Caroline, don't take what I say personally," Justin said gently. "*You* may be the kind of person who'll be content with the more traditional way, and that's okay. I don't think anyone should be forced in *either* direction. I think the important thing is to have the freedom to choose. I mean, take Theodora. They have three children and for years she did nothing but look after the children,

51

give dinner parties, etc., etc. Then one day she exploded and decided she'd been horribly oppressed and was never going to cook another meal. She went out and got a social work degree. But the irony was that Frank really hadn't been oppressing her at all, as she used to claim. They were both just doing their thing, as society had told them—he going out and working, she staying at home."

"Are they happy now?" Caroline asked hopefully.

"They've worked things out. Things were a little shaky between them for a while." He smiled. "You always want things to have happy endings."

"I know that's bad," Caroline said.

"No, it's perfectly natural . . . certainly at your age."

His reference to her age broke the spell. Until that moment she had felt they were talking almost as equals. They walked toward the car. It had gotten colder. "I didn't see why that other couple, the younger one," Caroline said suddenly, "why they got married at all."

"Well, he explained that—she'd had that false pregnancy."

"Well, I didn't see why she didn't go to find out if she was really pregnant before they got married. She could have had an abortion, anyway."

"Abortion wasn't legalized then. Maybe the play *is* dated in that way. But even so, not everyone wants to race off and have an abortion."

"No, I didn't mean that," Caroline said hastily.

"I don't think there's anything wrong with it," Justin said. "Legalized abortion is a great thing, but it's still a complicated issue." Seeing she remained silent, he said, "I'm sorry. Did you have one? I'm not being critical."

"Me?"

"Well, lots of girls your age do."

"Oh, no, I . . . didn't have one," Caroline said. Partly she was pleased at the idea that he regarded her as someone who was experienced enough to have had affairs and abortions, but in another way he seemed to be placing her in some vague sociological group—teen-age girls of today—and that made her want to protest and assert her innocence as a form of individuality.

He dropped her off at her house. They sat in the car a minute. "Thank you," Caroline said stiffly. "I had a good time."

"So did I. . . . Can you make it upstairs all right?"

In the confined area of the car, with their shoulders almost touching, the physical sense of him which she had had at the theater returned even more strongly. Perhaps he was aware of this, or perhaps he was just leaning over to open the door for her. In any case he started bending toward her, but Caroline, confused, drew back; a moment later he did too. His drawing back made her feel deprived, as though someone had offered her a present and then suddenly yanked it away. After a moment Justin reached out and tentatively touched her shoulder. "It was a nice evening," he said. "I enjoyed it."

His sudden air of awkwardness, of seeming not to know what to do, affected Caroline. She sat there in a daze. Then, startling herself as well as him, she leaned over and kissed him quickly on the cheek. He smiled, but there was a troubled expression in his eyes.

"I'll see you in school Monday," he said.

She nodded and slipped out the door, before terror at her own boldness could overtake her.

A month and a half after Caroline went to the theater with Justin—it was almost Christmas vacation—he didn't appear for chemistry class one Monday morning. It was a ten-o'clock class so that most teachers, even those who sometimes got caught in traffic, would have arrived on time. The secretary from the main office came in and wrote: "J. Prager will not be in today. This will be a study hour." Everyone cheered. There was an exam due back on which most of the students felt they had not done well.

Caroline, trying to go over her French composition for the next hour, wondered why Justin wasn't coming in, whether he was sick again. She found herself unable to stop thinking about him. But at about a quarter of the hour, ten minutes before the class was over, he walked in. "Just go on studying, kids," he said. "We'll do the exam the next time." He looked very haggard and pale. Caroline felt worried. Please don't let anything bad have happened, she thought, watching him anxiously.

As soon as the class was over, she went up to him. "Is everything okay?" she asked.

He motioned that she should wait until everyone had left. Then, closing the door, he said, "Ariella's disappeared."

"What do you mean?"

"I don't know." He laughed grimly. "I guess I'll go down to the morgue this afternoon."

"When did she disappear?"

"Friday. She's done this before, but never for this long. Three days—"

Caroline didn't know what to say.

"Carrie, don't say anything to anyone, okay?"

He had never used her nickname before. At school all the teachers called her Caroline. That and the intimacy of his taking her aside alone to confide in her made her heart start beating more rapidly. "Is Noah all right?" she asked.

"He's all right. He's with Ariella's parents. . . . Actually, I was wondering, could you possibly pick him up there after school? I have a faculty meeting later. Here are the keys. Just bring him back to the apartment. I'll be back at five or six."

All through the day Caroline thought of nothing but Justin. In the last month or so she had started having dreams about him. Waking up from one of them, she had thought with dread: Maybe I'm falling in love with him. Her main concern was that no one, especially Justin, should know about this. How lucky that she was so good at concealing her feelings! But still, she was humiliated by it. It seemed so schoolgirlish, developing a romantic crush on a teacher. She could never in a million years tell Maggie—she would laugh her head off. When had it started? The time they'd gone to the theater? The time in the kitchen when he'd been recovering from his illness? But she felt, really, it had been no single time. It was more that when he spoke to her, he always seemed not to mind her shyness, her hesitancy, always seemed to listen to her most stumbling remarks seriously, as though hearing not just what she said but what she wanted to say. Was it just her imagination that, when he drove her home after baby-sitting, he lingered longer than was necessary in the car, seeming to savor, as she did, those quiet snatches of time together?

The last class of the day was art class, Caroline's favorite time. She had been working on a series in black and white since her art teacher, Ms. Hopkins, felt she was neglecting form for color. In the beginning Caroline hadn't liked Ms. Hopkins. She had thought she was stiff and too rigid, and when she had been to see a show of her drawings at a Soho gallery she had been disappointed. But lately she had realized, when she had begun to put together a portfolio for Parsons, how much she had learned from her, almost despite herself. Absorbed in the final drawing of the series she'd begun the week before, the worry about Justin receded.

"Caroline, what's happening with that portfolio?" Ms. Hopkins wanted to know.

"I finished it. . . . I think it's the best I can do."

"Bring it around some afternoon—I'd like to go over it with you. Would you mind?"

"No, only—"

"I know! You're afraid I'll take out some of the ones you like and sneak in a few of *my* favorites. . . . But listen, have you thought of maybe just one from this series?"

"I just don't know if they really—"

"They're exercises. . . . No, I know they aren't as 'perfected' as some of the others, but I like it when your stuff has that stumbling look. Sometimes there's a glossiness that—"

Caroline smiled. "I feel like I'm always stumbling."

"None of that. . . . You can feel it when something new is stirring, I know it. Didn't you feel it today? You looked so absorbed, you didn't even see me pass by."

Caroline was aware that had been true. She loved that feeling, when she seemed to be outside time. "I want to see your new show," she said. "My mother wants to see it too."

"Well, don't expect too much," Ms. Hopkins said, obviously pleased. "Speaking of stumbling!"

"I thought you knew more what you were aiming for," Caroline said. "You sound like you do."

"Oh, that's the teacher in me. . . . I don't even know if that always helps. It's easy to intellectualize." She looked at Caroline's drawing again. "I'm so glad you stopped where you did. The others got too busy, don't you think?"

Caroline sighed. "I tried to stop, but I was afraid they'd seem too . . . sort of deliberately Oriental."

"That's okay—let them be what they want." She smiled. "So bring the portfolio in next week, okay?"

On the way to Ariella's parents' house Caroline leafed through the portfolio in her mind, wondering if she'd made the right choices, afraid there were too many that were the same. It seemed only a second until she was at East Sixty-seventh Street, near The Rockefeller University, where Ariella's father worked. It was a very modern apartment building with terraces. Caroline went up to 15J after being "announced" by the doorman.

She was greeted by a small woman with fluffy auburn hair who smiled at her. "I'm Mrs. Gruenthal," she said.

"I'm, uh, the baby-sitter," Caroline said. "Caroline Lenox . . . Justin said I should bring Noah home."

"Oh, did he? He didn't call us about it."

"He has a faculty meeting."

"Well, we could have kept him here. There's no reason, I mean, until Ariella . . . Has he heard anything? Well, I'm sure he'd have let us know if he had."

"I don't think he has."

Mrs. Gruenthal led Caroline inside. Noah was playing in the living room. "Darling, the baby-sitter's here," she said.

"Hi, Carrie!" Noah said cheerfully.

"Noah was just having a little snack; would you like something too?" she said. "I hope Ariella won't mind. I didn't have any fruit so I had to give him some cake. She's so careful with his diet."

Caroline said she would have cake and a glass of milk.

"Aren't you lucky to be so slim!" Mrs. Gruenthal said. "Ariella and I have always had a weight problem. I think it must be hereditary. I'm so glad Noah seems to be more like Justin in that respect."

"Ariella doesn't seem fat," Caroline said, and then thought that might have sounded rude, implying that Mrs. Gruenthal was.

"Oh, she hasn't been for years. But she still *thinks* of herself as fat, and she's so careful about what she eats. . . . I just don't understand this thing, do you?"

"Pardon me?" Caroline said, her mouth full of cake.

"Her going off like this. . . . Now I know Justin said she was depressed over the job thing and Ariella's never

57

been—well, she's not the most stable, especially since Vera. . . . Though it amazes me—I'm so pleased that"—she lowered her voice so that Noah, who was at the far corner of the living room, couldn't hear—"as a mother she's been . . . well, Noah is such a dear! Poor Justin! After the last time, he looked so—I think that's what led to his getting mononucleosis. He was so worn down and thin-looking. I just don't know what to make of it."

Caroline nodded.

"Did she seem odd to you? I gathered you baby-sit for them a lot? I mean, lately, does she seem any different?"

Caroline had been thinking about that all day. She remembered how Ariella always seemed to her very highly strung, talked a lot, confided in her. "She didn't seem any different to me," she said.

"I feel—I know I shouldn't, Otto says how bad this is, but I feel it must somehow be our fault. I mean, somehow we must not have given her something. She's always been so volatile. And even after all that analysis!"

Noah came over to them. "Is Daddy home?" he asked.

Caroline glanced at her watch. It was almost five. "Maybe we should go," she said. "Justin gave me his keys and I don't know if he has another set."

But when they arrived home, Justin was lying on the couch, his arm over his eyes. He started when they came in, as though he'd been asleep.

"I was afraid you might not be able to get in," Caroline said.

He sat up, yawning. "No, I—we keep a set of keys with some neighbors, an extra set."

Noah ran into the apartment yelling, "*Batman* time!" He rushed past them into the bedroom, where the TV was.

"Stay a minute, Carrie," Justin said.

"Okay," Caroline said. She took off her coat and sat tentatively at the end of the couch.

He glanced at her. "Well, I've found her."

"Where is she?" Caroline asked.

"She's in Connecticut with a friend."

"Oh."

"Actually I've been trying there all weekend, but they must've left the phone off the hook." He grimaced. "God, I hate those games! It's so stupid and unnecessary."

"Who is her friend?"

"He's a writer."

Caroline thought about her father's use of the word "friend" and wondered which kind of friend this was. "Why do they leave the phone off the hook?" she said.

"God knows. . . . I guess they both have a certain love of intrigue."

"Are you going to tell her mother?"

"Her mother?"

"Well, her mother said she thought you would let them know if you found her."

"Oh, right, I should. . . . Yes, maybe I'll do that now, if you don't mind." Caroline remained sitting on the couch while Justin called. All he said on the phone was that Ariella was coming back, that she'd needed to get away and had gone to spend the weekend in the country.

"You didn't say anything about her friend," Caroline observed after he'd hung up.

"No . . . well, there wouldn't be any point in that. They're upset enough already."

"Would that make them more upset?"

"It would if they knew him."

"Why?"

He sat down beside her. "Look, Carrie, obviously I'm not exactly in a position to be objective. Ariella would say he's a writer and feels things more deeply and all of that.

59

But what I see is that he drinks too much, which means she does too when she's with him, and that he seems even more unstable than she is, which, unfortunately, is going some."

"Is she in love with him?"

"*She* thinks so. . . . Maybe that's unfair. In *some* way she is, but—I suspect deep down she realizes he isn't someone she could live with over the long haul. She's tried it and it never worked. . . . And she's afraid if we get divorced, I'll want custody of Noah, and that scares her."

"Would you?"

He nodded. "She sees it as a way of punishing her. It's not. It really isn't. I think when Ariella is all there, she's a terrific mother, very warm and direct, but she's *so* damn irresponsible! Like this weekend. She goes off, without telling *anyone!* If she wants to see Stef—fine. Let her say so. But pulling this *again*, just disappearing, getting everyone frantic. Other times she's left the gas on, supposedly by mistake, with Noah in the apartment. She's been in auto accidents with him. In one the whole car went up in flames! She managed to keep her head and threw him out the window so he wasn't hurt, but her whole body, her legs, were scarred for about a year from her ankles to her thighs. . . . It's her life. I can't do anything about her self-destructiveness. It's just that for Noah. . . ."

The image of the flaming car with Noah in it remained in Caroline's mind. Horrified, she didn't speak for a while. "It seems so strange," she said then, almost to herself.

"The accident?"

What seemed unbelievably strange to her was that someone married to Justin could want to have an affair with another man. "Just—the whole thing," she said.

Something in his expression made her feel he knew what she'd been thinking. Quietly he said, "I guess those happy endings you like just don't seem to be so possible in real life." After a moment he went on, still speaking slowly. "Well, let's face it, most people my age have had a lot of things that haven't worked out. I have work I enjoy, a son I feel very close to—" His voice broke.

Caroline was so stunned by his breaking down that, without thinking, she reached over and put her hand on his. "Don't feel so badly," she said. "Really. It'll work out. I'm sure they'd give you custody. They'd have to! You're so good with Noah!"

He put his other hand up to screen his face, as though still not trusting himself to speak. Finally, he said, visibly trying to collect himself, "I'm so sorry, Carrie, truly."

"Why?" She drew her hand back.

"Dumping all this on you. . . . It's good of you to listen." He looked up at her. "You always seem to somehow—well—understand and not judge . . . or maybe that's just my illusion. Is it?"

She frowned. "I don't know." It was odd to think of him having an illusion about her. "I think maybe I do judge," she admitted.

"In what way?"

"Well, with Ariella . . . I do feel what she does is bad. I don't see how she can . . . But I guess I've never . . . been in that situation," she retreated abruptly.

"I imagine you'd be different if you loved someone."

She felt her face flush. "I don't know!"

"Haven't you ever been?"

For a second she was tempted to say: Only with you. But she hesitated. "I guess not." She smiled painfully. "You thought I had—had affairs and things, didn't you?"

He looked surprised. "No, why do you think that?"

"When we saw the play that night, you said— You asked if I'd had an abortion."

"Oh, that," he said. "Well, I knew you less well then.

61

Anyway, I don't think innocence is anything to be ashamed of. I mean, it can be just fear or stupidity, but I think it can also come from a sense of values about things, wanting to wait for something worthwhile."

She nodded, pleased at this interpretation. "Do you think you—didn't wait?"

"Well, it's true, we were only in college. I guess in retrospect we were too young." There was a pause. He frowned. His eyes, fixed on her, were kind but worried. "Carrie, I feel guilty about you somehow."

"How?" A horrified thought passed through her mind that he was going to say he was guilty that he had made her fall in love with him.

"I feel like I've somehow dragged you by brute force out of that quiet, self-contained world you live in."

Though he didn't say this in a critical way, Caroline winced. It seemed to her that since she had been three, teachers had been describing her as "self-contained." By now it was as much a part of the way she knew she struck other people as the freckles that appeared on her nose in summertime. "Everyone says that, about my being self-contained," she said wryly.

"Aren't you?"

"I guess I am. . . . I do daydream a lot."

"It isn't bad."

"Yes, it is," she said.

"Why?"

"Because the real world is there and one ought to go out and learn about it."

"Well . . . ought. I don't know about ought."

"Maggie says I'm going to be disappointed."

"You know," Justin said, "I love Maggie. I think she's terrific, but I think somehow you—you're too much under her sway in some ways."

"It might be from not having a sister or a brother,"

Caroline said. She had thought about this herself. "Wanting someone to look up to."

"Do you see your father much? You said your parents were divorced."

"Once a year," Caroline said.

"Why not more often?"

"He lives in Paris."

"How come? I mean, why does he live there?"

"He makes documentary movies. I guess he got successful there and, well, he likes it."

"Has he remarried?"

"He has a girl friend."

"Do you write back and forth?"

Caroline looked down. "Well, I used to, but . . . The thing is, he just doesn't like writing letters, so, well, it's hard just to write to someone if they don't write back. . . . Mother says he's not the type to have had a family, that he's more sort of bohemian and I have to accept him for what he is or else I'll feel hurt."

"But you feel hurt anyway?"

"Sort of. . . . Well, not so much now. But when I was younger . . . I guess I used to wish he'd come back to America or he and Mother would remarry. I guess lots of kids whose parents are divorced wish that."

"Do you like his girl friend?"

Caroline thought a moment. All the questions he was asking belonged to a part of her life that she usually kept tucked away and thought of as seldom as possible. It was so much easier for her to be the "good listener," to hear someone else's confidences, than to share her own. "I feel funny with her," she admitted. "I can't tell if she likes me. She says she thinks children are—I forget what word she used, but anyway she doesn't want any. . . . I think it was bourgeois."

"Is that the worst of all possible sins?"

"For her, maybe."

"That's a pity about your father."

"You mean, about him not writing?"

"About everything."

"That's just the way he is. He can't help it."

"You always defend him," he said reflectively.

"Well, I don't think it's necessarily selfish to not want children. I've talked to Mother about it a lot. She has this friend, Myra Gittelson, who doesn't have children or want them, but Mother really wanted a child. She says she only minded about my father leaving so soon because she had to go out and support us and she wasn't trained for anything special, because he wasn't making enough money so he could give alimony or anything. . . . But she still says she doesn't regret having had me."

"I don't see how she could," Justin said. "I think she's tremendously lucky."

There was a pause during which his words seemed to hang in the air.

"What do you think will happen now?" Caroline asked hesitantly.

He sighed. "I don't know. I guess we'll have to come to some kind of agreement. I just hope it won't be too bloody."

"Will you still want me to baby-sit?" She tried not to sound anxious, to keep a ring of desperation from her voice.

"Sure. . . . I mean, well, if I go out. I can't tell what will happen, but I'll call you."

"Okay," Caroline said, unable to resist adding, "I would miss Noah—if I didn't see him again."

"He'd miss *you* tremendously. Well, we both would. Don't worry. We'll work it out." He shook his head. "God, I feel like I've been up all weekend. I couldn't see straight all day."

"You should go to bed early," Caroline said.

"I think I will."

Noah came racing into the room. "I want a cheeseburger rare," he said.

"Would you like one too?" Justin asked.

"Okay," Caroline said. She didn't want to leave. She went in to call her mother that she'd be home late, then perched on the stool next to Noah to watch Justin cook the cheeseburgers.

"Mommy eats them raw," Noah said. "Yuck!"

"I like mine rare," Caroline said.

"Raw meat is all right if it's fresh," Justin said.

"But it *looks* yucky," Noah said. "It looks *alive*."

Caroline knew what he meant.

"Mommy's coming back tomorrow," Noah told Caroline. "She visited a friend. When can *I* have a sleepover date?" he said to Justin.

"Whose house do you want to sleep over at?"

"Michael's."

"It's okay with me. . . . But don't you think you might miss us in the middle of the night?"

Noah laughed at the absurdity of this. "Why should I miss you in the middle of the night? I'll be asleep!"

"Well, some kids do. They wake up and feel scared."

"Those are babies!" Noah said scornfully.

"Does Michael's mother know about it?" Justin asked.

"Yeah, he told her. . . . Only she said I have to bring a sleeping bag."

"Well, you have one, don't you?"

"Daddy, you didn't put enough Bosco in!" Noah said. "I need more."

"Noah, don't put in too much. It's not good for your teeth."

"I want it to be as dark as *that*," Noah said, pointing to the wooden breadboard hanging on the wall.

"You could drink it straight from the bottle," Justin said.

"Okay," Noah said, reaching for the bottle.

Justin took the bottle away from him. "That was meant to be a joke, pal," he said.

Caroline finished her cheeseburger and reluctantly said good-bye; she wondered what would happen now.

4

Todd had told Maggie to meet him in the lobby of 360 Central Park West at 12:30; they were going to spend the afternoon together. Maggie had been waiting for ten minutes and he hadn't appeared yet. She wondered if she'd gotten the number wrong. Was it really 306? But just as she was wondering if she would have time to go to 306 to check, he appeared.

"Hi," he said. "Sorry I'm late." He had a large black portfolio under one arm.

"What's that?" Maggie said.

"Some drawings," he said. A man of about fifty-five, heavy-set with ginger-colored hair, passed by and waved at Todd. "See you," he called to Todd.

"See you," Todd said.

"Who was that?" Maggie wanted to know.

"That's Herman Blachly."

"Yeah, but I mean, who is he? Like, where do you know him from? What *is* this thing you do Saturdays?"

By now they were outside on the street. Todd suggested they stop at a delicatessen nearby and have lunch since it was almost one. "I go to this life drawing class," he explained over corned beef sandwiches and beer. "We meet every week at someone else's house. That way we don't have to pay to rent a place."

"Who's in the class?"

"Well, there's Herman, whom you saw, and there's Mimi—she's at Barnard, she's an art major. There's Tia, who's a housewife. Well, actually, she worked in a bank, but now that her baby is due, she quit her job. And there's Joe Fenster, who teaches at Queens and has four kids and lives in Pelham."

"He comes all the way in from Pelham every Saturday just for this? You artists!"

Todd laughed at her surprise. "Yeah, well, it's a great class. We all love it. I'd come in from Pelham too."

"It's just life drawing?" Maggie said. "You mean from real models?"

He nodded. "Only, well, this might seem a little unusual, but what we decided was—see, models cost money too, so we decided we would all take turns posing. Each week one of us poses and the others draw him—or her, as the case may be."

Maggie stared at him. "All of you? Even Herman?"

"Even Herman."

"But what about what's her name, the one who's pregnant?"

"She poses too. Actually, that's been very interesting because she posed about a year ago when she wasn't pregnant and then when she was just beginning to show, around her fourth month. Now she's due in three weeks. It's interesting to see how her body has changed. I guess I'd never seen a pregnant woman in the nude before."

Maggie found herself wondering how many nonpregnant women he'd seen in the nude.

"Doesn't she mind?" she said.

"Mind what?"

"Well, she must look horrible, with her belly all sticking out like that."

"She looks beautiful," Todd said dreamily.

"Oh, come on! She can't!"

"She does. . . . Maybe this is partly from an artist's point of view, but the lines of her body are very"—he groped for a word—"very round and appealing."

"I don't know," Maggie said. "I guess I haven't seen any pregnant women in the nude either. . . . But how come men pose too?"

"Well, that's what's interesting about this. . . . Like,

take Herman. You'd think, would it be that interesting to draw a fifty-eight-year-old slightly paunchy man in the nude? Well, it was. I think the sketches I did of him are probably the best I've done."

"Is Herman an artist too?"

"No, he— Well, actually, to earn a living he runs a sporting goods store. He's one of those people you'd probably have contempt for, Maggie."

Since she had learned to talk, it seemed to Maggie people had been accusing her of being dogmatic; she was used to it, but still, hearing a comment like that come boomeranging back at her was disturbing. "I don't think I'd have *contempt* for him necessarily," she said.

"The point is, he has to support his family—his wife doesn't work and they have two kids. . . . But he loves painting so he does this to keep his hand in."

Maggie took a swig of beer. "What about the Barnard girl?"

"What do you mean, what about her?"

What Maggie meant was: Is she pretty, is she sexy, does she have a boyfriend, do you like her, lust after her, have you ever gone out with her? But all she said was, "What's she like?"

"You mean to draw or as a person?"

"Either."

"Well, to draw I guess she comes closest to being what a traditional model would look like—sort of full breasted with rather narrow hips."

Maggie decided she hated the Barnard girl. She hated girls with narrow hips. "What is she like as a person?"

"Hard to describe. Kind of conventional. Frankly, I don't think she draws that well. She's very—well—held back in some way. I mean, she has the technical know-how, but not the—Well, she lacks some kind of divine spark, I guess I'd say if that doesn't sound too pompous."

Maggie was slightly, but not entirely, relieved. "I'd like to see your drawings."

"I'll show them to you when we get home." They had planned to go to his house afterward. "Would you mind if we stopped off at Lindsay's just for one second?"

"Your sister?"

"It's a little out of the way, but Mom wants me to pick up a plant Lindsay's been growing for her. They're both nuts about plants. Maybe the kids will be there—they're terrific."

"How old are your sister's children?"

"Well, now, I guess Harriet is around three or maybe four and Casey's only two. . . . Lindsay had Casey at home because she thought it would be good for Harriet to see it. She said she thinks little girls grow up thinking of the birth process as this very frightening, painful thing, and to see that it isn't is important."

Lindsay and Lance lived near Columbia University, on 114th Street and Broadway. "It can get kind of noisy," Todd said, "but they like the atmosphere, all the bookstores and stuff. . . . I guess it was partly they who convinced me to go to Columbia. Lance went there. Where did you say you applied?"

"Well, my science teacher, Justin, went to Cornell and started getting his doctorate there, and he thinks for what I'm interested in, they have the best program. I've applied to Princeton and Yale too."

"How come he didn't get his doctorate, if he liked it so much?"

"Well, he somehow . . . I think it was he got married and decided to try teaching and found he really liked it and I guess once you get away from research, it's hard to get back into it. You have to give it all you've got."

Todd smiled. "That shouldn't be a problem for you."

"No, it shouldn't be," Maggie agreed. "I guess I'll have other things to worry about, though."

"Like what?"

"Well, Justin thinks people—men *or* women—who become completely obsessed with their careers become dull, narrow people. . . . Maybe that *is* a danger."

"I don't think *you'll* ever be like that," Todd said in his reassuringly calm, decisive way.

"I think I might," Maggie confided. "I mean, when I get into something, I tend to forget about everything else. Daddy says the world could go up in flames and I wouldn't notice."

"That's good, though."

"In a way."

"I know what you mean about not wanting to be too narrow," Todd said. "Mom didn't become a lawyer till we were in school, and she wanted Lindsay to wait till she was established before she had kids. But Lindsay said sort of what you've been saying—that she didn't want to be *just* a lawyer, she wanted to have kids too, so she went ahead and had them."

"Has it worked out all right?"

"It seems to have. . . . Well, Lance really loves kids too, so I guess they don't regret it. Lindsay says if it weren't for the population thing she'd have four."

"Four!" Maggie said, horrified.

"She says it's a terrific experience."

"You mean giving birth to them or raising them?"

"Both, but I guess more raising them. . . . I can understand that. I guess I wouldn't want as many as four, but I'd certainly want two."

Maggie looked at him, puzzled. "Would you really?"

He was puzzled at her being puzzled. "Sure. . . . Well, I wouldn't want to go through life not knowing what it's like to be a father. I think maybe I'd wait till I was older than Lindsay was, though. She was just twenty-three. Not from the career point of view. I guess I'd just like to have ten years after college to do different things and not be tied down."

Maggie sighed. "I don't think I'll *ever* have them."

"Why not?"

"Well, the thing is, this might sound like a weird reason, but my mother didn't do anything, she was just a mother and she was terrific. I mean, she loved it and I think if you're going to do it, that's the way you should do it. . . . But I don't think *I* could ever do that."

"That's sort of reactionary of you," Todd said, looking surprised.

"I guess," Maggie said.

"Maybe when you fall in love with someone, it'll be different," he suggested. "Lindsay said she never especially liked the idea of babies as such, but the thought of her and Lance being able to create a person together seemed pretty great."

"I don't know," Maggie said. In the abstract she could see what he meant, but she doubted she would be like that. On the other hand, she'd never been in love.

Lindsay came to the door. "Hi Toddie," she said. "Are you Maggie? Hi! Listen, would you believe it, we're still having breakfast. Want some coffee?"

"Breakfast?" Todd said. "We had lunch already."

"Okay, okay, I know, it's disgraceful, but we were up working till three."

"Sure, sure," Todd said.

"We were. . . . He never believes me," she said to Maggie. "Lance is in the shower and the sitter took the kids to the park, so you'll have a rare moment of peace and quiet."

"What do you mean? It's always peaceful around here," Todd said.

"Peaceful? Look, I'd call my kids beautiful, I'd call them brilliant, but peaceful, no. . . . Hey, let's see what you did today. Was it Tia who was posing?"

Todd took out his portfolio and opened it up. Lindsay and Maggie looked at the drawings of the pregnant woman.

"Todd . . . Jesus, you're good," Maggie said, impressed.

"He's a genius. I know he's my brother, but it's true."

"I didn't like the way this one turned out," Todd said, looking embarrassed.

"Show Maggie the ones you did of Herman," Lindsay said.

"Those are at home," Todd said. "I'll show her when we get there."

"How about the ones of Mimi?"

The ones of Mimi, who Maggie remembered was the Barnard girl, were under the ones of Tia. Mimi sat, cross-legged, staring intently at the person who was drawing. She had the kind of breasts that Todd, if what he had said about his reaction to the pornographic movie was true, could have described as "big blobs of silicone."

Lindsay was looking over Maggie's shoulder. "You know, I've finally figured out what I hate about that girl," she said. "She has *no* hips! I think men *like* hips. Lance says he likes mine. He even says he likes my potbelly."

"What's this I hear?" Lance said, coming into the kitchen. He was very tall, with sandy hair and freckles. "Am I being quoted out of context?"

"We were talking about your admiration for my potbelly," Lindsay said.

"Of course I admire your potbelly," Lance said. "I always have. It was one of the first things I noticed about you."

Lindsay gave him a suspicious glance. "I didn't have one when you first met me."

"You had an incipient one."

"By the way," Lance said to Maggie, "I'm Lance."

"Hi," Maggie said.

"They've already had *lunch*, can you believe it?"

"Well, Todd has to get up early for that class, doesn't he?" Lance said. "I forgive him."

"Look, Lynn, where's the plant? I told Mom we'd bring it to her."

Lindsay got up. "I have it all ready," she said. "But listen, promise me, don't let Mom overwater it. That's what happened last time. She starts feeling sorry for the soil. Now with this plant it has to be watered just once a week. . . . Todd, are you listening?"

"I'm listening . . . once a week."

"And tell her it *must* have sun. She can get one of those special lamps if necessary, but don't let her stuff it in the corner of the dining room and pray for some mystical thing to keep it alive. . . ." To Maggie she said, "Mom has this thing about talking to plants, encouraging them, you know? Which is okay, *if* you also give them enough sun and don't water them to death."

Todd took the plant, which was wrapped up in brown paper.

"Be careful with it!" Lindsay called as they exited, Todd's portfolio under Maggie's arm. "Don't drop it!"

"Maggie'll help me," Todd said. "She's strong."

They took the subway down to Greenwich Village, where Todd lived with his parents. "She's very nice," Maggie said.

"She talks a lot," Todd said. "Yeah, I like her. . . . As sisters go, I'd say she's one of the better ones I've run across."

Todd's family lived on the tenth floor of a small apartment building. Maggie looked around as they walked in. It was a sunny, cheerful apartment with plants and brightly colored rugs and simple wooden furniture. Used as she was to the apartment she lived in with her father, she found it a surprise. She and her father lived on the third floor; their apartment, save for electric light, was al-

74

ways very dark. Neither of Maggie's parents had ever believed in furnishing a home in any *House Beautiful* sense. All the furniture, which was mainly ancient except for the analytic couch, looked as though it had been flung haphazardly from a bag and left to rest where it fell. Maggie thought this indifference to aesthetics was odd, given her father's interest in art, but he claimed that was not true. Genuine art, art that hung in museums, that was collected, was one thing, he said. But furniture, practical objects, were of no interest beyond their utility. A table was to eat at, a chair to sit on.

"Here, Mom," Todd said as his mother came out to greet them. "From Lindsay. . . . Don't overwater it and give it lots of sun."

"She always says that," Todd's mother said. "I *never* overwater them! Lindsay seems to think I sneak in and water them in the middle of the night. . . . But you can't let the soil get *parched*. . . . Hi, Maggie, it's nice to meet you." Todd's mother was of medium height, with short brownish-gray hair. She was dressed in a bright-green pant-suit and wore a blouse with turtles on it. Todd's father, who came over to take the plant, looked like Todd. He had the same greenish, sympathetic-looking eyes and the same curly auburn hair, although his was grizzled with gray.

"How did it get to be four-thirty?" Todd's mother said. "Where did the day go?"

"You were on the phone with your mother for half an hour," Todd's father reminded her. "You answered that letter to George and Helen, you had to go to the health food store for those things for the meat loaf—"

"Maggie, you'll stay for dinner, won't you? I know I shouldn't do this, but I'm trying this meat loaf for the first time. Lindsay gave me the recipe. She's into all this health food stuff, which is okay as long as it tastes good. Food that doesn't taste good doesn't deserve to exist, is what I think. . . . But this sounded more reasonable—I mean, it's not one of those bean sprouty deals."

"Sure, I'd be glad to stay."

They sat in the living room and listened to music. Todd's father went in to set the table and make the dessert. "The dessert you can count on," he said. "I've made it before. It's a kind of Indian pudding."

Maggie felt suspicious of Todd's parents. Had he told them, "Look, folks, I'm bringing home this girl and she's a raving feminist," and had they, forewarned, deliberately planned for Todd's father to set the table and make the dessert? Had they deliberately planned that precisely such a pleasantly unforced kind of egalitarian mood would prevail? Perhaps the moment she left, Todd's mother would don a ruffled apron and Todd's father would settle into an armchair and bark for his pipe and slippers to be brought at once.

"I hear you gave Todd a hard time at that debate," Todd's father said at dinner.

Maggie smiled sheepishly. "Not *that* hard, I'm afraid."

"Maggie," Todd's mother said, "would you tell me just one thing? You know, Todd has this problem when he gives speeches. He hears a humming in his ears, he says. . . . Now did you notice anything funny about the way he sounded?"

"Not at all," Maggie said sincerely. "He told me that, but I never would have known otherwise."

"You see!" Todd's mother said to Todd. "I knew that was true."

"Yeah, but it still bothers me," Todd said. "It's not just that no one else can tell. *I* can tell."

"It's psychological," Todd's father said. "Todd said your father was a psychiatrist, Maggie. I went to an analyst several years ago. It was a very interesting, important experience for me."

"Well, my father says almost anyone can benefit from a

good psychoanalysis. He says not everyone *needs* to go, but everyone could benefit from it."

"*I* could benefit from it," Todd's mother said. "That's for sure. . . . One day when life settles down to a nice, tranquil routine I'm going to treat myself to a long, peaceful analysis."

"It's not peaceful," Todd's father said.

"I don't see why not," Todd's mother said. "Lying down on a soft couch, closing your eyes, taking off your shoes, telling about your childhood and your dreams . . . it sounds *wonderfully* peaceful."

"Anyway, our lives are never going to settle down," Todd's father said.

"Of course they are! I've decided already—at sixty everything is going to be different."

"She was just fifty last month," Todd explained.

"That gives me ten years of wearing myself to a frazzle," Todd's mother said, "and then I'll be ready for analysis."

After dinner Todd's parents went out. Todd took Maggie into his room. Like the rest of the house, it was, by Maggie's standards, amazingly neat. There was a bed with a blue cover neatly spread over it, a desk, amazingly cleared of papers, and a chair to read in.

"Where do you keep all your stuff?" Maggie wanted to know.

"What stuff?"

"Just things . . . things you've collected." Maggie collected stamps, coins, books on whales, rocks. Her entire room was a mass of boxes, papers, folders. "You even make your bed," she said accusingly.

"Well, Mom says I have to. She doesn't believe in household help."

"That doesn't mean you have to actually *do* it."

"Well, I don't know . . . I don't like sleeping in a bed that's all rumpled up. Also, I like to be able to find things," Todd said. "If everything was lying all over the place, I'd never be able to find something when I needed it."

They lay on the bed together and kissed for a long time.

"Maggie, do you think—would you mind taking off your overalls?" Todd suggested.

Maggie hesitated. Her overalls were to her what a suit of armor might have been to a knight. It was not just that they were durable and roomy—they were a form of protection. In them no one could see her; she felt comfortably sexless. Still, under the circumstances, they seemed a hindrance. She took them off. Without them she felt naked.

Todd slid his hand up under Maggie's red turtleneck and down the rest of her body. "Oh, Maggie," he said.

"What?"

"I can see why you always wear overalls," he said.

"Why do I?" She was genuinely curious.

"Well, with your figure . . . men would be pestering you all the time on the street."

Maggie was surprised. Her many reasons for being attached to her overalls had never included that particular one. "You know, this isn't fair," she said stubbornly. "*You* should take something off too."

"Okay," he agreed amiably. "What should I take off?"

"Your shirt," she said after a moment's thought.

Todd took off his denim shirt and tossed it on the floor. Maggie looked at him. He had white skin and the same soft curly hair on his chest that was on his head. It felt nice. She had always thought she would find hairy men too apelike, but Todd's chest hair was distinctly appealing.

"I wish I could draw you sometime," Todd said. "Would you mind?"

In some way Maggie felt she did mind. The thought of

the man artist drawing the woman model seemed a classic sexist situation. "Maybe sometime," she said cautiously.

When they broke out of the next kiss, Todd was breathing rapidly. "Maggie," he said, "do you think we . . . I mean—"

"I didn't bring my diaphragm," she blurted out. Actually, she had thought of wearing her diaphragm, but that had seemed like it might be too calculated, as though she were planning for this very eventuality.

He shook his head. "I guess I should have—well, that seemed so deliberate, as though I was expecting this to happen."

"Weren't you?"

"Well, I guess I did think it was a possibility, but I wasn't sure. . . . Maybe it's better this way, though."

"In what way?" Maggie wanted to know.

"Well, we know we will do it eventually. . . . Maybe it's better not to rush into it too precipitously."

"I feel horribly horny, though," Maggie confessed.

"I know," he sympathized. "Me too."

"Maybe we could, you know, caress each other? Would you like to?"

"That sounds good."

"Are you sure?" Maggie said.

"About what?"

"About what I just suggested . . . I mean, I read somewhere men don't like that. It's intercourse or nothing."

"*I* never heard that," Todd said. "I think it sounds like a great idea. Do *you* want to do it, though?"

"Sure," Maggie said. She felt a little drunk and strange, as if the room was whirling around and around, although she had drunk no alcoholic beverage at dinner.

When it was over, they lay limply in each other's arms, pleased with themselves.

Maggie was thoughtful. "I think maybe sex is going to be better than I expected."

"Didn't you expect it to be good?"

"No, I always thought it *sounded* awful."

"I always thought it sounded pretty good."

"Did your sister sleep with her husband before they got married?"

"Sure."

"Here? I mean, did they do it in your parents' home? Did your parents mind? I heard sometimes parents mind with girls more than with boys."

"No, they never minded. . . . I guess they figured they were going to do it, so why not at home? They're pretty liberal, though, as parents go. I mean, I know they did wonder when Lindsay and Lance were going to get married because they went together for around five years— they met in her freshman year."

"Why did your parents care if they got married?"

"Well, in that way I guess they are conventional. . . . Or maybe it's just that they've been happy and so they don't see marriage as a bad thing."

"It's weird that your parents are so happy," Maggie said.

"What's so weird about it?"

"How long have they been married?"

"I guess around twenty-eight years."

"In my school *nobody's* parents have been married that long . . . *nobody's* parents are happy."

"It can't be *that* bad."

"That's the way it is," Maggie said. "Really. I'm not exaggerating."

"Well, Mom and Dad do say they think they were lucky. They met when they were just out of college, when Dad was in law school, and well, I guess it just turned out okay." It was clear that he didn't find this half as remarkable as Maggie did.

"But what about when your mother went back to work?"

"What about it?"

"Didn't your father get mad because she didn't make supper every night?"

"I guess I shouldn't say this," Todd said, "but, frankly, my mother is not such a great cook. I think Dad was kind of relieved."

Maggie sat up. "Maybe next Saturday you could come to my house," she said. Now that she knew that next Saturday was definitely the time she would finally lose her virginity, she decided that it would somehow be pleasanter on home ground.

"Okay," Todd said. "Will your father be there?"

"He usually goes out with his girl friend."

"Does she ever sleep over?"

"No," Maggie said, putting her overalls on again. "It's sort of weird, really, because they've been seeing each other for almost ten years. When I got to be a teen-ager, he used to say he wouldn't be home Saturday, and if I wanted to have a friend stay over, I could. . . . But she never stays at our place."

"How come?"

"I think it's probably some Oedipal thing," Maggie said, lacing up her sneakers. "He probably thinks I'd go into paroxysms of jealousy or something."

"Would you?"

"I don't *think* so. Maybe when I was little, I would have, but not now."

Maggie's father always said "the young" thought that only they were entitled to be interested in sex, and they supposedly thought everyone over thirty should be celibate. Maggie thought this was a gross slander. As far as she was concerned, people could screw till they were eighty, if they felt like it.

When she got home, she took her diaphragm out of her

bureau drawer and looked at it solemnly. All week, whatever she did, she could think: This is the last time I'll do this as a virgin. That would be interesting. It would make it kind of a special week. Her last chemistry class as a virgin, her last subway ride as a virgin. She wasn't at all certain she was going to enjoy intercourse, but anything, no matter how horrendous, was worth going through in order to pass out of that awful state.

It was definitely something to look forward to.

5

The Friday school ended for Christmas vacation Justin called in the afternoon and asked if Caroline could baby-sit that Saturday night. "I'm sorry to let you know at the last minute," he said.

Caroline said that was okay.

When she got there—it had just started to snow—Justin explained that he was going to see Ariella. She had, he said, taken an apartment near her parents, and they were going to talk over the whole custody issue.

"Is it a nice apartment?" Caroline asked.

"I haven't seen it yet. . . . It sounds fine—a bedroom and a living room. Her parents are paying for it. I was kind of surprised she agreed to that."

After he left, Caroline went into the bedroom to watch a movie with Noah. It was *The Yearling* with Gregory Peck. She had read the book when she was younger, but had never seen the movie. Noah and Caroline sat side by side on the unmade mattress, watching the small color TV, which was propped against the wall. At one point she got up and walked out of the room.

"Where are you going?" Noah called.

"His mother is going to shoot the deer," said Caroline from the next room. She waited until there was the sound of a shot. Finally Noah called, "You can come back, Carrie. It's all over."

When she returned cautiously to the room, he said, "They didn't even show it."

"I don't care," Caroline said. "It's the idea of it."

"It wasn't a person."

"I don't care!" Caroline said. "Why did she do it? Why didn't she just chase the deer away?"

"She was mean," Noah explained. "Anyway, that was the story. If she didn't shoot him, there wouldn't be a story."

"Yes, there would," Caroline said. "There would still be the story of how he found the deer and took care of it and how he had to give it away." She didn't see how shooting the deer had made it a better story.

"I don't mind seeing movies like that if you're here," Noah said. "Then I don't get sad so much." He leaned against her.

Caroline pulled him closer. "Me too. . . . It's awful watching them alone."

"You promised you'd finish the book for me."

"Maybe next time. It's a little late." She realized she had let him stay up way past his bedtime partly because she wanted to be with him longer. Once he was asleep, she felt restless and uneasy. She thought of watching a movie on the late show but she felt too tired. She had been up until midnight the night before writing an English paper, and she had expected Justin would return early. Also, she thought she would feel uncomfortable sitting alone in the room with the unmade mattress. She wondered why Justin hadn't had Ariella come here to discuss whatever they were going to discuss. Then she decided he must have not wanted Noah to hear, especially if they ended up arguing.

She went into the living room and sat down on the couch. It was an especially comfortable couch, covered with soft corduroy, with pillows at both ends. Caroline turned off all the lights in the living room except for one in the corner and they lay down on the couch. She pulled the afghan that was folded up at the bottom of the couch over her and closed her eyes.

When she woke up, the sun was streaming in the window. Noah, in his pajamas, was standing next to the couch. "How come you're still here?" he wanted to know.

Caroline sat up, stiff. "What time is it?" she said, yawning.

"Eight o'clock. . . . Is Daddy here?"

"I don't know," Caroline said.

"Let's check." He went with her down the hall and quietly opened the bedroom door. Justin was asleep, the covers pulled over him.

"Do you want any breakfast?" Caroline said.

"I had it already. I just have cereal. . . . Do *you* want some?"

Caroline had a bowl of Product 19. She thought of calling her mother, but remembered she was away that weekend.

"That's what Daddy always has," Noah said. "He says it's good for you—but it doesn't *taste* good."

"I think it does."

"I guess grown-ups always do."

Caroline decided she should stay until Justin woke up, partly because he hadn't paid her yet. "Do you want to watch TV?" she asked.

"I can't till Daddy wakes up because the TV's in there."

"Oh, that's right."

"I let him sleep till ten on Sunday and till nine on Saturday," he explained. "That's the rule."

"I see," Caroline said. "Well, what should we do, then?"

"We could go out," Noah said. "It snowed. Look!" They went to the window and looked down at the snowy park.

"Okay," Caroline said. "Go get your boots and stuff, okay?"

It was a beautiful morning, sunny, with a clear, vividly blue sky. No one else was in the playground. Sitting in the sun, Caroline was actually warm in her parka. Noah didn't seem to mind that there were no other children. He ran around, trying the swings, the slide, even making some snowballs. Caroline began thinking of a children's book she had thought of writing and illustrating for Noah. It was going to be about a little boy whose mother goes away suddenly. She had planned pictures in her mind of Noah and Justin doing things together, and had even made some preliminary sketches, but she wasn't sure how to set up the story. Whenever she thought of the book, she thought of it as a group of pictures. It was harder for her to imagine the words that would show the bond between the little boy and his father.

"Do you have a Kleenex?" Noah asked, coming over.

Caroline shook her head. She saw his nose was running. "We could go back," she said. "It's after ten."

When they returned, Justin was in the kitchen making breakfast. He was wearing blue jeans and a shaggy gray sweater; he was barefoot. "Hi!" he said. "Want some breakfast?"

"We had it already," Noah said. "Can I watch TV?"

"Sure. . . . How about some hot chocolate?" Justin said to Caroline. "That's what you're supposed to have when you come in from the snow."

"Okay," Caroline said. She loved hot chocolate. "I'm sorry I didn't leave a note about our going out this morning," she said. "I forgot. Were you worried?"

"I saw you from the window," he said. "Your parka is such a nice, bright color, you were easy to spot."

"How come you didn't wake me up last night?"

"Well, I got in pretty late and it was snowing like the dickens. And you were so sound asleep. I wished I could've opened up the couch—it turns into a real bed—but I was afraid I'd wake you. I called your house but no one answered."

He sat the hot chocolate down in front of her. There was real whipped cream on top. "Was the apartment nice?" Caroline asked.

"Ariella's? It's okay. I don't especially like those ultra-new East Side places, but it's good sized, with a terrace. She'll sleep in the living room when Noah stays over, and he can stay in the bedroom. . . . I think we reached a kind of compromise. It's only one block from her parents, and she says if she ever has the desire to bolt, she'll leave him there."

"So you'll have joint custody?"

He nodded. "Frankly, I don't think I have much choice, and she feels it's a sign of trust; it's important to her."

"Where would she bolt to? To that friend in Connecticut?"

"Probably. . . . I don't think he'd be too fond of the idea of her dragging Noah up there anyway."

"Is he a famous writer?" Caroline said. "Would I have heard of him?"

"He's not as famous as Ariella hopes he'll be some-day," Justin said dryly.

"Why does she hope that?"

"Why?" He looked surprised. "Isn't that every wom-an's fantasy? To be the mistress or wife of someone famous?"

"I don't know," Caroline said. "I think maybe I'd rather be famous myself."

He laughed. "Well, I think Ariella would like that too. But, given second choice, I think she'd pick being the woman behind the famous man, as her mother was. That may have been part of our problem. In fact, it definitely *was* part of our problem."

"That you aren't famous?"

"That I started getting my doctorate and Ariella— Well, what happened was I stopped at one point, to teach, actually expecting to go back, but then I found I really loved it. I mean, the kids at Whitman are terrific, very bright, and I guess, without ever saying it, after a couple of years I realized I didn't especially want to go back. But I remember one evening my former doctoral professor came to dinner and I said how much I was enjoying teaching and that I knew now I'd never go back for my doctorate. I'll never forget the look on Ariella's face. She looked stricken. She said, not in front of him, of course, 'I never expected to be married to a high-school chemistry teacher.' "

"But you still didn't want to go back?"

"You mean, after discovering she felt that way? Of course not! Look, Carrie, you can't run your life to suit someone else's myths. That would have been a disaster. And I happen to think that particular game is one which never works either way. If the man succeeds, the woman ends up feeling: I'm just your appendage, why didn't I get *my* doctorate? Why are *you* famous and not me?"

"Is it because her father is famous that she felt that way?" Caroline asked.

"Maybe partly . . . though when we got married, he hadn't won the Nobel prize. . . . Actually, ironically, Ariella's father is about as unworldly an individual as you could find. I remember her mother yelling at him to at least buy a new suit when he went to Stockholm to get the prize. He wanted to go up there with the same pair of baggy slacks he's worn for the last fifty years. He just happens to be a guy who lives, breathes, and eats science—that's his world."

"He sounds nice," Caroline said.

"He is. I like him a lot."

As she was about to leave, Justin said, "Carrie, next week I'm going to see Ariella again. There are a few things we still have to discuss. . . . Do you think— Why don't you bring a suitcase and plan to sleep on the couch? Would that be okay? I don't know when I'll get in and I don't want to keep worrying about you all evening, about your getting home too late."

Caroline's mind instantly darted ahead to what nightgown she should bring. She didn't have a nice bathrobe, and she wondered if she should go out and buy one with her baby-sitting money. At home she rarely wore a bathrobe, but maybe it was a good thing to have. "Yes, that would be okay," she said.

"Good. . . . Well, I'll see you around eight, then. . . . Have a good Christmas."

"You too," Caroline said.

She did buy a bathrobe, a red velour one with lace at the collar and small buttons going up the front. She felt it went with her favorite nightgown, one her mother had given her for Valentine's Day which was pink with small red hearts on it. The robe was warm because it had long sleeves and reached to the ground, but it was pretty, like the nightgown.

She was saved from having to explain to her mother about sleeping at Justin's by the fact that three days before the event her mother said, somewhat hesitantly, "Carrie, I'll be away again this weekend—is that okay?"

"Oh, sure," Caroline said. "You seem to keep going away lately. How come?"

Her mother looked a little embarrassed. "Well, it's just, Malcolm's mother died and left him this very lovely little farm—well, it used to be a farm—in the Berkshires, and he's trying to decide whether to keep it. It does need a lot of work. . . . Is it all right, though?"

Caroline had only been half listening. "What?"

"I mean, you don't mind or feel lonely that I'll be away? You seem so busy lately that I thought—"

"Oh, no, it's fine," Caroline said. "I don't mind."

More than not telling her mother about staying at Justin's, she felt awkward lying to Maggie when the matter came up quite offhandedly. Usually she told Maggie everything that happened and didn't happen in her life, but this she wanted to keep to herself. She was a little afraid of having the piercing light of Maggie's irony turned on her feelings about Justin.

When she arrived at the Pragers' apartment, the couch had been folded out as a bed and sheets were spread on it. "Voilà," Justin said. "Actually, it hasn't been used as much as we thought when we first got it, but a few friends have stayed over. I think it's pretty comfortable."

Caroline sat down on it. "It seems fine," she said, feeling awkward. She looked around the living room. "Don't you have a tree?" she asked, surprised.

"A tree?"

"For Christmas."

"Oh . . . no, I guess with all the . . . confusion I forgot this year."

Caroline found that almost shocking, that someone, especially with a child, would have forgotten to get a tree. She thought Justin seemed like a good parent, but that omission seemed to her to verge on the unforgivable, confusion or not. "Where did you put Noah's toys?" she asked.

"In his room."

"I think you should have gotten a tree," she said.

He smiled. "Trees are nice, aren't they? I like them too. I always missed having one as a child because of being Jewish, but Ariella and I decided we weren't *that* Jewish."

After Justin left, Noah took Caroline into his room to show her all his new toys. His favorite seemed to be one from his grandparents, the Bionic Man, which came from a special kit. They played a few Bionic Man games, with Noah giving most of the orders. Then, at eight-thirty, he went to sleep. He wanted all the presents lined up right next to the bed. Caroline put the present she had gotten him next to the others. She wanted him to discover it when he woke up in the morning.

Then she worked some more on the book she was making for him. She had decided she would leave him the drawings and that together they would write the words. All week, before going to bed, she'd been refining the sketches. In some the boy and his father looked just as she wanted; she had caught something of Noah's expression as he played and read. In others he seemed to her to look too old. But now she abandoned herself to the pleasantest part, filling in the color. She'd brought her set of Dri Marks and had already planned the basic shades in her mind. She worked carefully, and slowly, enjoying the warmth the colors brought to the black-and-white sketches. Doing an area of pink-and-yellow wallpaper took the better part of an hour, but she didn't mind. She wanted to get it just right, aware that it was as much for herself as for Noah that she was doing it at all.

At eleven-thirty she decided to go to sleep. Taking the small blue suitcase into the bathroom, she locked the door, put on her nightgown and robe, brushed her teeth, and then washed her face. At home she usually took a bath before she went to bed, but she had known she would feel funny taking a bath at the Pragers' and had taken one at home before she left. Then she went back into the living room, took off her robe, and got into the bed-couch.

Really, she didn't want to go to sleep. She wanted Justin to see her in her nightgown and robe and was afraid that in the morning Noah might want to go outside again and she would have to get dressed. But the thought of sitting until he came home, expectantly, seemed too calculated. She lay down and closed her eyes. Once she did, it was easy to entertain herself with fantasies about Justin. Her mother used to say that she had movies running in her head all the time, and it was true—she often missed her bus stop because she was so intent on her thoughts. Now, the time seemed to pass in a flash as she elaborated various encounters between the two of them, inventing dialogue, moving both of them in her mind like the most docile of puppets.

When the key turned in the lock, she started. She felt guilty, lying there in the dark, awake, and closed her eyes and tried to breathe as though she were sleeping. Justin passed by the couch and pulled the blanket, which had half slipped to the floor, over her. Then he went into the kitchen. Caroline lay there for several minutes, listening to him rustling around. Then, unable to restrain herself, she got out of bed and went into the kitchen.

"Hi," Justin said. "I hope I didn't wake you. . . . Your blanket had fallen off."

"No, that's okay," she said.

He was pouring himself a glass of beer. "Would you like some?"

Caroline hated the bitter taste of beer, but she wanted to seem grown up. "Yes, thank you."

"Is dark okay? That's all we seem to have."

"Sure. . . . Is it late?" she asked with what she hoped was convincing ingenuousness.

"Not especially. Half past twelve. We all went out to eat. They wanted to go hear some music after, but I bowed out."

"Who is they?"

"Oh, Stef came in. He was staying over."

Caroline was startled. That seemed very odd to her. "Don't you mind seeing him?" she asked.

"Not so much anymore. I'm inured to it anyway. . . . When Ariella began her campaign to be a sexually liberated women, her goal for us as a couple was a sort of open marriage—we were both supposed to have lovers and bring them home, all have dinners together, etc., etc. All very open and aboveboard."

"Did that work?"

He laughed. "Well, it led to certain situations which in

retrospect I guess had a certain comic, if not ludicrous, quality. Frankly, I think Ariella's taste in men leaves something to be desired. I mean, they may have been great in bed, but as conversationalists! She seemed to have a penchant for unemployed silversmiths with hair to their shoulders."

Caroline wondered anxiously whom he had brought home and what *they* had been like. "Weren't you jealous, though?" she asked.

"Of course I was! Look, it's a system that would only work if human beings weren't human. Ariella used to say that sleeping with someone should have no more significance than going to the movies with him, but I think that leaves human emotion out of the picture. Maybe in the best of all possible worlds people wouldn't suffer from jealousy or fall in love, but as it is . . ."

Caroline considered this. "Do you think that would make things better?"

"Not really. . . . Do *you*?"

She blushed. "I don't know." She looked at him. "You seem in a very good mood," she said.

"I'm in a fantastic mood, Carrie. I feel like some gigantic weight's been lifted from my shoulders. It's ironical, but Ariella's running away this most recent time really has turned out to be for the good. Otherwise I think it would have all dragged on and on. . . . I was always so fearful of how Noah would react, and he seems perfectly fine! We probably should have done it years ago."

Caroline thought how then she would never have baby-sat for them. "I put Noah's present by his bed," she said. After a second she added, "I got him a carrot." She was hesitant about mentioning the book.

"A carrot?" He looked startled.

"I mean, it's a doll really, but it's shaped like a carrot, but it has a face and everything. I just liked it."

"That's sweet of you. He was kind of inundated, as you

could probably see from his room." He looked at her contemplatively. "That's a nice nightgown."

"My mother got it for me," Caroline said.

"That kind of old-fashioned thing suits you." He continued to gaze at her, somewhat more appraisingly than usual. Although that was what she had wanted, it made her uncomfortable.

"I like the kind that go to the floor," she said.

"Hmm?"

"With nightgowns," she stammered. "More than the short ones, I mean."

"Oh, right." He yawned. "Well, I guess I'll turn in. How's the couch? Comfortable?"

Caroline didn't want to admit she had not even been trying to fall asleep. "Yes, it's very comfortable," she said. She went back to the living room and got under the covers. The room was still dark.

Justin came in. "Do you have enough blankets?" he said. "We have some extra ones, if you like."

"No, I'm fine," Caroline said.

He bent down to tuck her in. She saw his face come closer. Then, before she had time to react, even with surprise, she felt his lips touch hers. He kissed her lightly but lingeringly and she could smell the faint scent of beer, which was more aromatic than bitter. Then he moved back. "Well . . . that was precisely what I wanted to avoid," he said wryly.

"Why?" Caroline said.

"There are a million reasons. You must know some of them."

"That you are married?"

"For one. . . . *And* I don't want to lose my job. . . . *And* you're awfully young."

Caroline was immensely glad that her birthday had been the week before, so that she could say, with all honesty, "I'm eighteen." Somehow eighteen sounded much

94

older than seventeen to her. Eighteen seemed comfortably close to twenty, to adulthood. After all, lots of people were married at nineteen.

"Eighteen is still pretty young," Justin said. He was kneeling beside the bed; she could see his face very well in the dim light.

"I don't think it's as young as it used to be," Caroline said. "I think nowadays, well, people mature faster."

"True." He was gazing at her reflectively. Then he brushed her hair back off her forehead. "Sleep tight, Carrie," he said, standing up.

"You too," Caroline said.

Lying in bed, she felt a little confused about what had just happened. She had offered herself to him and he had turned her down! Hadn't she? It seemed to her she had, in spirit anyway. What if it wasn't scruples that had made him do it, but just lack of interest? But he *was* interested, she was sure! All those long conversations and glances and confidences. Did he just do that all the time? To all their baby-sitters? Or rather, since she knew she was their only baby-sitter, would he have done it to anyone who had baby-sat for them? She loved him and it would kill her if it turned out to be just her imagination. It wouldn't be fair! In a sudden burst of what seemed almost like rage, the feeling was so intense, she wished she could just go in and seduce him, but she wasn't sure how it was done, what was said. And the thought that he might just be distastefully surprised held her back as much as anything. Still, in her mind she kept imagining variations on it in which he was delighted, overcome, and in which he exclaimed frequently that it wasn't her imagination at all, that he loved her and wanted her and had ever since she had first baby-sat for them. Finally, exhausted, she fell asleep.

In the morning she got dressed in the bathroom again. She had brought what she considered her nicest sweater, a deep-blue cashmere which her father had sent her when she had turned sixteen. At breakfast Justin said, "That's my favorite color, that shade of blue," and Caroline felt how lucky it was that she had brought the sweater, not even knowing that ahead of time.

They all played Monopoly together after breakfast. Caroline was the worst. She was terrible at all games. Her mother liked bridge and sometimes played with friends, and Caroline had once tried joining her, but she always found her mind wandered and she forgot the trump card. It was the same with chess, which Maggie had tried to teach her, and with almost all sports. In gym sometimes the volleyball would hit her on the head because she was standing there dreamily, forgetting that she was in a volleyball game. She wondered if Justin let Noah win on purpose. She didn't think that was good with children. She remembered getting mad when her mother did that when she was younger.

Near noon Justin said, "Carrie, would you do me a favor and take Noah over to Ariella's parents? They're expecting him for lunch and I just feel if I don't make some inroads into these papers, they'll drag out into the rest of vacation. Why don't you come back and have lunch with me?"

Caroline got Noah into his snow pants and jacket and boots and scarf and mittens, and herself into her parka and fur-lined gloves. She had forgotten to bring boots, but she had heavy shoes.

Ariella's father answered the door this time. Caroline had wondered what someone who had won the Nobel prize would look like. She had been expecting a tall, imposing man with penetrating eyes, a little scary, whereas Mr. Gruenthal was small, barely her own height, and was dressed in a turtleneck, baggy slacks, and sneakers. He had frizzy gray hair and a genial expression. "I'm so glad you came, Caroline," he said, ushering her into the living room. "We've wanted, Blanche and I have wanted, to thank you for taking such good care of Noah through this difficult period. . . . Justin's told us all about it."

"Well," she said, sitting down, "I like Noah a lot."

"And he obviously likes you. He talks about you all the time."

"He's so bright," she said.

"Oh, he's a remarkable child," Mr. Gruenthal said, "a *very* unusual child. He can comprehend concepts which are astounding. I taught him chess, and right away he opened with the queen's gambit! Instinct!"

Caroline wasn't sure what the queen's gambit was, but she gathered it was a good move to have made.

"I gather from what Justin says that you're a very brilliant young woman," he said, smiling at her.

"I think you probably mean Maggie," Caroline said. "She's my friend."

"Oh yes, I know about Maggie. . . . But aren't you the artist?"

Caroline was bowled over at acquiring such a formidable title and by the fact of Justin's having mentioned her drawing to his father-in-law. "Yes, I—I'm afraid I'm not too good at science, though," she said.

"Noah seems to have a remarkable grasp of science," Mr. Gruenthal said. "Of course, I hate to get my hopes up. Ariella did too, and then somehow, around in high school, I believe, she gave it all up. Of course women tend to—"

"Tend to what?" Caroline asked.

"Well, I was going to say tend to give things up. . . . I do think there's some truth in that, but especially with science. I've had some brilliant young women, even on the post-doctoral level, but somehow they seem to lack a certain . . . I don't know what it is, ambition, tenacity, whatever . . . which you need, I'm afraid."

Caroline wondered how he felt about Justin just being

97

a high-school teacher and if he was disappointed. "I guess Ariella would like to teach," she said.

"Yes, well . . . I just don't know with Ariella. It sometimes seems like she seeks out these fields where the chance of success is absolutely minimal. I don't know if Ariella has the discipline to hold down a teaching job, even if she does get one. You know, teaching isn't an easy thing—it's preparing every night, it's being dedicated. She ought to know that, being married to Justin. I would imagine he must be a marvelous teacher, is he?"

"Yes, he's very good," Caroline said, not wanting to admit that in Justin's classes her mind wandered more than in almost any other. She knew that was probably due to the subject matter, not to his teaching ability, since so many of the other students seemed to look forward to his classes.

Outside it was freezing cold. The sun had gone in, and a harsh wind was blowing from the river. Caroline waited a long time for the bus, hopping from one foot to another. Her feet felt icy, especially her toes; tears slid down her cheeks from the iciness of the wind.

She didn't know what would happen when she got back to the Pragers' apartment, but she felt as though there was some unfinished business from the night before between herself and Justin. Surely he would explain, surely he would say something! The lines in her head that she had written for him went along the lines that he had come to realize he was madly in love with her, that although she was only eighteen, he found her amazingly mature for her age, what did age matter after all, when they had so much in common, when they could talk together so easily. But she was terrified that he might be able to say the opposite, even that he didn't want her to baby-sit for them anymore.

When she got there, Justin was sitting on the couch, a pile of papers on the floor. Handel's *Water Music* was playing in the background. "That's my mother's favorite piece," Caroline said, taking off her parka.

"I love Handel," Justin said.

Caroline shivered. "It's awful out!" she said. "I think it's going down to zero."

"Come over here and get warm," he said.

After a moment's hesitation she went over and sat next to him on the couch. She hugged herself. "Brr."

"You poor thing . . . I'm sorry, sending you out like that."

"That's okay," she said, looking at him expectantly. And then he took her in his arms and kissed her. Unlike the kiss the night before, it was deliberate and no longer casual. When it was over, Caroline felt so dizzy she thought she was going to faint.

"Carrie," Justin said. The expression on his face was vulnerable and uncertain; it made him look younger.

She just looked at him, waiting.

"When were you eighteen?"

"Last week," she admitted.

He sighed and shook his head.

"It doesn't matter," she insisted. "Really. I don't think people's age matters."

He kissed her again; he was holding her so tightly she could hardly breathe. Then suddenly he let her go. "Listen, Carrie," he said with an obvious struggle. "I think you better go home."

"What?" She stared at him with horror. "I don't want to," she said stubbornly.

"Well, if you stay, we'll make love . . . and I think . . . it probably wouldn't be a good thing."

"Are you afraid you'd be taking advantage of me?" she said, hating this conversation beyond anything.

"Yes."

"That's stupid."

He looked at her for a long moment, as though the

conversation were difficult for him too. "You might fall in love with me," he said. "I'm afraid—"

"So?" She wished she didn't sound so belligerent, but couldn't help herself. "I know you're not in love with me," she said. "You don't have to be."

"Look, it's a tremendous mishmash," he said. "I'm very fond of you. I'm attracted to you. I just don't want you to feel—"

"Let's just do it!" she burst out, almost in anguish. "We can talk about it later."

Justin hesitated. Then, "Okay," he said quietly.

The bedroom was dark and messy, as it always was. Justin took off his clothes. He did this casually, as though he had done it hundreds of times in Caroline's presence before. Caroline watched him. She didn't know if she was supposed to take her own clothes off or what. Then Justin, naked, began helping her off with her sweater. He eased her jeans down over her hips.

"Where did you find such a lovely body?" he said when she was naked.

Caroline didn't know what to answer to that. Her heart was beating so loudly she had trouble hearing what Justin was saying.

"We don't have to do it, if you don't want," Justin said. "We'll just do what you want."

"Okay," Caroline said.

"Don't be scared, Carrie."

"I'm not," she lied.

She was glad he didn't know, she *thought* he didn't know, not only that she had never slept with anyone, but that she had never done *anything* with anyone, except a few attempts at kisses by boys on dates. She let him caress her body and kiss her and felt as though she were on a roller coaster that was moving forward at its own inexorable speed; she trusted him completely.

"Do you want me to?" Justin asked finally.

Caroline nodded, unable to speak.

"Are you ready?"

She wasn't sure if he meant psychologically or physically. "How do I know?" she said.

When he was inside her, she felt a sense of triumph, as though finally they were equals. She had gotten him here, she had seduced him, so it seemed to her. And now he couldn't go back, he would have to love her. She was sure, based on nothing at all, that he was loving her, that as they moved together it was more than fucking. She let her hands move over his body, feeling amazingly reckless, almost drunk.

"Darling," he said; he had called her his darling.

"I love you," she admitted, hoping he wouldn't mind—it was too late for him to mind!

"Carrie, are you close?"

Her mind was so blurred that his words didn't mean anything to her; they seemed to come at her from a great distance, as though in some foreign language. She opened her eyes and saw his face so near. "It's all right," she said. "Go ahead."

Even without coming, the feeling of him as he came made her almost weak with joy. His body was glazed with sweat. She hugged him close to her, fiercely, wanting him never to withdraw, to stay in her forever.

"Did it hurt?" he asked.

"No," Caroline said, because she knew she couldn't explain that it had but yet hadn't.

He took her in his arms. "You're so sweet, Carrie."

Caroline had hoped he would say something about her being sexy, not about her being sweet. But since he said it in a positive way, as though he thought being sweet was something good, she didn't feel too bad. She had been afraid he might roll over and go to sleep, but he kept her in his arms and kissed her near her ear. Did he do that because he always did it or because he knew she would like it?

"Who were the people you brought home?" she said, an attack of retroactive jealousy sneaking up on her.

"Oh . . . Various women."

"Were you in love with them?"

"Not especially."

"Why did you do it, then?"

"I guess my pride was wounded by what she was doing and I wanted to retaliate. . . . I mean, they *were* women I found attractive; it just wasn't . . . a kind of grand passion."

Caroline didn't know how she felt about this. She knew she would have been still more jealous if they had been grand passions, but in another way she didn't like the idea that he had done this with women he didn't care for especially, that he was *capable* of doing that. She wished he had slept with only one person other than her and that person had been Ariella. Maybe because she knew her, it made it less threatening.

"Did you not even sleep with Ariella before you were married?"

"Oh, we did a couple of times just before . . . a trial run. . . . Carrie?"

"What?"

"Do you—do you have any—do you use any form of birth control?"

"I never had to before."

"Well, maybe you should. . . . Would you mind going to a doctor and getting something?"

Her heart leaped. Was he implying they would do it again? She tried to sound detached and calm, as though it were a purely theoretical discussion. "Do you think the Pill's safe?" she asked.

"Why don't you ask your doctor?"

The doctor Caroline went to was a woman, Dr. Eichhorn. She had raised the topic of contraception several times, to Caroline's chagrin. She knew it would be embarrassing to go and see her just for that purpose.

"It's not really fair, I know," Justin said, "for the woman to have to be the one responsible . . . but there aren't any good methods by which the man can do it, except sterilization, and I don't think I would want that."

His calling her, indirectly, a woman thrilled her. She felt at least ten years older than she had an hour earlier. As for it not being fair, it seemed to her it was more than fair. There had to be risks and dangers—otherwise it wouldn't make sense.

"How did you find it?" he asked softly. "Was it disappointing?"

Caroline shook her head. She would never have told him what it had been like, not in a million years. He would think she was a romantic idiot. If only he hadn't heard her say she loved him! Why had she said that? "It was interesting," she said gravely after a moment's thought.

"Only interesting?" She knew he was teasing her.

"Well, it was good," she expanded guardedly. She knew it was impossible, but she wanted him to say that for him it had been wonderful, different from all those other times with those other women that he had found "attractive," different from the way it had been with his wife. "Did *you* like it?" was what she ended up saying.

"Like doesn't seem the right word somehow."

"Is it okay— Did you mind that I'm a virgin, that I was?" she corrected herself.

"I would have been surprised if you weren't."

"Why?"

"Well, you just seem— You don't have a very worldly air."

"I don't?" She couldn't help sounding disappointed.

"I think it's probably better to grow up slowly. . . .
Am I wrong? Have you gone out a lot?"

"No," she admitted.

"I feel flattered—that you chose me," he said.

This astounded her. She had never thought of herself
as having chosen him. It made her seem so powerful! "Do
you think Noah will mind?" she asked suddenly.

"Because he's in love with you?"

Caroline laughed. "He's not in love with me!"

"Of course he is!"

"I didn't mean that. . . . I mean, just, well, because he
wouldn't be used to it if I stayed over."

"I think kids take things in their own way. Ariella had
a friend who was having her lovers sleep over and she
had this eleven-year-old daughter. It turned out the
daughter just thought her mother was literally sleeping
with all these men, that is resting in the same bed
throughout the night."

"I just wouldn't want to upset him," Caroline said
softly.

"Well, of course not. I wouldn't either. . . . Look, I've
given so much thought to Noah and how he'll react to everything, maybe *too* much. I don't think this would harm
him. . . . But Carrie?" His voice had a more anxious
tone.

"What?"

"Will you promise me not to mention this to anyone
else? Not to your mother, even?"

"My mother!" Caroline thought how her mother was
the very last person she would mention this to.

"Well, not even to Maggie, then . . . because, well, I
don't want to be paranoid, but if anyone were to find out
about this at school, I don't think it would go over very
well."

"I won't tell anyone," she promised.

"And maybe, well, this may seem unduly cautious, but

104

maybe you shouldn't come up and talk to me at school. We can speak on the phone."

Caroline thought of the song from *Oklahoma* which their class had put on last year about all the things the woman was supposed not to do or people would know she was in love. Don't sigh and gaze at me. She forgot all the other things.

"It's not that I want to create some tremendous mystery about this . . . but I think we have to be practical."

"Sure," Caroline said. She had not thought beyond this afternoon. The idea that they would become lovers, that she would have a right to hold him, touch him, kiss him, that they would lie in this bed together not just once but many times, was a dazzling thought.

He kissed her. "I'm going to shower. . . . Do you want to too?"

"Not right now."

Caroline lay in bed, looking around the room. She remembered the day she and Maggie had come to deliver the papers and how she had looked at the books and Justin had said, "What is this, the Gestapo?" How strange if someone had said to her then: In three months you'll be lying in this bed. How disbelieving she would have been! And she thought of how awkward she had felt watching TV with Noah, and wondered if it had been due to some premonition. All the things that had happened, all the casual conversations in the kitchen, the night they had gone to see *Who's Afraid of Virginia Woolf?*, all those things now struck her in retrospect as having been part of some divine plan. Even her deciding to get a new bathrobe. She had never thought, not even for a minute: I will need a new bathrobe because I might be going to bed with Justin. And if anyone had suggested such a thing to her a week ago, she would have felt angry and embarrassed. But now even the new bathrobe seemed part of the plan. Even the snow. Even Handel's *Water Music*.

It was still snowing out, or perhaps hailing. Caroline pulled the comforter up to her neck and lay comfortably, sleepily, in bed. The sound of the snow hitting the air conditioner blended with the sound of Justin taking a shower and made a soft, roaring sound, like the ocean. Lying there, trying to keep from falling asleep, Caroline decided that this was the happiest day of her life.

6

Maggie had changed her mind. All week, as she had expected, she'd felt excited at the thought that by the end of Saturday evening she would no longer be a virgin. But by the end of the week the thrill of saying to herself, "This is the last time I will do this as a virgin," had worn off. More than that, she had now come full circle and decided they should simply have gone ahead and done it the week before, contraceptives or not.

It now seemed too planned out. It was certain, Maggie decided gloomily, setting the table—Todd was coming to dinner with her and her father—to throw a pall on things. She had already inserted her diaphragm thinking that when the moment came she might be too nervous to get it in right. Even now she wasn't quite sure. That very evening she had put it in and taken it out half a dozen times, like a woman rearranging her hairdo before deciding it looked best the way she had done it the first time. She wondered if you were supposed to feel it. She was acutely aware of it inside her and wondered if that meant it was not where it was supposed to be. They said that if a man felt it, he didn't like the feeling. Well, that would be Todd's problem; she had enough to worry about.

Her father was in the kitchen trimming the steak. Some years after Maggie's mother's death, Maggie and her father had had a confrontation on the subject of cooking. For five years they had had an excellent housekeeper, but she had finally quit to take care of her aged mother. After that there had been several unsatisfactory attempts at housekeepers, until finally they both decided it was easier to have no one. A young man named Jonas came once a month to go over the rugs and do the windows. Maggie's father said it eased his liberal conscious to have a strapping young man doing windows instead of an ancient, frail lady, like the one they had had who used to save old tea bags to use a second or even a third time. But about cooking they had a problem. They both loved to eat and they were both terrible cooks. Maggie's mother had been an excellent cook and so had their former housekeeper. For years Maggie's father had gone around saying that anyone could learn to cook, it was just a matter of following a recipe. But over the last few years that maxim, like many others, had bitten the dust. Finally it was agreed that Maggie's father would do steak and Maggie would do hamburgers, that on Sunday they would send out for Chinese food, and that when they both couldn't take it any longer they could eat out at a neighborhood restaurant. Tonight was a steak night; Maggie was responsible for the potatoes and the salad.

Both Maggie and her father had an attraction for gadgets—their kitchen was a store house of Hammacher Schlemmer bargains. Whenever he protested about the corn holders she had bought, she could retaliate by bringing up the stainless steel apple corer. If she suggested disposing of the device that squeezed lemon juice without getting the seeds on your plate, he could counter with the egg separator which was never used because there never seemed to be any need to separate eggs.

At seven o'clock Todd appeared wearing a suit. Maggie looked at him, alarmed. Her only attempt at looking different had been to shower and put on a clean pair of overalls and turtleneck. He was even wearing a tie!

"Uh, come on in," she mumbled, feeling it wouldn't be polite to say something negative about his suit and tie, though, in fact, she hated suits and ties and felt no man should ever wear them under any circumstances.

"I'm very glad to meet you," Maggie's father said, coming out to greet Todd.

For the next half hour he took Todd around the apartment, giving him the requisite tour of all the African art objects, what tribes they had come from, their ritual uses. Maggie, who had heard this lecture more times than she cared to remember, went into the kitchen.

The steak was thick and tender; the potatoes were just right. Maggie's father opened a bottle of red wine.

However, what started off as an amiable, friendly dinner soon disintegrated into an argument.

They began discussing the role of John F. Kennedy in history. Would history remember him as a good president, a bad president, or, possibly, a great president? They started off with the fact that a new revelation about Kennedy's sex life had appeared in the paper.

"Now *that* I completely discount," Maggie's father said. "As they say, I'd rather have a president who was screwing women than screwing the country . . . but I can never forgive him for getting us into Vietnam."

Todd's opinion was that getting into Vietnam, which he agreed had been a bad thing, had had a kind of historical inevitability about it. It was based on the attitude of Americans toward Asia, toward Asiatic peoples.

"Now there's where we part company," Maggie's father said. "A president's role is to lead, to educate, not to give in to every idiot belief of the citizens of this crazed country."

But Todd, emptying his third glass of wine, didn't give way. With the same steady, calm persistence with which he had demolished Maggie's arguments at the debate, he held his own against Maggie's father. It suddenly struck Maggie that something about what was happening here was being done for her benefit. Some attempt to show her who was the better man was going on. She didn't feel at all flattered; she felt horrified. How unfortunate that instead of taking part in the argument she had been sitting quietly. Her not taking part had put her in the position of

The Woman, the silent, admiring audience, and if there was one role in which Maggie could not bear, even for an instant, to think of herself, it was the silent, admiring audience.

"This is very good wine," Todd said, pouring himself another glass. Maggie looked at him warily. She wondered if he was getting drunk.

"*I* think so," Maggie's father agreed. He seemed invigorated by the argument. "At first it struck me as a little light, but when you get used to it . . . I really came on a find the other day, though. . . ." And he proceeded to lead Todd into the sewing room and show him a new case of another kind of red wine. "I'd like you to try this one," he said. "I'd be curious how you find it compares."

"Daddy, we've finished eating," Maggie said. "We don't need another bottle."

"Nonsense! Of course we do. . . . I have a very fine brie that cries out for a bit of Bordeaux to go with it." He opened the new bottle as Maggie brought in the cheese and grapes.

When he finally left for Nina's, Maggie decided that she was as completely uninterested in making love as any person could possibly be. She felt mad at Todd for actually being interested in all her father's theories about art, about politics, about wine. It wasn't fair! Here when *he* held forth, just because he was fifty, just because he was a psychiatrist, everyone thought it was terrific. When *she* held forth, everyone said she was dogmatic.

Todd smiled at her. He had taken off his jacket and tie. "Hi."

"Are you drunk?" Maggie said suspiciously.

"I'm pleasantly high," he confessed.

They walked toward her room. "Your father is an interesting person," Todd said. "You and he seem to have a curious relationship."

"What's so curious about it?" Maggie demanded defensively.

"Well, it reminds me in a way of this play we read last term in school, *The Tempest*. He reminds me of Prospero and you remind me of—what was her name?"

"Miranda," Maggie supplied.

"That's right. . . . The whole ambience, the two of you living alone together in this peculiarly close way."

"It's *not* peculiar!" Maggie said. "Anyway, Miranda is such an idiot." Maggie and her English teacher at school had spent three years in an unsuccessful interchange about Shakespeare's plays. It was Maggie's opinion that Shakespeare's heroines, from Ophelia to Miranda to Cordelia, were all either benighted ingenues who couldn't think their way out of a paper bag *or* crazed maniacs like Lady Macbeth. Her teacher had said over and over that Maggie was missing some of the subtlety of Shakespeare's characterization, but Maggie felt this was utterly untrue. Everyone else felt they had to bow down when the name Shakespeare was uttered. Only she, like the child in "The Emperor's New Clothes," had the honesty to see the truth.

"I didn't mean you were *like* Miranda," Todd said soothingly. "I just meant—"

"No, I know," Maggie said.

They were in her room. "The other thing which is—well—an interesting discrepancy," Todd said, "is the contrast between your father's radical views and the . . . style in which you live."

"Just because he has money doesn't mean he has to do some dumb thing like join the Republican party!"

"I didn't say he should join the Republican party. . . . I just said it was an interesting discrepancy."

Maggie was in no mood to discuss interesting discrepancies. She sat on the floor and looked at Todd. He sat down beside her. "What shall we take off this time?" he asked with a grin.

"Oh, let's just take *everything* off," Maggie said gloomily. "We might as well get it over with." She flung her clothes in a heap on the floor. In a rare attempt at neatness she had stuffed various things under the bed and in the closet. She had even changed the sheets. She lay down, watching Todd, who was not in such a hurry and who seemed to have a curious desire to hang rather than fling his clothes.

He lay down next to her. "Maggie . . . relax."

"I *am* relaxed!"

He leaned over to kiss her. After that things moved forward a lot faster than Maggie had expected.

"Okay, let's do it," she said finally. An object, which she assumed to be his penis, nudged its way forward slowly and somewhat tentatively into her vagina. "Is it all the way in?" Maggie asked after a moment.

"I *think* so," said Todd.

"But it doesn't hurt," Maggie said. "Maybe it's not in the right place."

"I don't think there are that many places it can go," Todd said.

"Don't you know?" Maggie said.

"Well, I've never done it before, so—"

"You haven't?" Maggie's eyes flew open.

"No," he admitted, surprised at her surprise.

"But that's awful!" Maggie said. "*One* of us should have done it before. We won't know if we're doing it the right way."

"I think between the two of us we can figure it out," Todd said dryly.

Maggie hoped that was true. She closed her eyes and let him proceed. She kept waiting for it to hurt. She had intended to pinch her arm as she did at the dentist to be able to stand what she had assumed would be the excruciating pain. But at most there was a mild discomfort, not even equivalent to having her teeth cleaned. She was so struck by this that she forgot to do much else. Then, coming to, she began stroking Todd's back and buttocks, which felt very smooth.

"Maggie," Todd said, "the thing is, I just don't know if I can hold back much longer."

"Okay," Maggie said. "Just go ahead."

"Is that okay? You haven't had an orgasm, have you?"

"You're not supposed to the first time," Maggie said. "Then you wouldn't have anything to look forward to."

She was impressed by the sounds of genuine passion he made as he came, even if he sounded, in some indefinable way, a little like a wooden porch chair, creaking. When he withdrew she looked at him suspiciously. "You've really never done this before?" she said.

"Uh-uh."

"Then how come you knew exactly what to do?"

"I don't think it's all that complicated," he said.

"Was it like what you expected?" Maggie said, eager to analyze it.

"It was good," Todd said simply.

That didn't satisfy Maggie. "No, but I mean compared to what you expected, what was it like?"

He smiled. "I don't think I tend to analyze things as much as you do, Maggie. Why not accept it for what it is? A good thing which gives every sign of becoming better."

Maggie sighed. "I *do* analyze things too much," she said. "Maybe I'll wreck it that way."

"You won't wreck it," Todd assured her.

"I hope not." Suddenly she felt more cheerful. "But you know what was really weird—it didn't hurt!"

"Is it supposed to?"

"Yes! Horribly." She looked down at the sheets. "There wasn't even any blood."

"Should there have been?"

She was amazed at his ignorance. "In all the books I've read girls bleed like stuck *pigs* after doing it the first time!"

"I'm glad *I* didn't read any of those books," Todd said uneasily. "Anyway, isn't it good that it *wasn't* painful or bloody?"

"Definitely," Maggie said. "I wonder why in books they make it sound so awful, always talking about thrusting and things like that."

"The books I've read make it sound pretty nice," Todd said.

Maggie was beginning to get excited, thinking about it. "Wouldn't it be terrific if it turned out we were really good at it?" she said.

"What do you mean—good at it?"

"I mean, well, if we really liked it."

"Well, sure," said Todd, as though the opposite possibility had never occurred to him.

"Hey, I'm starving. Do you feel hungry?"

"Sure."

"You know what I feel like having?" Maggie said, leaping up. "A hot fudge sundae!"

They went into the kitchen and Maggie rummaged around for a double boiler. "I hope we have vanilla ice cream," she said, checking the freezer. "Actually it's ice milk because my father has this cholesterol thing. . . . Is that okay?"

"Fine by me."

"We have a terrific kind of syrup," she said, searching for the bottle. In the kitchen, amidst the syrups and jams, her father kept Valium and Librium in case a patient needed some immediately. "It's bittersweet. I think that's the best. . . . We may have a problem with the cream, though. Daddy doesn't use cream in his coffee anymore. He says it's too fattening. . . . No, hey we do have it. That was smart of me."

"I'll whip it," Todd said. "Do you have a beater?"

While he whipped the cream, Maggie heated up the chocolate sauce. "I wonder if sex makes you hungry," she said reflectively, watching the syrup start to bubble. "Of course, hot fudge sundaes are always good."

"It probably does burn up a lot of energy," Todd said.

"Does it? . . . Maybe for the man. . . . I don't see how a woman can burn up that much just lying there."

"Well, you can burn up psychic energy."

"Can you? Yeah, I guess." She brought the syrup over and poured it over the ice cream. On top of the whipped cream she put a maraschino cherry on each portion.

"This is good," Todd said, delving in.

"I feel so sorry for Daddy," Maggie confessed. She popped the cherry into her mouth. "He's always on a diet! If he'd just lose weight once and for all, then he could go back to eating things like heavy cream."

"He *does* smoke a lot," Todd observed. "I would think as a doctor—"

"*And* as a psychiatrist," Maggie supplied. "Yeah, well, he says since he sits all day, he has to have something to do. . . . I guess that's something of a rationalization. Nina smokes a lot too. They're both always trying to give it up and then breaking down again. Frankly, I don't think they'll *ever* give it up. . . . He can't even play tennis anymore, he puffs so much!"

"Did he use to?"

"Yeah, he was pretty good. . . . We used to play together till I started to beat him. We used to play doubles too." She sighed and leaned back. Every bit of the hot fudge sundae had disappeared. "I'm lucky I'm tall," she said.

"In what way?"

"Well, I can eat more. . . . I don't think life would be worth living without hot fudge sundaes and lox and heavy cream and things like that—do you?"

"I don't know if I'd go *that* far, but I would miss those things."

She was staring at him almost in a trance. "I can't get over your not ever having done it before!"

"Why can't you?"

"Well, I guess I just assumed you had. You seemed so self-assured."

"I did?" He looked pleased.

"I'm glad I didn't know before tonight, though. Before it might have bothered me, but now I'm sort of glad. I mean, it's like we're starting from the same place. I think that's good." She was silent for a moment. "Todd, there's something I should tell you . . . but it's really terrible, I mean, for what it reveals about my character."

"What is it?"

"That movie we saw that first night. I lied. It really *did* make me horny."

"Well, me too," he said, as though this was to be taken for granted.

"But you said you didn't think it was sexy!"

"I didn't want you to think I was a male chauvinist."

"That's awful, though!" Maggie said indignantly. "You mean you were just pretending? *Are* you a male chauvinist?" She felt as though she had unwittingly slept with a supporter of George Wallace.

"Of course I am," he said teasingly.

"Todd! Please don't joke about that. . . . I'll never sleep with you again if you are."

"I'm not," he said promptly.

"Are you just saying that so I will?"

"Maggie, come on. . . . Do I really seem like a male chauvinist to you?"

"No, but maybe you've just been putting on a big act to get me into bed with you. Maybe you psyched me out and thought, That's the way I have to act to get her."

"Well, let's put it this way: I wasn't unaware of what

your convictions were . . . but I do think I'm a feminist. . . . And I just thought you were beautiful."

"I'm not beautiful!" Maggie said. "Seriously. Todd, I don't want us to get off on the wrong foot. Will you promise me never to lie about anything? Even the way I look?"

"Maggie, I do think you're beautiful. . . . That wasn't a lie."

She decided not to argue with him. They went back to her room.

They got into bed together and lay side by side in the dark. In about five minutes Todd was asleep. Maggie was too excited to fall asleep. She felt ecstatic. She felt like leaping around in the apartment. Finally she decided to get up and listen to music in her father's study, where it wouldn't awaken Todd. She put on a bathrobe and went quietly down the hall into the study. She put some Bob Dylan records on and lay back in the reclining chair, listening. She liked listening to music in the dark. It was like eating in the dark—it made it seem special.

She was surprised when, at two o'clock, her father came home, the Sunday *Times* under one arm.

"Mags! What are you doing up?" he said.

"I couldn't get to sleep," she said. She felt a little awkward. Not that she thought he'd object to Todd being there, but she had just assumed he would stay at Nina's and not return until the following afternoon. "How come you didn't stay at Nina's?" she asked.

"She has to visit some friends early tomorrow," he said. He started for the kitchen.

"Daddy . . . Todd and I had some hot fudge sundaes and we didn't do the dishes. We'll do them in the morning, is that okay?"

She felt as though by this indirect statement she was informing him that Todd was still there. "That's fine by me," he said. "I liked him, Maggie. That was an interesting discussion we had. So, he'll be here in the morning?"

"I think so," Maggie said.

"Good. There are a few extra points I thought of later this evening that I wanted to make." He disappeared into the kitchen.

Maggie knew he would sit over a glass of wine and read the Sunday paper. She felt it was cheating to read the Sunday paper on Saturday night.

She wondered, for the first time in her life, if her parents had been happy together. She hoped they had. She knew they hadn't had the kind of relationship Todd's parents seemed to have. Her mother had had her sphere, which had included the house and Maggie, and her father had had his sphere, which included his work. But there had never been a sense that these were equal spheres. Her mother would always say, if she brought a friend home from school, "Be quiet, your father's with a patient," as though what went on behind the white soundproof doors were some occult mystery only the gods on Mount Olympus were privy to. Whereas her father, with his "anyone can cook" remarks, had always seemed to her to take a kind of affectionate but disparaging tone toward her mother. Well, I hope they loved each other, Maggie thought, in some way.

When she returned to her bedroom, Todd was still sleeping. He slept on his back, one arm thrown out to one side. He looked beautiful. Maggie decided her father had been wrong—naked men were beautiful. She crawled in beside Todd and in a little while fell asleep herself.

In the morning Todd wanted to have breakfast before they made love again. He said he needed food for strength. Maggie would have liked to do it before breakfast, but she decided if she had waited over seventeen years to do it at all, she could wait another half an hour.

"What do you eat for breakfast?" she asked when they were in the kitchen. The dirty dishes of the night before were still there.

"Well, on Sunday we usually have scrambled eggs and bacon and toast," he said.

Maggie frowned. "With bacon you're out of luck. We probably have eggs, though."

"Let me make it the way Dad does, with cottage cheese—do you have any?"

It turned out they did. Maggie made coffee and toast and set out black currant jelly, her favorite, on the table. "There's a store I go to on Lexington that has two hundred kinds of jam," she said, "and almost as many kinds of honey. I thought I would try every kind of honey, but they taste pretty much the same. They're all good though."

Before making love again, they showered together. Freshly clean, they fell back into bed.

"I just had a great idea," Maggie said.

"Yeah?"

"I think maybe each time we should do it a different way. Then, when we've tried *all* the ways, we can decide which ones we like best. They say you can get in a rut if you just keep doing it the same way over and over."

"Well . . . but we've only done it this way once," Todd reminded her.

"That's true." Maggie thought a moment. "You think we ought to just sort of concentrate on one or two until we really know them well and then go on to the others? Like swimming?"

"Swimming?"

"Well, you know, when you're learning to swim, first you learn the breast stroke, then the crawl, then diving. But, like, you master one before you go on to the next. Is that what you think?"

"I think we should just do whatever we feel like," Todd said.

This time Maggie decided to concentrate more. It seemed to her that the first time she had spent the whole time being surprised it didn't hurt. Now she tried moving around more. She stretched her knees up so the soles of her feet were resting on Todd's buttocks. She explored his back and discovered he had a small hairless patch at the very bottom of his spine which was very soft and smooth, like an Achilles' heel. She didn't have an orgasm this time either, but it seemed to her she started to. "Did you mind my diaphragm?" she asked. She had forgotten all about it.

"Mind in what way?"

"Well, feel it."

"Not especially. . . . I think it's nice of you to have one. . . . I mean, they say it's pleasanter for the man."

"Pleasanter than the pill?"

"No, pleasanter than condoms."

"Oh . . . those," Maggie said. "They sound awful. . . . Well, I guess I'll go on the pill now."

"I don't think you should," Todd said.

"Why not?"

"Well, I don't think it's safe. There've been all those reports."

"Yeah, but those are just people with histories of blood clots and women over forty."

"I wouldn't take a chance," Todd said.

"What's it to you, anyway?" Maggie said offhandedly. "I mean, so I die of a blood clot at forty-two?"

He looked pained. "Maggie, why do you say things like that?"

"Like what?"

"Like that I shouldn't care what happens to you. You sound so cynical."

"I do?" Maggie had just thought she was being practical.

"Of course I care what happens to you," he said. "How could I not care?"

"You mean, because I'm the first person you've slept with?"

"Because I love you."

Maggie stared at him in horror. "You can't love me!" she said. "We've only known each other for a little while."

"Why do you look so horrified?"

"I don't know," she admitted.

"You're a funny girl."

"I *am*," Maggie said. "Really, Todd, I'm weird. I mean, you just don't know me."

"I think I know you pretty well."

"No, I'm much weirder than I *seem*, even. . . . You better hold off about deciding you love me till you know me better."

"Do you feel it ties you down somehow?"

"I don't know. It just makes me nervous. . . . Anyway, we can still sleep together. I don't think you have to love someone to sleep with them."

"No, but it's nicer that way," he said wistfully.

"I thought that was just what they said."

"Well, maybe they say it because there's some truth in it. . . . Maybe I'm more of a romantic than you."

Maggie looked at him, perplexed. Something about the conversation made her uneasy. "Why don't we play chess?" she said.

"Okay." He smiled at her. "Don't worry, Maggie— being in love isn't supposed to be so bad."

"Yes, it *is*!" she said. "It's supposed to be awful!"

"Where did you get that? From another of those books?"

"Todd, seriously . . . it makes people miserable; it does. I'm not joking."

"There's nothing to be said for it at all, huh?"

"Not compared to all the bad things." She got out the chess board. For her twelfth birthday her father had bought her this set of carved red and white pieces. Naked, they started to play.

"Daddy should be getting up soon," Maggie mused.

"I thought he was sleeping at Nina's."

"No, he came home last night."

"Well, then, shouldn't we—?" He indicated their naked bodies.

"Oh no, he never comes into my room. It's okay." She stared at him pensively. "You know, I think Daddy's wrong," she said.

"About the Vietnam War?"

"About men's bodies . . . I think they *are* beautiful."

"Well, women's bodies have a certain *intrinsic* beauty," Todd said.

"You sound just like him!" Maggie said. "No, I can see—I mean, I think breasts *are* nice . . . but men have very nice behinds and backs and legs."

"Anything else?" Todd said, grinning.

"Well, let's face it," Maggie said, "penises do take some getting used to, but they're not as bad as I expected." She continued staring at him dreamily. "When I was little, I always used to wonder what the point of pubic hair was, but now I think it's sort of nice."

"It's your move, Maggie."

She took his knight with her bishop. "What's odd is how they always say penises are hard . . . when really they're soft."

"I think that's like the blind men and the elephant," Todd said.

"In what way?"

"Well, you mean it *feels* soft, the skin . . . whereas when they say it's hard, they're referring to it in another context!"

"They are, huh? . . . Look at that, isn't that strange?

Just because we were talking about him, he perked up. Does that always happen?"

"He doesn't get talked about that much. . . . Do you want to call it a draw?"

"I don't really . . . but I will."

When they came into the kitchen an hour later, Maggie's father was preparing his breakfast. He was in his undershirt, slacks, and slippers. On a large stainless steel tray he was arranging radishes, herring, a fresh roll, some scallions, and a container of margarine. "There's fresh coffee," he said, "if you kids want any."

"You make it too strong," Maggie said.

"Coffee *has* to be strong. . . . By the way, Mags, I read that paper you left for me. Very interesting, very interesting indeed. . . . Has she told you about this project she's working on?" he asked Todd.

Todd shook his head.

"Well, you know last year Maggie did this project which won a nationwide prize . . . and this year her science teacher, Justin, has her doing some experiments as a special project. Justin once said to me he felt that if he ever got another student like Maggie in his entire experience of teaching, he'd be amazed."

"Daddy, will you cut it out?" Maggie said.

"Why should I cut it out?" He appealed to Todd. "I'm quoting the simple and objective truth."

"Go on, take your stuff into the living room," Maggie said, shooing him away.

"Look at that," Maggie's father said, mock aggrieved. "Will you look at how she treats her aged father? I ask you—is that kind?"

"Daddy!" Maggie said warningly.

After he had left, Todd said, "I'd like to see that paper sometime."

"Oh sure," Maggie said offhandedly.

"I showed you my drawings," he reminded her.

"Who posed yesterday?" Maggie said.

"At the class? I did, actually."

It had only recently occurred to Maggie that since everyone in the class posed, Todd must also. She didn't care for the idea at all. All those repressed, horny women staring at his body for three hours! "Don't you feel funny?" she said.

"At what?"

"Having them stare at you . . . all those women."

"Well, it's funny . . . I think it's like what Lindsay said about coed dorms. She said the first time she went into the bathroom and saw a boy peeing, she almost fell over, but the fiftieth time, she didn't even notice."

"As long as none of them propositions you," Maggie warned.

"Tia's thirty-six," he said.

"So? Older women like younger men," Maggie said.

"Yeah, but she's married."

"When did that ever stop anyone? . . . Anyway, how about Mimi?"

"I think Mimi's probably frigid," Todd said.

"Just because she has such a gorgeous body?"

"I don't happen to think her body is so gorgeous. . . . No, just because that's how she strikes me."

Maggie was curious. "Do you spend a lot of time thinking about women that way?"

"What way?"

"Like whether they're frigid or not?"

"Well, I occasionally speculate about it."

"What did you think about me? . . . I mean, when we first met?"

He smiled. "I thought you seemed very intense and passionate . . . but I wasn't sure if that extended beyond intellectual matters."

"Did you hope it did?"

"What do you think?"

By late afternoon Todd had to go home. Maggie lay down and took a nap from four to six. When she woke up, it was dark out. She went to call Caroline.

Caroline's mother answered the phone. "No, Carrie's not here, Maggie," she said in her soft voice. "She's at the library."

"But the library's not open on Sunday," Maggie started to say. When these words were about half out of her mouth, the thought occurred to her that maybe Caroline was not at the library, but had just told her mother she was. "Oh, I guess—she's at the—there's one downtown," she stammered.

"I believe that's the one she said she was going to," Caroline's mother said.

"Well, listen, could you have her call me as soon as she comes in? It's important."

"Of course," Caroline's mother said, sounding a little surprised.

Caroline called at seven. "How come you told your mother you were at the library?" Maggie said.

"What did you call about?" Caroline said, not answering that question. "Mother said you said it was important."

"I can't talk about it on the phone—you've got to come over."

"But Maggie, it's freezing out."

"I don't care. Take a cab. . . . You've *got* to come over!"

"Is it that important?"

"Yes!"

Caroline came over by cab. Maggie told her father Caroline was coming. "Ah yes, how is Little Blue Eyes these days?" he said. "I haven't seen her in quite a while."

"Daddy, will you quit calling her Little Blue Eyes? . . . She's not that little and her eyes aren't even blue! They're gray."

"Sometimes I worry about Little Blue Eyes," he said thoughtfully.

"Why? What's there to worry about?"

"Someday she's going to look up at some man with those big eyes and before you can say Jack Robinson, she's going to be knocked up."

Maggie hated the expression "knocked up." "Daddy, will you cut it out? Teen-age girls are not that naive these days, and don't tell me about some dumb patient you once had. Caroline knows all about sex, as much as anyone."

"I like Caroline, Mags, I do. . . . The way she blushes and casts down those long eyelashes on her cheek. She's a real old-fashioned girl."

Maggie sighed. Like all their arguments, this one was getting nowhere. When Caroline did arrive, she took her immediately into her room and closed the door firmly. Sometimes she wished her bedroom, like her father's office, was soundproof.

"So, what is it?" Caroline said. Her cheeks were pink from the cold. She looked pretty.

"We did it!" Maggie exulted.

"Who? Did what?"

"Todd and me! We slept together. . . . And Carrie, it was great! It really was."

"That's nice," Caroline said with a weak smile.

Maggie was disappointed, even hurt. She had expected more of a reaction than that. "Well, I just thought I'd tell you," she said.

Caroline frowned. "I'm sorry, Maggie. . . . I just—I just—" And then, to Maggie's horror and amazement, Caroline burst into tears.

Maggie patted her helplessly on the shoulder. "Don't cry, Carrie—please don't." She wondered if Caroline was jealous about her having slept with Todd. "You'll do it sometime too," she said.

"I—I have done it," Caroline gasped.

Maggie's eyes opened wide. "Who with? I mean, with whom?" she stammered, grammar momentarily deserting her.

Caroline tried to stop crying long enough to talk. "With Justin," she whispered.

Maggie sat back. For once she was at a loss for words. "Oh . . . wow," she said finally.

"Please don't tell anyone, Maggie," Caroline begged. "I wasn't supposed to tell you, even. Okay? Not even your father or Todd?"

"Okay," Maggie said. "But—what about his wife?"

"They're getting divorced . . . not because of me. They were just— That's just how it happened."

Maggie sighed. "Oh, dear," she said, but a second later Caroline was off again, sobbing onto Maggie's shoulder. "Listen, Carrie, don't feel bad, really. It'll work out," she said. She wasn't at all sure what she meant by "work out," but she wanted to make Caroline feel better. "Everything'll be okay. I'm sure it will."

7

"Well, I think this is enough science for one morning," Gordon Troupe said, coming over to where Caroline had been standing quietly in one corner of the laboratory. Maggie, Justin, and Todd were behind him, talking animatedly about something that Caroline knew she wouldn't be able to understand. This weekend trip had been Justin's idea. He had wanted to take Maggie up to Cornell and have her meet Gordon Troupe, the professor under whom he had begun getting his doctorate right after college. Now that he and Caroline had been sleeping together for two months, Justin seemed less nervous about letting people know about their relationship. He was still very strict about their conduct toward one another at school, but he had decided Maggie could be trusted.

The idea of a whole weekend sounded nice to Caroline, and she was relieved that her mother, who thought she and Maggie were going up alone, had voiced no suspicions. But the trouble was that all the talk so far, since they had arrived Friday night, had been about science. To Caroline, science was like a foreign language. Even when Justin explained the simplest concepts like a cell or a gene—concepts Noah, at seven, seemed to have no problem in grasping—no matter how many diagrams were drawn, no matter how simple the language used to explain the ideas, none of it made sense to her. In spite of herself, she felt jealous of Maggie.

Maggie was glowing this weekend, aware of her unequivocal status as "the star." Caroline had never questioned Maggie's position as the intellectual superior of the two of them. Deep down, though, she felt that it just wasn't possible to judge artistic talent in the same objective way you could judge scientific ability. How would Picasso or Mary Cassat have done on college boards, and what difference did *that* make? Still, seeing all these men—Justin, Todd, Gordon Troupe—buzzing around Maggie, and seeing Maggie effortlessly holding her own, talking about concepts Caroline knew she couldn't have mastered if someone had held a gun to her head, all of this made her feel angry and sad in about equal proportions.

"There's a nice Italian place near here," Gordon Troupe said. "Do you like Italian food, Caroline?"

She felt he was bending over backward to be nice to her. "Yes, I like it," she said politely.

At dinner, despite the vow to stop talking about science, it kept weaving into the conversation. Caroline took small bites, not feeling at all hungry. She tried to drink a whole glass of wine, hoping it would make her feel more relaxed.

"Are you—I'm sorry, I forget—applying to Cornell too?" Gordon Troupe asked her.

"No, I'm, uh, going to college in the city," Caroline said.

"Barnard?"

"No, Parsons. . . . I applied to Barnard too, though."

"Yes, well, Osiah Spector is at Barnard. He used to be here. He's head of the biochemistry department."

"I'm not that interested in science," Caroline admitted.

"Oh, take a course with Osiah, though. He's a remarkable teacher. I've never seen anyone like him for making the most abtruse concepts as clear as glass. I wish *I* had that gift."

Caroline knew she would never take a course with Osiah Spector because she would get into Parsons. Why should she even be interested in science? Why was it so important to know anything about cells and genes? They were there and they did whatever they were supposed to do. Justin couldn't understand why she wasn't curious about how the world worked. He, like Maggie, thought that she had hangups about science. She got angry when he suggested this. What did *he* know or care about famous illustrators or rare books, which it happened she loved? But she never accused him of having hangups about it.

After dinner they went to a student hangout where there was dancing. It was crowded and noisy. Gordon Troupe excused himself and said he had to get home; his wife was waiting. Maggie, to Caroline's surprise, said she wanted to dance. She got up with Todd and went out on the packed dance floor. Caroline looked at them with dismay. She had never thought she would live to see the day when Maggie, of all people, would strike her as looking sexy, but she had to admit that this particular evening she did. Maybe it was the effect of her affair with Todd. Maybe it was the fact that, instead of overalls, Maggie was wearing a pair of snug-fitting jeans and a blouse made of patches that were not totally opaque. Maggie was not an especially good dancer, but she leaped and wriggled around with enthusiasm while Todd watched her with a slightly bemused smile on his face.

"Do *you* want to dance, Carrie?" Justin asked.

Caroline shook her head. She was terrible at dancing.

The wine, far from making her relaxed, just made her dizzy and uncomfortable.

When a round of dances had ended, Maggie and Todd came over to them. "Come on, eggheads, on your feet!" Maggie shouted.

Justin stood up. "That's a challenge that has to be met," he said. He stood up to dance with Maggie, and Todd sat down beside Caroline.

"I guess I have to learn to dance," Todd said.

"Don't you know how?"

"Not really. . . . Maggie says she thinks I'd like it if I knew how. I'm not so sure."

Caroline looked at him. She thought Todd was very nice. She really liked him and felt at ease with him. It was hard for her to imagine, though, that he was so fantastic in bed, the way Maggie said he was. Of course, allowances had to be made for Maggie's penchant for exaggeration, but usually Maggie's exaggerations were on the negative side rather than on the positive; there had to be some truth in it.

Todd was nice, but the trouble was, compared to Justin—well, there was just no comparison. This bothered Caroline a lot. If you took any one of Justin's qualities—his looks, his sensitivity, his intelligence—then the discrepancy between him and any other man was simply staggering. But if you took all of those things together, then the difference was so vast as to be alarming. Caroline felt that all women, comparing Justin to their own husbands and boyfriends, must be aware of this and envy her; it made her nervous. She glanced at Justin and Maggie dancing. Maggie was tossing her dark curls around and her eyes were flashing. Justin was a better dancer than Caroline had assumed. She had been hoping he would be terrible.

Todd began talking about something and Caroline pretended to listen. Doing this gave her a chance to keep her eyes glued to his face and not to watch Maggie and Justin. But the quick glimpse of them she had gotten made her feel as though someone had thrown a large black bag over her head. It made her think of Mondays at school. For over a month now she had been staying at Justin's Sunday night, telling her mother she was staying at Maggie's. She had invented some excuse about working on the school yearbook which her mother seemed to believe with ease. Often they would be up half the night making love, and she would feel exhausted at school, after carefully arriving separately from him so no one would suspect anything. She knew her grades didn't matter anymore, so that even if fatigue made her unable to concentrate in class it would have no especially dire results. She would see Justin standing in the hall, laughing or talking to other teachers or students, but if he chanced to glance at her, his face would instantly assume a totally detached, blank expression, as though she were some not-very-bright student whose name he couldn't quite remember. She knew he did it on purpose, but each time he did she felt chilled to the marrow, as though in that expression, that coldness, were some truth about their relationship which was belied by whatever might have happened the night before in bed. A terrible swell of anger and even hatred toward Justin would well up in her, so that once, standing at a window, she had had a sudden desire to smash her hand right through the glass. Even the impulse—having thoughts like that—disturbed her.

The evening passed both quickly and slowly. At times it seemed to Caroline that she had spent her life sitting there, trying not to watch Maggie and Justin. But then suddenly it was after midnight and Justin was suggesting they all return to the college inn where they were staying and go to sleep, since they were to get up early the next morning and see some waterfall.

Back at the hotel room, Caroline sat on the edge of the bed tense with anger. She remembered a conversation she had once with Justin about differences between men and women. He had said that he felt the fact of men being, in most cases, physically stronger than women made some difference. "I mean, face it," he said, "if I wanted, if it ever came to that, I could give you a pretty hard time." At the time she hadn't cared one way or the other, but now she felt a horrible resentment of this fact, which she felt was certainly true in their case. She would have liked so much to fight him physically, to cause him physical pain! The realization of her own helplessness infuriated her.

She had assumed Justin would notice something of her mood, but perhaps because the light was dim or he'd had a little too much to drink, he didn't seem to. He came over and sat beside her, putting his arm around her. "That was a nice place," he said. Then, deliberately, he turned her face toward him and kissed her. It was a long, lingering kiss and before she knew what was happening his tongue was inside her mouth and he was pushing her, half playfully, half roughly, back onto the bed. There were none of the usual prolonged kisses and caresses. Instead, he simply moved her so that she was positioned more squarely in the center of the bed, worked her panty hose down, and entered her immediately. Normally she would have taken his urgency as a mood or a proof of his attraction to her, but now it just seemed a further indication that he was simply playing out his fantasies about Maggie. She was just a stand-in, a convenient substitute. Despite this, she felt herself responding to him against her will. It was ironic. In the beginning of their affair, when they had made love, it had been an effort for her to respond to him physically as much as she felt she should. Now it was the opposite—trying to be cold and detached, she felt her body react in spite of herself, as though it were hooked up to some entirely separate set of connections.

When it was over, he brushed his hand lightly over her hair. "That was good," he said, his voice quiet and affectionate.

After a moment Caroline said, "I wasn't in the mood."

"Weren't you?" He sounded surprised.

"No . . . I didn't feel anything."

"The hell you didn't!"

"I didn't."

By now his voice had turned cold and angry. "Then you've developed into a very convincing actress."

"You just wanted to go to bed with Maggie. . . . You were just using me."

"With Maggie?" He sounded amazed.

Caroline nodded.

"Carrie, how can you— My God, you know how I feel about Maggie. I think she's marvelous, but not in that way. I don't have the least desire to go to bed with Maggie." Then, almost as an afterthought, he said, "Anyway, even if I did, I wouldn't."

That sentence seemed to Caroline to undo everything else. "What do you mean even if you did, you wouldn't?"

"Well, I mean . . . look, everyone has occasional fantasies about members of the opposite sex. That doesn't mean you act on them. That's only human."

It seemed to Caroline it wasn't human at all; it was inhuman.

"You must too," Justin said. "Don't you?"

"No."

"Well, you will," he said. "Look, if anyone should be jealous, it's me."

"You?"

"Of course. . . . I get worried about it. If you're this beautiful at eighteen, Lord knows what you'll look like at twenty-eight. You should have seen Gordon staring at you during dinner. He looked like you could have led him off with a ring through his nose. . . . In any case, I think it's delightful that Maggie's found someone. Seeing the mighty Margaret fallen is a pleasant sight."

"Fallen how?" Caroline asked.

"In love. . . . And, you know, it's fantastic the way he handles her."

Caroline thought "handles" sounded manipulative. "Do you think that's what it is?"

"Oh, maybe it's not deliberate . . . But in any case it seems to work. Maggie's like a porcupine. If you go at her directly, she pokes out all her quills."

"I feel like there are so many things I can't do," Caroline said, talking as much to herself as to him. "I can't understand science, I can't dance. . . ." In the dark her anger had drained away, leaving her limp but sad. She felt as though Maggie had only been part of what was troubling her, the part that it was possible to talk about. The rest, the other fears which seemed to get stronger as they became more involved with each other, she wouldn't have known how to articulate. And she felt, as well, that that side of her might disgust him—that, whatever he said, he wanted partly to see her as the naive, golden-haired adoring schoolgirl, and that there was enough truth in that for it to be convenient for her to hide the rest.

Justin kissed her neck. "What people can do doesn't matter," he said.

"Yes, it does."

"No, it's what they're like, the effect they have on other people. You're so much more responsive to people than Maggie, the way you draw them out."

But that, too, struck her as partly false, the "good listener" who sat patiently as he poured out his troubles with his wife and his marriage. Maybe it had just been a way to trap him.

"Darling, listen, I'm sorry about before."

"No, that's all right."

"I didn't . . . I thought when I kissed you, you seemed—it seemed as though you were in the mood. And you looked so lovely tonight. I guess all evening I kept thinking of our coming back here and—"

"I know," she said quickly, not wanting to talk about it anymore.

"You say you didn't feel anything and yet you seem—I guess I just can't believe it's all an act. That doesn't seem like you."

"Maybe you don't know me that well," she said suddenly.

"Maybe."

And then, as though horrified at the whole evening, she flung her arms around him and held him as close to her as possible. "It isn't an act," she said. "It isn't. I don't know why I said that."

"Sweetheart." He held her tightly, as though to calm her. And she let herself be calmed.

A few weeks later she and Justin met his eldest brother, Chester, for dinner.

"He's a little stuffy," Justin said. "But he's a good person. You'll like him. . . . He and Ariella never hit it off at all."

"Why not?"

"Well, he thought she was too unstable. I mean, he does tend to look at things from what he feels is my own best interest. Being ten years older, I guess he still thinks of me as the kid brother who can't manage for himself."

"Does he know about me?"

Justin nodded, but looked uncomfortable.

"What does he think?"

He hesitated just a moment. "Well, he thinks you're a little young."

Young! Her death knell. She would have powdered her hair gray on the spot to get away from that predictable, damning adjective.

They met Chester at a seafood restaurant in the East Seventies. He was waiting there, having a drink at the bar when they arrived. He looked like Justin, Caroline thought, but was stouter and looked more than ten years older; his hair was graying at the sides. He was a general practitioner and lived with his wife and four children in Bangor, Maine, which sounded to Caroline somewhat exotic and far away. His having a wife and four children and being a doctor had turned him, in her mind, into a kind of arbiter of social values. She wondered if he disapproved on principle of the fact that she and Justin were sleeping together, even leaving aside her age.

Chester picked up the evening *Post*, which was lying on the bar next to him. "Hi, Justin. . . . You must be Kathleen?"

"Caroline," Justin corrected him.

They went to sit at a table. Chester and Justin ordered lobster. Caroline wanted to order lobster, but she was afraid that wearing a bib might make her look even younger or would suggest youngness, so she ordered shrimp instead.

"You know, I just don't know how you can stand this city," Chester said. "Really . . . every time I come back, it looks filthier than before."

"It's the only place I could live," Justin said with a smile. It was clear this was an argument that they had had over the years, never won by either side.

"I can see it maybe for young people . . . but as a place to bring up children! . . . Did *you* grow up in the city, Caroline?"

She nodded.

"I don't know," he said, shaking his head. "No grass, no trees, no fresh air."

"There's Central Park," Caroline said.

"Well, maybe with a girl it's not so bad . . . but I think boys need the out-of-doors. . . . Even girls, though. Suki—she's my oldest daughter—if she hadn't been able to ski all through her adolescence, I don't know *what* she would have done."

"Is she still going with that boy—I forget his name?" Justin said.

"Mace? No, she threw him over. Well, you know how they are at that age—a different one every week."

Caroline wondered if this was an indirect comment on herself; she knew Suki was close to her age. She looked at him sideways.

"Of course Nan's completely different," Chester added hastily. "She's still in love with horses. I think if she could marry a horse, she would. . . . Do you ride, Caroline?"

"No, I . . . I'm not that athletic," she admitted.

"I thought city kids were always being shipped off to camp to learn those things," he said.

Caroline didn't want to explain that her mother had not been able to afford to send her to summer camp. Even the art lessons she had taken since she was ten had been a sacrifice in terms of the family economy. And yet getting up early Sunday mornings to go to class had been the high point of the week for her. She looked forward to it, even during school and at other times when she was supposed to be concentrating on something else. "We always liked the city in the summer," she said.

"Did Ariella ever get a job?" Chester asked when the lobsters arrived.

Justin shook his head. "She's still looking."

"She won't find anything," Chester predicted. "It's a crazy time to look for a job. . . . Though I did hear that some places are taking women just so— Hey, did I tell you about Miriam? They made her assistant to the dean! It's fantastic. She has her own office, her own secretary." He looked pleased at his wife's accomplishments.

"That's great," Justin said. "Is she still liking it?"

"Loves it." Turning to Caroline, he said, "My wife never did that much—or, well, I should say she did a lot, but mainly in connection with the kids, our house. . . . And suddenly she landed this job and in four years she's really worked her way up. I have to admit when she first got it, I wondered how she'd manage. It turns out she's a real whiz at organization. Her boss came to me and said, 'Till your wife came here, I couldn't find a damn thing.'" He cracked open a lobster claw.

"Would you like to try some of mine, Carrie?" Justin

said. He placed a tender-looking tidbit on the side of Caroline's plate.

"Okay," she said, feeling he was being like a mother with an underfed child. Would he cut her shrimp for her next, and butter her bread?

After dinner Justin excused himself and went to the men's room. Caroline, left alone with Chester, began yanking off bits of her napkin and rolling them into small balls in her lap.

"Justin tells me you want to be an illustrator of children's books," Chester said. He was still wearing his bib with the red lobster painted on it.

"Yes, I might," Caroline said, staring at the lobster. "I like to draw and I like children," she said softly.

"I'm sorry, I couldn't hear you."

"I like children," she said louder, feeling it was a banal remark to have made in the first place and sounded even more so on repetition.

But he just smiled genially. "Yeah, they're terrific, aren't they? It's a pity Justin and Ariella didn't have more. One is really—well, not enough."

"But with Vera . . . I guess that's difficult . . ." Caroline said.

"Oh, sure, it was no one's fault. . . . Well, though, I do think if Ariella hadn't been so stubborn. There are ways a woman can— If she'd been willing to take it easy during her pregnancies instead of running around like a chicken with its head cut off. . . . Do you know Ariella?"

"A little," Caroline said.

"She's a very— Well, she does have a certain intensity, I suppose I should grant that, but it's so diffuse! She doesn't seem to know how to get it all together."

Caroline cleared her throat. "They're not living together anymore," she said.

"Pardon me?" He looked startled.

"She has a boyfriend in the country."

"Oh—yes . . . that's been such a messy thing." After a moment he added, "It's been good for Justin that you—that he has someone."

"We're in love," she said, scaring herself and making him, as she saw by his face, distinctly uncomfortable.

"Yes, of course," he said.

"I mean, it's not just," she plunged on recklessly, insanely, "we're not just sleeping together. It's more than that."

He was frowning.

"We might even get married some day," she said, wanting to leap at his throat, to eradicate that smooth expression on his face.

"That would be . . . yes," he said. He lit a cigarette.

"I'm not so young," she said. "Anyway, it's only ten years."

"Oh, I don't think you're young," he said hastily, obviously lying.

"I'm not! So you don't have to worry."

"Worry?" He looked puzzled.

"I mean—" Her face was blazing, as though she had a fever. "Justin said you thought I was a little young."

"Well, I may have . . . I think I meant for you, young from that point of view."

She didn't know what he meant. In fact, she wasn't sure the whole conversatin had been a good idea and was relieved when Justin returned. "Why don't we walk a little?" he suggested. "It's such a lovely night."

Outside he took Caroline's hand as they walked Chester back to his hotel. Caroline didn't know if he deliberately wanted to show some connection between them, but, in any case, it made her feel better. She let them do all the talking, feeling exhausted from her confrontation with Chester at dinner. Perhaps she had only made it worse, confirming him in his belief that she was awkward and childish and not right for Justin.

140

In bed later she was more aggressive than she had ever been, as though trying to prove to both of them that the time when she had been a virgin was light years away in time, that she was not the naive, idiotic schoolgirl she was sure she had appeared to Chester. "Carrie," he cried out, almost as though in pain as she moved slowly above him. They were both drenched in sweat.

After they had finished and she was lying curled up with her head on his chest, Caroline said, "Would you pay to have me for a mistress?"

She had meant this as a kind of joke, but Justin didn't answer. She repeated the question.

"I don't understand why you should ask something like that," Justin said.

Caroline thought a moment. "I guess because I'm insecure," she said.

He drew her closer. "You should never feel insecure just after we've made love," he said.

"Only before or during?" Caroline said.

But it was clear that to him the idea that she should be insecure, especially sexually, was too unlikely to be taken seriously. Probably he thought she was begging for compliments.

She had thought she would fall asleep immediately, but somehow she couldn't. Justin had—she could tell by his even, quiet breathing—but Caroline still felt ill at ease, as though the residue of the evening had churned something up in her which refused to settle down. Suddenly she got out of bed and got dressed. She moved quietly so Justin wouldn't hear her. She wanted to go home! More than anything she felt like being in her own house, in her own bed, by herself. It seemed terribly important. On a piece of paper she wrote: "I have to do some studying tomorrow so I thought I'd go now." Rereading it, she was aware of how inadequate it sounded, but she couldn't think how else to put it. She placed it carefully on her pillow and tiptoed out of the room.

Their apartment was empty; her mother was away for the weekend again. But somehow that didn't bother her. In the past she had usually felt anxious being alone there—it wasn't as good a neighborhood as the one in which Justin lived. But now she felt peaceful and secure, as though she had just escaped from some danger. She made herself a drink of hot milk and honey and sipped it peacefully, glancing through a magazine her mother had left on the table. Then she got into her flannel pajamas, ones she would never have worn with Justin because they were neither sexy nor romantic. As an afterthought, she took the phone off the hook and placed it carefully under a cushion to still it's bleeping protest.

She went right to sleep and had no idea if it was shortly afterward or a long time later that a loud, ringing sound began penetrating her sleep. For a moment she was confused and thought it was the alarm. But it's Sunday, she thought groggily. And didn't I take the phone off the hook? Then she realized it was the doorbell. Slowly she got out of bed and walked to the door, a feeling of foreboding in her stomach. She put the chain on and cautiously opened the door two inches. It was Justin. He was soaking wet. "What the fuck is going on?" he said furiously.

"Is it raining?" Caroline said as she undid the chain.

"Carrie, listen—" He walked inside and closed the door behind him. "What happened? Why did you go?"

"I just felt like being by myself," she said, knowing this sounded barely more adequate than her note.

He grabbed her suddenly and for a moment she thought he was going to hit her. Instead he just held her so tightly it hurt. She would feel the water from his hair dripping down her neck. "Carrie, don't play games," he said in a muffled voice. "Okay? I just can't take it right now."

When he let her go, she was silent. "I didn't mean it that way," she said finally.

"How did you mean it, then?"

"I told you . . . I just wanted to be here, by myself."

"Well, you're coming back with me right now."

"I'm not!"

"Then I'll stay here."

She looked at him defiantly. Despite being frightened at how angry he was, she felt a secret thrill of power at being in her own home, as though that proved something. "There's no double bed," she said. "It will be crowded."

"Okay, it'll be crowded, then."

He went into her room. She loved her room. But, as he looked around it for the first time, she felt she was seeing it with his eyes and felt it might seem schoolgirlish—the Marie Laurencin print on the wall, the white furniture, the patchwork quilt, the fox from F.A.O. Schwarz that her mother had bought her for her eighth birthday which lay, his head resting on his tail, curled at the foot of her bed. Her easel stood open with a half-finished drawing scotch-taped to it.

"What a nice room," he said, but a little ironically.

"You see what I mean—the bed is small," she said, pointing.

"Yes, I see that," he said. He took off his clothes except for his underwear. Not knowing what else to do, Caroline got back into bed. "I like to sleep near the wall," she said.

"That's fine," he said.

She turned facing the wall, her back to him. He curled his body around to fit hers, spoonlike. Then, slowly, he slid his hands up under her pajama top and began softly stroking her breasts, going around the nipple. She could feel his erect penis pressing into the cleft of her buttocks. After a moment she said, "But we did it already."

143

Justin sat up so violently the mattress tilted off the bed. "Oh shit," he said.

"What?" she said, shrinking back.

"Carrie, look, what are we having—a love affair or some kind of— What does that mean, we did it already? Like, he's at it again, there he goes."

"I wanted to be by myself," she said quietly.

"Why?"

"What do you mean why?"

"Maybe we better just end the whole thing," he said. "I feel like maybe what you want really it to return to this neat little room with everything in place and just daydream your way through the next ten years with no one around to disturb you."

"No," she protested.

"Maybe I'm wrong," he said. "I feel in your head you have some romantic image of love and anything else scares you. . . . *Am* I wrong?"

"No, maybe you're right," she said softly.

"I can't figure it out," he said, frowning. "When I make love to you, you seem so there, like that's where you want to be, but something seems to happen in between."

"I feel like all we're doing is screwing!" she said. "You just need someone and I'm there, so—"

"Carrie, believe me, sex is one of the more available commodities in our present age. That's *not* why I'm here."

"Why are you?"

"Because I need you and I want you, not just physically. . . . Do you believe that?"

She hesitated. "Sort of."

He laughed. "Sort of!"

Caroline looked down, her words coming slowly. "You need me for now," she said, "but I don't know about after that."

"After?" He frowned.

"After school is over, after you're divorced." She stared at him desperately.

"I just can't tell about 'after' right now. I know how you feel. But it's still all so close, the thing with Ariella, the—"

"Are you still in love with her?" she demanded.

"No," he said quietly. "Not anymore . . . really. But I can't— I am in some way torn. Can't you just trust to letting things go as they will?"

But why didn't he realize what she feared was that, in giving herself to him, she would give up everything, that there would be nothing left of her? She thought of a supposedly humorous Mother's Day card her mother had once received from a friend. It had been a series of drawings. In the first a mother dog was lying on the ground, waiting as her puppies came over to suckle from her teats. In the second she was lying contentedly as they drank. In the third the puppies, their bellies full, were trotting off with smiles on their faces; where the mother had been was just a pile of bones. That was how she feared love would be for her; she was frightened by the intensity of her own feelings. It was different for Justin. Like Maggie, he had that self-confidence, that sense of an inner core which made it possible for him to give himself to someone and not fear total disintegration. "I just feel afraid," she said vaguely.

He was staring at her. "Carrie, don't pull out now. Don't leave me. Please."

At those words something came unstoppered in Caroline. The thought of losing him terrified her. She flew over and buried her face against him. "I won't," she said, her voice muffled. "I don't want to—ever."

He stroked her as she clung to him. "It's going to be okay," he said. She could feel his body shaking. "Let's go to sleep now. I think we're both tired."

This time the curve of his body around her seemed

comforting rather than threatening. She had been sure she wouldn't be able to sleep with the two of them in such a confined space, but in a moment she was unconscious. In the morning, waking up before him, seeing the sun streaming in the window, the night before seemed light years away. Caroline lay there, watching Justin sleep, and wondered why she had been so afraid.

8

On Friday nights Maggie and her father usually went to the Carnegie Hall Cinema. It showed revivals, which they both liked. The only trouble, Maggie's father said, was that he always felt at least a hundred and ten years old because no one who went there, besides himself, had been born before 1950. After the movie they went to The Russian Tea Room, which was right around the corner, for a late supper.

This particular evening they had seen a romantic comedy called *Love in the Afternoon*. In it Gary Cooper, a debonair, fiftyish man-about-town was having an affair with Audrey Hepburn, a lovely twenty-year-old cellist. Audrey Hepburn lived with her father, Maurice Chevalier, a plump, twinkly-eyed white-haired man who was a private detective. Gary Cooper hired Maurice Chevalier, not knowing he was the father of the girl he had been seeing, to find out more about her because she seemed to keep such strange hours, only appearing to make love at certain hours in the afternoon. Actually, this was because Audrey Hepburn had to meet with the orchestra where she played the cello, but Gary Cooper thought it was because she led some sort of mysterious double life.

"The scene I loved," Maggie's father said as they came out, "was that one where Chevalier realized it was his daughter what's-his-name was having an affair with."

"Gary Cooper," Maggie supplied.

"That look on his face when he said, 'Do you love her?' That was just marvelous!"

Maggie was touched. She assumed her father had identified with Maurice Chevalier and was saying, indirectly, that he would be concerned if she ever had an affair with a man who didn't love her. That made her think of Justin and Caroline—not that she suspected Justin didn't love Caroline, but because of the disparity in age. "Daddy," she said when they had ordered, "how would you feel if I had an affair like that?"

"Like the one in the movie?"

"Yes, I mean with a man who was older like that?"

He drank from his vodka and tonic. "Not very happy, I don't think."

"Why not?"

"Well, the life span on relationships like that is, unfortunately, fairly limited. . . . And they also have certain intrinsic problems."

"Such as?"

"Well, I'd say they work pretty well when the woman is in her twenties and the man is in his forties. It's when she gets to be thirty or forty, and he gets to be fifty or sixty, that the trouble begins."

"What kind of trouble?" Maggie wanted to know.

"Sexual problems, for one. . . . Most women start coming into their own sexually in their thirties and by fifty most men are slowing down."

"That's just sex, though."

"*Just* sex?" He smiled.

"Well, that's just *one* thing."

"A pretty important one usually. Okay, it's not just that. Here's how it goes. She meets him and she's a little slip of a thing, miniskirts, adoring, whispery voice. He seems to her to know everything. Ten years later her voice has gotten louder, her skirts longer, he doesn't seem to know everything anymore. . . . Take this patient of mine."

Maggie felt she should have known there would be a patient. She ripped off a chunk of bread. "Okay, I'll take her."

"She's thirty; she met this guy when she was twenty. He was forty-three, divorced his wife and four kids. For ten years things were pretty good. Now, she comes to me and tells me he said to her, 'I've created a monster.' I love that phrase. First of all: 'created.' Now he didn't *create* her. But you see the Godlike fantasy behind that, the whole Pygmalion idea, 'I will take this shapeless blob of warm wax and shape it as I will.' Then: 'monster.' Why monster? Because now she's an attractive, self-possessed young lady with a successful career—hence a 'monster.' "

Maggie sighed. Her chicken Kiev had just been set down and she poked it with her fork, watching the butter ooze out. "Does it *always* have to be that way?" she asked.

"Always? Well, maybe not always. . . . I'm just talking about what's likely."

"Daddy, the thing is, there's something I wanted to ask you about. . . . Actually it's a secret."

He held his hand up. "No secrets. All day long I hear nothing but secrets. I only want to hear what is public knowledge."

"It's about this friend of mine, actually it's Caro—"

"No names! Miss Smith. You have a friend, Miss Smith."

"Okay, I have a friend, Miss Smith, and she's seventeen years old, eighteen, and she's having an affair with a man who's about ten years older. . . . How do you think that will work out?"

"Well . . . eighteen, twenty-eight. That's a different story. I thought you meant twenty, thirty years, that kind of gap. Ten years isn't much. Maybe at eighteen, but not five years after that." He took a forkful of blini, being careful not to let the caviar fall out. "Mags, there's something I wanted to talk to *you* about."

"Yes?" Maggie felt apprehensive. She wondered if it was something about Todd and herself, if he somehow felt that having an affair wasn't good for her in some way.

"The thing is, you'll be going away to college soon and Nina—Nina wants to get married."

"To you?"

"To me . . . and, well, would you mind?"

Maggie thought a moment. "Actually, I always wondered why you didn't get married a long time ago. It wasn't because of me, was it? I mean, you didn't hold back because you were afraid I'd mind?"

He smiled slyly. "On the contrary, sweetheart, you were my perfect excuse. But now my perfect excuse is leaving home and—"

"You mean you don't want to yourself?"

"I don't especially see the point. . . . Apart from having children and beating the tax man, why do it? But for Nina, well, it means something to her and I don't have any violent objections."

"Where will you live?"

"Oh, in our place. That part of it shouldn't present any problems. Nina thought—well, June happens to be the thirteenth anniversary of when we met. Nina is very sentimental—she keeps all these things written down in a little black book. She knows the exact evening we met. Anyway, would June strike you as okay? You'd be out of school then."

"June's fine," Maggie said. "Would it be a big fancy wedding?"

"No, just a bunch of friends. I'll leave it all to Nina. I just want to live through it."

On the way home Maggie thought of what difference this would make in her life, if any. Her old fantasy of living with her father after college had faded.

It was true that now she had met Todd, the idea of being at Cornell, a five- or six-hour drive away from New York, wasn't quite as appealing as it had seemed six months earlier. He had said he intended to buy a second-hand car and would drive up every weekend, but she knew he would probably be studying some weekends and in winter, with all that snow, would a six-hour drive seem worth it?

Still, despite herself, she felt a little sad at the thought of her father getting married. She didn't think it was an Oedipal thing. It was just that she had always thought of him as the inconoclast, the free spirit, and here he was giving in like everyone else. She could understand it perfectly well. Nina was of the generation of women who felt that getting married was necessary. She couldn't blame her for that. She knew Nina was economically independent—she had a job doing public relations for a theatrical agency. Maggie's father had always said he didn't want a woman who would be dependent on him in that way—it bred discontent. Of course he had several patients he could present as examples of that. Maggie remembered one who, the day she inherited a large sum of money from her mother, told her husband of twenty years that she was divorcing him. According to Maggie's father, he had been amazed. "If I'd had the money, I'd have left you fifteen years earlier," she'd said. "Thank God I have it now."

This was one of the many reasons it was inconceivable to Maggie to marry unless you were in a position to support yourself. When she heard from her friends that some of them had mothers who didn't know what their husbands earned, that some of them were given checking accounts into which their husbands placed small sums for them to draw on for household expenditures, Maggie felt as horrified as when she had heard of various practices by slave owners prior to the Civil War. She remembered how, when her mother wanted a new stove, she would ask her father and he would say, "All right . . . but then we won't be able to go to Puerto Rico this spring" or "You won't be able to get a new winter coat." At the time it had never struck Maggie that there was anything but practicality in this, but now, looking back, she didn't like the way it had been between her parents. If she lived to be a hundred years old, she vowed, no one would ever tell her that in order to have a new stove she had to give up a vacation or a winter coat. Just let them try!

"Margaret, I think you deserve a drink," Justin said.

She had just gone up to him after class to tell him that the letter from Cornell had arrived; she was going there on a Merit scholarship. "Okay," she said. It was the last class of the day. "Thanks a lot, Justin, for everything you did. I really appreciate it."

He smiled. "Come on, Maggie. No false modesty. They were lucky to get you and you know it."

Maggie smiled back. With Justin she always felt she could be herself and, frankly, she thought he was probably right: They *were* lucky to get her. "I hope I'll like it," she said.

"I think you will. . . . You mean leaving New York?"

"Not so much that. . . . Partly, but, well, I didn't know I'd meet Todd when I applied. It's so far away. He's going to Columbia."

"He can drive up, can't he?"

"Sure, he's planning to. It's just—" What Maggie was reluctant to say was that she was not at all certain of her own capacity for long-range fidelity. Before she had met Todd and slept with him, she had never thought of men at all except as interesting people to talk to. Now suddenly it seemed as though she had begun thinking of every man, even little men in dry cleaning stores, in terms of their sexual capacities. It made her nervous.

"Look, if worse comes to worst, you can transfer to Columbia," Justin said. "They don't have a bad department."

"That seems cowardly, though," Maggie said. "And after you went to all that trouble."

"Don't be silly—it was no trouble."

He opened the car door and she got in beside him. Just as they stopped at the corner for a red light, Caroline passed by. She had a dreamy look on her face and clearly didn't see them. Justin honked and rolled down his window. "Hey, Carrie!"

She turned around, startled.

"Want to come for a drink with us?"

"Oh . . . no," Caroline said quickly and rounded the corner.

Justin rolled the window up again. Maggie wondered why Caroline had said no. She knew Justin had told her not to reveal to anyone at school that she was having an affair with him, but with the two of them it seemed odd. Maggie had felt funny with Justin ever since she had known of his relationship with Caroline. She felt that in different ways she was about equally jealous of both of them. She was jealous of Caroline because she had always felt that *she* came first with Justin. When he had said that he felt as though his own scientific career was being fulfilled vicariously through her, she had been immensely flattered. It was not that Caroline's sleeping with Justin really changed any of this, but it seemed to dim her unequivocal position as his "favorite" in some way.

And then she felt jealous of Justin because in the four years Caroline had been her friend, she had grown accustomed to Caroline's naive, unquestioning approval, the way she would say, "Maggie says . . ." as though the simple fact that Maggie had given utterance to something gave it a kind of validity. This, too, had not entirely changed, but Maggie felt that some of Caroline's admiration had shifted to Justin. She didn't like to think that having love affairs would endanger a friendship between women in any way, but she couldn't deny that something between herself and Caroline had subtly changed, perhaps on her part as well. They still confided in each other but not about everything, and they were no longer each other's only confidantes. Maggie knew this was inevitable, but something about it made her sad too.

They stopped at a small bar on Third Avenue. Justin ordered a beer and Maggie had a screwdriver.

"Do you feel excited about graduating?" Justin asked.

"In a way," Maggie admitted. "Did I tell you—my father's getting married."

"Congratulations."

"Thanks."

"You don't look so happy about it."

"Well, it's not that so much. . . . No, I guess it's okay. I just think it's kind of dumb."

"Getting married?"

"Umm . . . I don't see the point of it."

"Not under any circumstances?"

"Well, maybe if a couple wants children."

"You don't think there's any point in a ceremony as such?"

She shook her head.

"I admit what's basic is a sense of commitment and you can have that outside marriage or not have it inside marriage . . . but I feel, well it's like all rituals—birth rituals, funerals. I think they fill some basic human need—I think if a couple isn't married and they have a bad fight, they're just that much more likely to say, 'What the hell, why bother?' Whereas if they're married, they'll hang in there and try to work it out."

"But why is that *good*?" Maggie said. "Why *should* they work it out?"

He laughed. "I'm going on the possibly old-fashioned assumption that there is a virtue in a long-lasting relationship."

"You mean in a moral sense?"

"No, not moral, just psychological. I don't think most people are suited for bouncing from one person to another. It's too tiring.

Maggie was puzzled at this. All the articles she'd read had said just the opposite, that people were, in fact, suited precisely *to* bouncing from one person to another and that anything else was artificial. "Well, *I'm* not going to get married," she said, taking a gulp of her drink.

"Ever?"

"Maybe at thirty or thirty-five. . . . I don't think it would be fair. I really want to get involved in my work. I don't know if there'd be enough of me left over to share with someone."

"Why not let the man decide that?"

Maggie felt that maybe she hadn't been really honest. "It's also," she said, "that I don't know if I *want* to share—I mean, I'm a little afraid if I had that kind of relationship with someone, the kind you're talking about, in or out of marriage, it would be a diversion . . . I wouldn't be as single-minded."

"I guess that's where we differ: I don't especially revere single-mindedness."

Maggie hesitated. "You don't ever regret not going on for your doctorate?"

"Sure I do. . . . Only, well, I have this friend, Ross Lindeman. He was getting a doctorate when I did, and he did finish. He's at Einstein now, he has his own lab, twenty people working under him. But it seemes like he spends every second applying for grants, getting frantic that someone will outrace him on a particular finding. . . . I don't think I'm cut out for that kind of life. I mean, even teaching. I love teaching, but I love other things too. I love music, I like bike riding, I like having a three-month vacation. I don't feel like narrowing everything down that way."

Maggie became solemn, thinking of herself as Justin's

frantic friend. "Does he—your friend—ever talk of getting out?"

"No, he loves it. He'd probably be miserable living any other way. I don't think it's a moral issue, Maggie, I really don't. It's a matter of finding what suits you."

"My father loves his work," she said thoughtfully, "but then he collects art too. . . . Maybe in some way he's more like you. Maybe that *is* a better way to be."

"Neither is *better*. . . . And where would the world be without people who had that capacity for absolute dedication?"

"True." She looked at him. "I guess I won't have a simple life, though," she said a little regretfully.

Justin smiled. "Not many of us do, in the end."

Suddenly the thought that he and Caroline were having an affair passed through her head. It still seemed strange to her. Maybe it was that she knew both of them so well, but thought of them as separate. Perhaps because of Caroline's natural reticence Maggie found it hard to imagine the two of them together, not only what they did in bed, but what they talked about, even.

She wondered if twenty years from now she and Caroline would look back on their respective relationships with Todd and Justin as just passing fancies or as the cornerstones of something lasting. She thought of how her father, referring to a woman he'd been engaged to in medical school, hadn't been able to remember her name.

"What are you thinking about?" Justin asked.

"Oh . . . time," Maggie said.

"It's funny. . . . Last fall I suddenly felt an acute awareness of the fact that I'd be thirty in a few years. What had I done to show for it, that kind of thing. I got really depressed. But now suddenly I don't care at all."

Maggie wondered if that was because of Caroline. She thought of her father's comments in The Russian Tea Room about relationships unraveling if there was too great an age difference. "I guess I don't think of you as being that old," she said. "You don't *look* that old."

"Twenty-eight isn't *that* old."

To Maggie it did sound quite old, but she felt perhaps she ought not to say that. "I mean, you don't have gray hair or anything. I do," she said.

"You?"

"Uh huh." She showed him a single white hair she had discovered the other day. "I guess I'm going gray early," she said. "My mother did."

"Eighteen does seem a little early."

"I'm not even eighteen yet! I won't be until July."

"I guess I don't think of you as being that young either. . . . You always had that serious 'I know exactly where I'm going' expression. It was kind of intimidating."

Maggie laughed. She loved the idea that Justin had found her intimidating. "I guess I better be going back," she said. "Though, actually, could you drop me at Caroline's, Justin? I left something there."

"Sure," he said.

Caroline wasn't at home, but her mother was when Maggie rang the bell. "Hi, Maggie! Goodness, it's been a while since I've seen you. You look marvelous!"

"Thanks," Maggie said. She liked Caroline's mother. Often, when Caroline went down to the store, they would sit in the kitchen and talk. Maggie felt that perhaps it was because she didn't have a mother, yet enjoyed talking to an older woman. She found it completely incredible that Caroline had not yet told her mother about Justin. She couldn't have conceived of having an affair and not having her father know about it. Maybe this way was more civilized and "normal," though.

"Caroline's down at the store," Caroline's mother said. "Have a cup of tea with me."

"Sure," Maggie said.

Although she had sat in this kitchen hundreds of times,

she was always amazed anew at the neatness of it. She could never recall having seen one dirty dish in the sink, not one spoon, even!

"Caroline tells me you've met a very nice young man," Caroline's mother said.

"Yes, he *is* very nice," Maggie said.

"I'd love to meet him sometime."

"Well, he'll be at graduation," Maggie said. "Maybe we can all go out to eat afterward."

"How did you meet him?"

"How?" For a moment Maggie couldn't remember. "Oh, let me think. . . . It was at a school debate. He was on the opposite team."

Caroline's mother sighed. "I wish so much Carrie had done more of that sort of thing in high school. She's never even gone to any of those school dances."

"Well, neither have I," Maggie said. "They're awful."

"Yes, but . . . Well, perhaps you're right. I'm just afraid at Parsons there won't be any real men."

"Don't worry," Maggie said. She knew Caroline would kill her if she mentioned Justin to her mother, yet she felt distinctly uncomfortable.

"Caroline's so talented as an artist," Caroline's mother said, "but it's just, well, I sometimes wonder if she's going to know how to cope with life. I mean, with men also. Men are so— Well, you know how it is these days. They expect a certain, they just *assume* a girl will fall into bed with them. It's become so cold-blooded, I just don't know if Caroline will know how to handle herself."

Maggie began fiddling with the saltcellar. "I think she'll do all right."

"Do you? . . . I sometimes feel she's waiting for Prince Charming to come riding along on his white charger and, well, that can be disappointing."

Maggie smiled. "Maybe he *will* come along."

Caroline's mother smiled back. "I think Prince

Charmings are in somewhat short supply these days," she said.

When Caroline came back from the store and saw Maggie sitting in the kitchen with her mother, a wary expression appeared on her face. Maggie knew she was wondering if by accident she had let anything slip about Justin.

"I came to get those books," Maggie said.

"Oh, they're right inside. . . . I'll walk you to the bus stop. Is there time, Moth? I'll be back in a minute."

"Go right ahead," Caroline's mother said, unpacking the groceries Caroline had set down. "There's no hurry."

As they were walking to the bus stop, Maggie said, "Carrie, you've *got* to tell her, it's just crazy."

"About Justin?"

"Yes! My God, it's so weird. I don't understand it. So she knows? What's she going to do? Have a nervous breakdown?"

"Maybe," Caroline said, smiling painfully.

"I think you underestimate your mother."

"It's not that," Caroline said. "It's just— Well, no, I know she has her good points, but about men she *is* a little—well, maybe I shouldn't say paranoid, but I just know she'll think I was seduced against my will, that Justin fed me some strong drink or hypnotized me and then slung me over his shoulder and carried me off."

"But you wanted it too!"

"Of course I did. I'm just explaining how *she'll* look at it. . . . And then, well, I don't think she thinks that highly of women living with men outside of marriage, maybe due to my father and his girl friend. She always gets this kind of supercilious expression when she talks about it, like those are women who don't have a very high opinion of themselves or don't have the willpower to hold out for marriage."

"Weird," was all Maggie could say. "You still ought to

tell her. Frankly, I think this is your golden opportunity."

"In what way?"

"Well, this whole bit of your living at home for the next two years. It's just—"

"It's because of the money," Caroline said hastily.

"Bullshit. If she wanted to raise the money, she could. She's hanging on to you."

Caroline sighed. "I know."

"Carrie, look, do you want to be one of those ladies who at forty is living with her sixty-five-year-old mother like in that movie we saw?"

"*Rachel, Rachel.* . . . No, of course not."

"Well, then you better get cracking. Because I have the feeling you'll keep putting it off and saying, 'Well, one more year,' or 'She can't take it now, maybe next year' . . . and your whole life can go by! I think Justin is irrelevant. You just ought to get out."

"But I'm her whole life," Caroline protested.

"That's the problem. You've been her perfect excuse," Maggie said thoughtfully.

"What do you mean?"

"Well, Daddy was saying that he thought of me as his perfect excuse because while I was at home, he could always tell Nina he didn't want to marry for my sake. . . . It's the same with your mother. Probably she's scared of people, of men, and, well, people in general, but as long as she has you, she doesn't really have to go out and form any relationships. . . . You know, really, Carrie, it might be terrific for your mother for you to move out. She might suddenly be forced to do things, start having affairs, even."

Caroline looked dubious. "I don't know."

"It's like a person who doesn't know how to swim. If they have some rubber tube to hang on to, they never learn. If you take the tube away, they have a chance to learn."

"Or drown," Caroline said.

"Look, I don't want to sound cruel, but you've got to think of *your* life," Maggie said, "not just hers. It's odd, but you know what you sound like? You're like some married man who meets someone he wants to marry, but he can't bear to leave his wife of twenty years for fear she'll disintegrate without him."

"There's something in that," Caroline admitted. "But it *would* be cruel, Maggie! That's what I can't get over. It *would* be. . . . But I know you're right. I *do* have my own life."

"I predict great things for your mother," Maggie said. "The month after you move out she's going to meet a scintillating widower with a yacht and a collection of Oriental art who'll sweep her off to . . . Paris."

"Not Paris," Caroline said, laughing. "That's where my father is. . . . How about London?"

"Okay, London," Maggie said, "to his country estate where she'll meet loads of interesting people, have a salon, ride to hounds—"

"Forget the hounds—she loves animals."

"Okay, forget the hounds. Instead she'll cultivate a huge garden. She'll sit on the veranda while the maid in her white apron brings out frosty pitchers of iced tea. When you come to visit, she'll say, 'Carrie, thank heavens you finally moved out. If you hadn't, look at what I would have missed.' "

The bus was coming. Caroline was listening to Maggie with a bemused smile. She gave her a hug. "Thanks for coming over," she said. "All that you said is . . . good."

"Do it!" Maggie yelled out of the open window of the bus. "Go home and do it!"

When the bus was in motion, Maggie sat back. There she was again, telling everyone how to run their lives. It was strange. To other people she seemed so self-confident and sure of herself. But lately it had begun seeming to Maggie that, although she did, in fact, possess these qualities, they were more willed than completely natural. Often with Todd she felt that whereas she could rant and rave, argue and shout, to some extent it was a papering over of all kinds of uncertainties and fears; whereas he, in his calm, unflappable way, had a vein of certainty, of really knowing what he wanted and cared about that she envied. Whenever she expressed her opinions, he listened with interest, he enjoyed arguing, but he never necessarily decided she had been right.

She recalled how, the week she had known they would sleep together, she had gone through the week saying, "This is the last time I'll do this as a virgin." Now with school ending, with her father marrying, she had that same sense of this is the last time. Had that been the last time she would sit in Caroline's kitchen talking with her mother? Everything seemed to be breaking up, and even though it was easy to tell Caroline that moving forward was crucial, necessary, all to the good, in fact it made Maggie uneasy. Previously she had always thought of New York as her home. Now she realized that was no longer necessarily true. She could choose to settle here, but she could choose to settle anywhere else as well. Her father and Caroline, who had been so important in her life, would inevitably become less important. She and Caroline would still stay friends, they would write, but it would be different. She would still be close to her father, but they would never go to the Carnegie Hall Cinema on Friday nights anymore. Yet she very much didn't want to turn to Todd in a mood of desperation, to seek through him to make up for these other losses, tempting as part of herself found such an alternative. She was used to being surrounded by people she felt close to, whom she loved, to whom she could talk. The idea of Cornell, so large, so impersonal, so far away from "home," was more than a little scary.

I want to be really strong, Maggie thought, gathering up her books to get off the bus. I don't want to just pretend to be. Let me be.

9

Despite herself, Caroline had not yet told her mother about Justin. She had lain in bed so many nights planning ways to introduce the topic, had rehearsed exactly what she would say to any one of her mother's supposed criticisms or reactions so often that it came as a shock to her that her mother still did not know. If only her mother were not so trusting! Any excuse Caroline offered about sleeping at Maggie's or needing to go to the library, her mother simply accepted without a second thought, having had no previous knowledge that Caroline was capable of duplicity. She had never even called Maggie's to check! Caroline sometimes wished she were the kind of girl who would carelessly leave her diaphragm around where her mother would find it to force a confrontation, just as a guilty husband might leave a lipstick-stained handkerchief in his pocket. But that was just not her style. She kept her diaphragm neatly secreted in one of the zippered pockets of her leather handbag and it would have been as much against her mother's grain to go looking in her handbag as it would have been for her to leave the diaphragm lying around.

It was so childish! At times she felt she was mainly scared that her mother would get mad at her, would yell and accuse her of being a "bad girl." At other times what she feared most was that her mother would burst into tears. She didn't know which reaction would be worse; both seemed equally terrifying.

She might have put it off forever except that one evening Justin said, "Carrie, there's something I think we should talk about."

Caroline's heart sank. She was petrified that he was going to say that now that the school year was drawing to an end, they should stop seeing each other, that their affair had served its purpose. "What is it?" she asked apprehensively.

He smiled. "It's nothing bad."

Caroline thought how when she was young and her mother would say, "Carrie, I want to tell you something," she would always ask, "Is it something bad?" until one day her mother, exasperated, had said, "Of course it's not something bad! Why do you always say that?" She sat watching Justin expectantly.

"I think we should live together next year, once school is out, in fact . . . don't you?"

She looked at him warily, as though suspecting a trap. "You mean, live together all the time?"

He nodded.

"We don't have to," she said hastily.

"I know we don't *have* to."

"I mean, I'd still sleep with you and all that."

He smiled wryly. "I thought you were the one who was a romantic."

"You think it would be good?" she asked.

"Well, *I* would like it," he said, "but I can't speak for you. If you want your freedom, I can understand that."

"Freedom?"

"I mean, if you want to see other men, whatever, you deserve a go at all that."

Other men! What would she possibly want with other men? "But maybe you'll get bored with me, seeing me all the time," she said frowning.

"Maybe you'll get bored with *me*."

Caroline smiled at the absolute impossibility of that.

"So, what do you say?" he said. "Do we take a chance?"

"Okay, sure."

Justin went over and cradled her in his arms, kissing the top of her head. "You're so sweet, Carrie."

"Am I?" she said enigmatically.

"Aren't you?"

"I don't know."

"I don't mean that's *all* you are."

Then she thought: Let him think I'm whatever he wants me to be. That's all that's necessary. Standing there, enclosed by his arms, she felt secure until a thought pierced through, like an arrow: Will he marry me in the end? Is this a step closer to that or a step farther away?

"Why are you frowning?"

Caroline didn't want to be like the little old woman who kept throwing things back in the sea and asking for more and more until she was left with nothing. What she wanted, deep down, was that final seal of commitment which to her was symbolized by marriage. Then he would really be hers! That would be the *real* proof. Still, she knew better than to spoil the moment by pushing him toward more than he was ready to give. "I guess I *should* tell my mother," she said, leaning back against him comfortably.

"Have you told her anything about us?"

"No."

"Well, I think the time has come."

Caroline's heart began to beat rapidly. Hearing Justin say so calmly "The time has come" made her realize it had, indeed, come. "I keep putting it off," she confessed.

"How would she feel about our living together?"

"Terrible."

"In what way?"

Caroline sighed. She found it much harder to talk about this with Justin, who didn't know her mother at all, than she had with Maggie. "She'd think you were taking advantage of me," she said.

"Taking advantage how?"

166

"Well, just by . . . I mean, just that we were sleeping together. She'd think you had made me or, well, promised to marry me, but really just wanted sex. . . . That's how she thinks of it."

Justin looked thoughtful. Caroline was very glad he didn't say he thought that was crazy of her mother. "Then I really should meet her," he concluded.

"Why would that help?"

"Well, for one, she'd see I wasn't such a monster . . . and that my intentions are highly honorable. . . . Are you afraid she'll still think the same thing even *after* she meets me?"

There was practically nothing that didn't frighten Caroline about Justin and her mother meeting. Usually she was pleased that Justin was physically attractive, but now she feared her mother would hold this against him, that she would assume he had millions of affairs. But, on the other hand, if he were ugly, she wouldn't have liked that either since she always said she didn't like men who were very fat or pockmarked or badly dressed.

"How do *you* feel about it, though?" Justin wanted to know.

"About our living together?"

He nodded.

Apart from having one eye on the distant goal of marriage, Caroline thought the idea of their living together sounded so incredible, so wonderful, that it was hard for her to conceive of it as a reality. To think of actually being able to have breakfast with Justin every morning, to see him every single night, to be in the living room while he was correcting papers, to take bike rides with him in the park! "I think I would like it," she admitted softly.

She knew from his expression that he understood all that she felt. "It'll be easy for you in terms of Parsons," he said. "The subway's right around the corner. You could get there in fifteen minutes."

Getting to Parsons was the least of Caroline's concerns at the moment. If she had been told that living with Justin meant she had to walk thirty miles each way in the driving rain she would have considered it a minor penalty to pay. "How do you think Noah would feel about it?"

"I . . . Well, I asked him."

"You did?"

"I thought . . . I mean, not that I wouldn't have done it otherwise, but I *did* want to know how he felt, and he said, 'Great, when's she moving in.' "

"Do you think he *really* feels that, though?"

"I do. . . . It wouldn't be a matter of excluding him, of our going off a lot and leaving him by himself. No, of course, I've thought of it a lot since he's been through so many changes this year . . . but he knows you; it isn't like some stranger moving in. You get along so well."

"I wonder who we would have as a baby-sitter if we went out," Caroline mused.

"We'll find someone. That won't be a problem."

"Not someone pretty," Caroline said quickly.

Justin laughed. "You don't have anything to worry about . . . but if you like, we'll get a stout Irish lady with gray hair and big brown shoes."

But then Caroline began thinking how, now that she would no longer be baby-sitting, she wouldn't have any extra money. She had read lots of articles in magazines about people living together, and they always stressed how important it was for the couple to share expenses. Pooling your resources, it was called.

"How much is your rent?" she asked Justin anxiously.

"I've been pretty lucky," he said. "It's rent controlled, so it's still under three fifty."

Three hundred and fifty dollars! With phones and electricity that would be four hundred! And that didn't even include food.

"Carrie, what's wrong? Why do you look so worried?" Justin asked.

"I don't know if I can pay for that," she stammered, "the rent and everything, I mean."

"Don't be silly—how could you? Where would you get the money?"

"I don't know," Caroline admitted. It was hard to explain to him what was also on her mind. She'd heard Maggie say so often that for a woman to be economically dependent on a man was a terrible thing; it ended up with the man becoming irritated and the woman becoming weak and clinging.

Justin took her hand. "Darling, let's take it one step at a time, okay? The main object at hand is for me to meet your mother. Let's handle that and then we can go on to all these other issues."

He was right; that *was* the main issue at hand. But now instead of just lying in bed at night thinking of telling her mother about Justin, Caroline thought about it every second of the day. If only there were some other way to do it! Couldn't Justin just call her mother up and say, "Hello, my name is Justin Prager. I'm having an affair with your daughter and I want to live with her." Deep down Caroline knew that such an approach was not exactly practical, but she continued putting off the dread moment. Then, one evening, it came up perfectly spontaneously.

She and her mother were in the kitchen, her mother washing the dishes, Caroline drying. Caroline picked up a glass and somehow, she wasn't sure how, it just slid from her hands and fell with a crash onto the floor. Her mother gave an exasperated sigh. "Carrie, sometimes you act like someone in love."

"I am," Caroline said without thinking, and then realized, with mixed relief and apprehension, that for good or ill the words were out and could not be retracted.

"Who are you in love *with*?" her mother said with an amused expression, as though she expected the answer to be the postman, Robert Redford, or something equally outlandish.

"His name is Justin Prager," Caroline said, having almost a sense of déjà vu from having repeated these words so often in her head.

Her mother looked stunned. "Isn't he the man you baby-sit for?"

Caroline nodded.

"What became of his wife?"

"They're divorced," Caroline said, although this was not really true since the two lawyers had met for the first time only the previous week.

"I don't think I completely understand this," Caroline's mother said. "Many times someone named Mrs. Prager would call up and say she was calling about baby-sitting."

"That was before . . . I mean, their getting divorced didn't have anything to do with me," Caroline said, willing her mother to accept this.

"Well, they always say no one can break up a marriage," her mother said reflectively. She bent down and put the broken pieces of glass in the wastebasket. "What about their child?"

"He—his name's Noah," Caroline said. "They have joint custody." She had the feeling her mother would think joint custody was odd. Her mother had a friend, a social worker, who said that it wasn't good for children to be "shuttled back and forth" between two homes.

Caroline's mother looked at her carefully. "You're in love with him?" she asked, as though just having heard that Caroline had been exposed to a disease for which no cure had been perfected.

Caroline nodded.

"And he—Is this a reciprocal arrangement?"

Caroline knew what the word "reciprocal" meant, but

the way her mother had expressed it sounded so dry and legalistic, her mind went blank for a moment.

"Does *he* love you?"

"I think so," Caroline said. She took a deep breath. "He thinks we should live together?"

"You and he?"

Caroline wondered if her mother thought Justin had meant that the three of them should live together and had a brief, agonized vision of how this would be. "Yes, us," she said.

"Where would you live?"

"At his apartment. . . . He, um, would like to meet you. Then we could—talk about it all."

"Yes, well, I think that *would* be a good idea," Carolines's mother said. She smiled. "This is quite a surprise, Carrie. You've never said anything."

"I'm sorry," Caroline said. "I meant to."

"You have been seeming unusually dreamy, but I thought—well, you're always somewhat like that. . . . It's curious—isn't he the science teacher at Whitman?"

"Yes."

"Science isn't exactly your best subject, is it?"

"No," Caroline said.

"Is he the one—I remember Maggie used to have a science teacher who helped her set up this—"

"Yes," Caroline said. "That's him."

"Maggie thought very highly of him, as I recall," her mother said. Clearly, this opinion of Maggie's weighed more with her than anything Caroline would say.

"Yes, he's a good teacher," Caroline said and then blushed, thinking this might seem to have some sexual connotation.

On the whole the conversation was going better than she had hoped. She had had so many dreads and fears that nothing could have lived up to them short of her mother taking out a pistol and shooting first Caroline and

171

then herself. Nonetheless, she felt decidedly weak in the knees; she sat down. Her mother was still looking at her with the same thoughtful, puzzled expression.

"Well, as long as it's not a question of marriage," she said, "I suppose I don't mind so much."

Caroline was surprised. "You'd rather have us living together?"

Caroline's mother smiled. "Well, I don't want to be cruel, darling, but arrangements like that have been known to break up. Not that marriages haven't too, but . . . I just think I'd go blind with rage if you were to marry him after a couple of pleasant encounters in bed."

"Why?"

"Oh, maybe I'm being old-fashioned and drawing too much on my own experience. But, you know, you're so talented in art, Carrie, and if you were to give it up for love or marriage or whatever, I couldn't bear it, I really couldn't."

"I won't," Caroline said softly.

"No, I don't think you will," Caroline's mother said. "I think you have a certain tenacity under that softness, thank God. . . . Also, well, he is older and that makes me uneasy, I have to admit."

"It's only—it's less than ten years."

"True, but at eighteen . . . No, maybe you treat each other as equals and it's all fine and dandy, but if it were that hideous kind of patriarchal 'Let me tell you what to do with your life,' I believe I'd strangle him."

"Justin isn't patriarchal," Caroline offered.

"Good!" Her mother stood gazing at her with a slightly uncertain smile. "Well, I guess in some ways this will make things easier for me."

"In what way?" asked Caroline, surprised.

Her mother was looking uncomfortable. "Well, actually, Malcolm and I have been talking for some time now about the idea of—well, living together basically. But I wasn't sure just how you would take it—I suppose that's why I kept putting off telling you."

"You mean he would live here?"

"Well, at first. . . . I mean, now, with you at Justin's, I suppose I could live there, though his place is a little small. I think I rather prefer ours, on the whole. . . . Or, I suppose we could get a new place altogether. I want to see how it goes, though. I mean, it may be a complete bust." She laughed, as though not expecting this would be the case.

"It seems so odd," Caroline said.

"Odd?" She smiled. "In what way?"

It wasn't just that Caroline had assumed that her mother would be devastated at losing her, it was that she had never stopped to think of Malcolm as someone in whom her mother was seriously interested. "I guess I thought you were just friends," she said.

"We are," her mother said promptly. "Of course, we're friends first and foremost. You can't go anywhere without friendship as a basis. But it's just that gradually, over the years—"

"Anyway, I thought he was married," Caroline said.

Her mother shook her head. "Darling, you really are amazingly self-absorbed, but I guess I can put it down to love or your age or something. Malcolm's been divorced for several *years* now. I told you. His wife took their daughter and moved back to Iowa."

"Oh, yes," said Caroline, vaguely remembering. Suddenly she stared at her mother. "Was that why you were away all those weekends?" she said. "Wasn't there a real house in the country?"

"There's a real house in the country," her mother said, laughing, "but it's true, talking about it, making plans, I suppose led us to thinking about—well, our nonweekend life. . . . I gather you didn't miss me too dreadfully, then?"

Caroline blushed. "Well . . ."

"All that guilt for nothing! Ah well."

"But do you think you'll *marry* him?" Caroline said, still dumbfounded.

"Don't rush us! We've only known each other fifteen years. . . . No, seriously, neither of us is the type to go stampeding into things, sweetheart. We'll see how it goes, that's all. But I think it will go very well. You know, some men don't begin to come into their own until they're aged a bit."

"Oh," Caroline said.

"But to get back to what I was saying, I'd love to meet Justin. If he's half the man Malcolm is, you're luckier than I can imagine."

Half the man Malcolm was! A paunchy little man with round gray eyes who was losing his hair! Caroline would have been furious if she hadn't been so relieved, or at least partly relieved, at her mother's "finding" someone. She had never had the faintest idea that her mother was still thinking about wanting someone or needing someone. She'd assumed she had written all that off years ago.

Her mother seemed to know just what she was thinking. Catching Caroline's glance, she said, "You can't imagine how nice sex can be when one doesn't need to prove anything."

Caroline felt slightly affronted, wondering if this applied to herself. "Oh, I'm sure," she said. But in fact, not only was she *not* sure, the very idea of Malcolm and her mother in bed together was something she could hardly imagine and, in fact, preferred not to think of. Obviously it had nothing to do with herself and Justin. How could it?

"I'm glad about Malcolm, Moth," she said, trying to make up for this reaction.

"He's very fond of you," her mother said. "He just

didn't want you to feel he was in any way . . . taking your place."

She had to buy a graduation dress. For occasions like this Caroline's mother was very concerned that she have the best. She gave Caroline one hundred fifty dollars in cash and said she should go to Bonwit's or Bendel's to buy the nicest dress she saw. Caroline went with Justin. It was the day of the evening they were to go out with her mother for dinner, but the excitement of buying the dress over-shadowed whatever anxieties she had about that.

All of the dresses were beautiful! Caroline went down the line, touching them carefully. They all had lace and bows and were beautiful pastel shades of pink and laven-der. Maggie always said she hated pastels. She felt they should be outlawed. She wanted to wear a shocking pink dress for graduation, but the rule was that it had to be a light color. Last year a battle had been fought and won by the feminist contingent among the students that the grad-uation outfit could be a pantsuit, but it still had to be a light color. Caroline was glad. She had never been to a dance, never had owned a really fancy party dress except the velvet ones her mother had bought her when she was little to go to the ballet. Finally she picked four of the prettiest dresses and took them into the dressing room. It made her a little nervous to see Justin sitting there. But she came out each time to show him how she looked in each dress. She had never thought men would be inter-ested in clothes, but Justin examined her gravely, even asking her to turn around so he could see the dress from the back. Caroline was glad he was there to help her de-cide, because to her each dress seemed more beautiful than the next. When she came out in the last dress, she said, "Which do you like best?"

"To tell the truth, I don't like any of them that much."

"You don't?" Caroline said in dismay.

"They all have too much junk on them . . . all that lace and stuff. They make you look like the cover of some junior miss magazine."

Caroline was puzzled. She had thought that was the whole object of such a dress.

"Show me where your size is," Justin said.

They went over together and he went through the dresses himself. Finally he took one out. "Why don't you try this one on?" he said.

"But it's so plain!" Caroline said.

The dress he had selected was pale beige, with a draped neckline and a full skirt. It was made of a soft, chiffonlike material, but it had no lace, no decoration, nothing! Still, when it was on, she had to admit it looked nice. The draped effect made her look fuller on top, and the skirt fell softly below her knees.

"I like that one a lot," Justin said without a moment's hesitation.

Caroline remembered how once she had gone with Justin when he wanted to buy a rug. He had looked through hundreds of rugs and had finally selected one, written out a check for several hundred dollars, and left the store. Once outside he had not seemed suddenly smitten with fears that the rug would not match the other furniture in the room in which it would be placed, or that it might not have been a good value or that some other kind of rug would have been better. That had been months ago and the rug was in the living room and he didn't seem to have had even one second's doubt about it! Caroline hoped that if she was reborn, she would be reborn as a person who could make quick, firm decisions like that and have no regrets afterward.

When she came out with the dress, the saleslady asked if it should be sent or if she would take it. "I'll take it," Caroline said, afraid it might not arrive in time. Justin took some money out of his pocket. He started handing it to the saleslady.

"No, *I* want to pay for it," Caroline said.

"Why? Let me. I want to."

"No, I don't want you to," Caroline said, embarrassed in front of the saleslady. When the saleslady had gone away with the dress and Caroline's money, Justin said, "Why wouldn't you let me pay, Carrie?"

Caroline hesitated. Partly, she felt her mother had saved especially to buy this dress and enjoyed the fact of being able to give it to Caroline. Partly she felt that for a man to buy a woman a dress placed her in that ambiguous, economically dependent position which was supposed to lead to such dire things. "I just want to do it," she said.

He seemed to accept this rather inarticulate explanation. "Anyway, it's a beautiful dress," he said. "It makes you look very sophisticated."

"Does it?" Caroline said, delighted.

"You looked around twenty-four in it, at least," he said, smiling because he knew that was the age she had picked as the perfect age to be.

After buying the dress, they walked through the park and had iced tea at the zoo. It was a beautiful day, especially for New York, hot, but with a cool breeze. Caroline, sipping her iced tea, reflected that now that school was almost over, she would no longer have to obey all those rules Justin had set down about her not being able to look at him or talk to him. Once school was over, she could look at him all day, if she wanted!

"Why are you staring at me?" Justin asked, smiling.

"I just feel like it," Caroline said. Her only worry was that she was too happy. Would she at some point in her life have to pay for this happiness? Would she have to die at twenty-eight of a brain tumor or be killed in a car crash? She decided that even those things, which seemed comfortably far away, would not be too great a price to pay. It made sense to her that there should be a price. Otherwise it wouldn't be fair. Why should she be happier than anyone else in the world? She was not especially virtuous, she hadn't performed any noble or courageous deeds. One day you'll die, she reminded herself, but even that awe-inspiringly gloomy thought didn't seem to right the essential injustice because one day *everyone* would die. That didn't explain why she, Caroline, had been selected out of all humanity to be given this incredible gift, this perfect happiness.

It was only when they were about to get on the bus that Caroline asked, "Where's the dress?"

"The dress?"

"I was carrying it in a box." She frowned. "I must have set it down somewhere."

"Probably when we stopped for that drink. . . . Let's go back."

But when they returned to the cafeteria, the box was gone and the attendant said no one had turned anything in to the lost and found. As they hurried back to Bonwit's, Caroline wondered if this were some kind of omen, some kind of punishment akin, on a more minor scale, to the brain tumor she had been worrying about earlier. But it turned out there was another identical dress in stock in her size. This time Justin paid for it. "Is that okay?" he said with a smile.

In an odd way Caroline didn't mind. It was true that now the dress had cost twice what it really should have cost. On the other hand, she had given both Justin and her mother the satisfaction of having bought her graduation dress; that seemed to have a kind of balance to it. They separated, agreeing to meet at seven-thirty, two hours later.

At home Caroline's mother had just taken a shower. Caroline came in to show her the dress. Her mother thought it lovely and not too plain. "You can wear it to parties and dances," she said with her usual practicality.

Caroline lay on her mother's bed and watched her get dressed. As a child she had liked to do this, and now she was especially eager for her mother to look her best for Justin. She felt a little as though she were fixing up the two of them. Deep down she was much more concerned about her mother's reaction to Justin than with Justin's reaction to her mother, but still she wanted her mother to look just right.

"Wear the blue silk dress," she said as her mother stood looking into the closet.

"Yes, that *is* a nice one," her mother said, taking it out. When she was finished, she looked very pretty. Her hair was in a French twist and she had on small pearl-button earrings. She smelled, as she always did, of lily-of-the-valley cologne. She looked neat and ladylike and feminine, Caroline thought, though she knew Maggie said the word feminine should never be used.

"Carrie, aren't *you* going to change?" her mother said.

"Should I?" She hadn't thought about it.

"Why don't you wear that nice skirt Sylvia Disch got you, the patchwork one?"

"Okay," Caroline said. She realized Justin had never seen her in a long skirt. It was a pretty one, made of patches, just like a quilt. With it she put on a plain white blouse. She had thought that telling her mother about Justin was her main fear, but now she decided that even worse was the fact that they were about to finally meet. Was her own presence really necessary? After all, *she* knew both of them. Couldn't they just go out to dinner by themselves? But Caroline realized that no one but herself would have considered this a very plausible idea.

Waiting for Justin, she prowled around the apartment while her mother spread cheese on small crackers and arranged them on a plate. She felt critical of their apartment; she felt she was seeing it through Justin's eyes. His own apartment, though not elegant, seemed intellectual in its messiness with magazines like *The New Republic* and *The New York Review of Books* lying on the coffee table. And there were nice things like the rug Justin had bought and the corduroy couch. Caroline felt the apartment in which they lived looked threadbare, genteel. Anyone could tell at a glance, she felt, that the drapes had come back from the cleaners two slightly different shades of green and that the hassock was placed where it was to cover a stain where something had spilled, that the carpet was a dark color because her mother felt that it would not show the dirt. The night he had stayed over she knew they had been too absorbed in each other for him to have had a chance to really examine the apartment. Now she felt more apprehensive.

When Justin rang the doorbell, an umbrella in one hand, Caroline looked at him critically. He was wearing a khaki-colored cotton suit and a shirt with fine green checks. She was afraid he looked too handsome. She wished he had not worn green, because that was a color that looked so good on him. "Hi," he said. "It looks like there might be some kind of storm out."

Caroline hoped the storm was not symbolic. She led Justin in to meet her mother. Then the three of them sat down in the living room.

"Maggie has mentioned what a good teacher you are," Caroline's mother said. At first Caroline thought she meant "Caroline has mentioned . . ." and then realized her mother had deliberately mentioned Maggie.

"Yes, well, Maggie is a very unusual student," Justin said, setting his drink down on the side table.

"I'm afraid Caroline is like me—her forte is more in the direction of the humanities."

"Well, I was a philosophy major myself in college,"

Justin said. "It wasn't until my last year that I decided to go into science."

Caroline hadn't known that; she found it interesting.

"*I* always liked philosophy," Caroline's mother said. "In fact, that was how I met my husband—in a philosophy class."

Caroline hadn't known *that* either. Despite her nervousness, she thought how interesting it was that both of them were saying things to each other that they'd never mentioned to her.

"I gather your husband is a filmmaker," Justin said, accepting a cheese canape from the platter.

"Yes. . . . He does, well, mainly documentaries," Caroline's mother said. "I think he's probably one of the leading documentary filmmakers in France. He's a very brilliant person, very unusual."

"It's a pity he hasn't been able to see Caroline more often over the years," Justin said.

"Well, you know, you can't change people," Caroline's mother said with a pained expression on her face. "People are just a certain way and, well, perhaps creative men don't have the— So much of their energy goes into their work." She had a slightly pleading expression in her eyes, as though hoping he would accept this.

"I guess I just can't imagine not having any interaction with one's child," Justin said.

"Yes, Caroline tells me you're very close to your son," Caroline's mother said.

"He's wonderful," Justin said. "That's why I'm glad that Ariella is living nearby. It always seems so difficult when parents are separated by great distances for whatever reason."

"Yes," Caroline's mother said. "Of course, nowadays it's different. Men seem to be more . . . well, involved with their children. It was different in our era. . . . I'm glad Caroline will be in the city. I would hate to have her so far away."

"Yes, I can understand that," Justin said.

There was a pause.

"It's terribly important to me that she go on with her art," Caroline's mother said, "because I, well, didn't and . . . It's not the thing of greatness, but one owes it to oneself to find out . . . how far one can go." In her quiet way she was breathless with emotion.

"Yes, I want her to go on too," Justin said. "My wife never . . . found anything and it, well, of course it was complicated, but if she'd had something—"

"of her own," Caroline's mother finished. "Yes, one *has* to. One simply has to!"

Caroline had been sitting, sunk in the armchair, listening intently to her mother and Justin talk. It was all very interesting, but at the same time the strain of hoping they were liking each other made her feel exhausted, as though, instead of sitting quietly in a chair, she had been running around and around the living room. She decided to blank out; it was a talent she had. She simply turned off the sound and sat there, watching both of them and not hearing a word either of them said. She thought how pretty her mother looked and how handsome Justin looked and how she loved both of them, and half an hour passed quickly by.

"I wonder if we should set out now," her mother said. "What do you think, Carrie?"

"What?" Caroline said, turning back into the conversation.

"It looks kind of ominous out," Justin said. In fact, the sky had turned pitch-black and streaks of lightning could be seen.

"Well, I *could* order Chinese food to be sent up," Caroline's mother said. "Carrie and I sometimes do that. Would that be all right?"

"It sounds fine to me," Justin said. He looked at the menu Caroline's mother brought in and indicated what he would prefer. Caroline's mother went to phone the order.

Justin looked at Caroline. "You can take your jacket off," she said formally.

"I think I will," he said. "It's a little sticky."

"Should I turn on the air conditioner?"

"No, it's not that bad."

She wanted so much to ask him what he was thinking, how her mother seemed to him, if he minded the hassock over the spot on the rug, or if he had noticed the drapes. But she was too aware of her mother, whose voice she could hear from the next room.

They ate at the small table in the end of the living room.

"Do you like to cook?" Caroline's mother asked Justin.

"Yes, I do . . . some things," he said. A kind of formality seemed to have returned.

"I wish Whitman had had some kind of home economics course," Caroline's mother said. "Of course Maggie would kill me if she heard that, but I do think girls should learn to at least boil an egg."

"I can boil an egg," Caroline said. These were among the only words she had spoken all evening.

"Yes, well, I mean . . . I was the same. When I got married, I could practically only cook spaghetti and omelets. I'm afraid it wore Roger's patience a bit."

Caroline hoped Justin did not take this as an indication that her mother was expecting him to marry her. "I think one can learn pretty quickly," Justin said. "It's like anything—when you have to . . ."

"I suppose you're right. What do you think about dessert? Carrie and I sometimes have this dessert—it's a little like a banana split, only on top of the ice cream you put honey and almonds."

"That sounds interesting," Jusin said.

183

"We only have tea, I'm afraid."

"I like tea," he said.

When Justin left at ten-thirty, Caroline went out in the hall with him.

"So . . . was that so awful?" he said, smiling.

In a certain way it had been, but it was over and it had worked out all right, so Caroline just said, "It was okay. . . . What did you think of her?"

"She's lovely. . . . She looks just like you."

People always said that, so Caroline was not surprised.

They embraced in the hall. Caroline thought that if she had been certain no one would interrupt them, she would have made love in the hall, but, as it was, she just pressed as close to him as she could, kissing him passionately, pretending he was inside her. "I love you," Justin said.

She wanted so much to go home with him! But she knew it would be better not to. "I'll see you tomorrow," she said, letting go of him reluctantly.

Back in the kitchen her mother was rinsing out the glasses of the before-dinner drinks.

"I feel most sorry for his child," her mother said, almost as though they had been in the midst of a conversation.

"Well, he's really very happy," Caroline said.

"No, but it's the children who suffer in these things," her mother said.

"*I* didn't suffer," Caroline said. She wanted somehow to tell her mother, now that their life together was coming to an end, that it hadn't been bad, that she hadn't minded things like not having been able to have music lessons or go to summer camp.

Her mother turned and smiled at her sadly. "Yes, you did suffer, darling, you did. . . . But it's all right. It seems to have worked out."

Caroline didn't know what to say. She wanted to ask

what her mother had thought of Justin, but she hadn't the courage.

"He's a very sympathetic person," her mother said, as though reading her thoughts. "I wonder why his wife . . . His wife was the one who left *him*, you said?"

Caroline hadn't wanted to tell her mother about Ariella's affairs because she knew she would disapprove so totally. "I guess she felt she married too young," she said.

"Well, there's something in that certainly," her mother said. "I suppose none of *your* generation will make that mistake. None of you seems to want to get married at all! . . . When I once asked Maggie about it, she looked at me like I was out of my mind."

"Maggie is different," Caroline said.

The morning of graduation Caroline cut herself while shaving her legs. She sat on the edge of the bathtub holding a cold, wet washcloth against her leg. More than the pain or the blood, she hated the idea that accidents like that could happen. Finally, after half an hour, the blood stopped. She covered the scar with several Band-Aids stuck one after the other in a line. It would show through her stockings, but there was nothing she could do about it.

The graduation ceremony passed in a haze for her. She hardly heard what the speaker was saying, though she gathered from the expression on Maggie's face that she thought it was a bunch of clichés, "the same old garbage," as Maggie had predicted. Caroline looked out into the audience. She was a little myopic, so that the faces tended to blur, especially the ones toward the back. She saw Maggie's father with his girl friend. They were talking to each other, and she was smiling. She saw Todd looking serious and attractive. Her mother, off to one side, had a proud, slightly tearful expression. Standing at the very back of the auditorium was Justin. He was standing next to another teacher. She glanced at him just for a moment. She had trained herself so carefully all year not to look at him that now her eyes darted guiltily away almost involuntarily.

After the ceremony they all went out to eat—Maggie, Todd, Maggie's father and his girl friend, her mother and Justin. They ate at one long table. Caroline did not deliberately blank out as she had when her mother and Justin had met for the first time, but she heard almost nothing that was said. She sat dreamily, poking at her food. She was used to talking and relating to all these people separately, and she was not sure how to be with them all together, which "self" she should be, the self she was with Justin or the self she was with her mother or the self she was with Maggie.

"Are you finished?" her mother said at the end of the meal, seeing that Caroline's plate was practically full.

"Yes, I guess I wasn't that hungry," Caroline said.

She was glad her mother thought the excitement of graduating was excuse enough for that. Justin was sitting next to her on the long, leather-covered bench. The only thing she had been aware of throughout the meal had been his leg and thigh pressed against hers, and the only thought she had had was wishing she could stay with him that night. But he had said that it wouldn't be fair to her mother and she had thought this was considerate of him, to think of her mother. After all, he had pointed out, in a few weeks they'd be together all the time. That was true, hard to believe but true, and Caroline forced herself to part from him at the end of the meal, feeling embarrassed even at the quick kiss he gave her with all the others there.

At home she felt sleepy and went to bed early, after taking a bath. She turned on the air conditioner in her room. She enjoyed the soft whirring sound it made, like an airplane about to take off. Now, looking back on it, it seemed to her that all the worries she had had about her mother knowing about Justin, about their meeting, had been like the worries Alice in Wonderland had had when she was first too small, then too large to fit through the door leading into the magic garden. It was only by nibbling on alternate sides of the mushroom that she had shrunk to the right size. Caroline felt that she was like Alice at that point, looking into the garden of adult life with its supposed pleasures and delights about to be tasted and experienced; it frightened her a little.

In the middle of the night the phone rang. Her mother always slept with her door closed and Caroline with hers open. She got groggily out of bed—the clock read three-twelve—and stumbled into the living room. "Hello?" she said warily.

"Carrie? It's me," Justin said. "Listen—Ariella's killed herself. I have to drive up there early this morning. I just wanted to let you know in case you tried to reach me. I'll call you as soon as I can."

Caroline put the phone back on the hook, got into bed, and fell asleep at once. When she woke up in the morning, she thought vaguely: I had a bad dream last night. What was it? But that was silly—to try and remember a bad dream. Then, on the way in to brush her teeth, she remembered that it had not been a dream after all.

She had driven into the forest down a secluded road, Justin said, closed up all the windows of the car, and turned on the gas. Because her boyfriend thought she was going to the city and her parents (who were taking care of Noah while Justin attended the graduation ceremony) thought she was still in the country, and because the road was so secluded, it was two days before the car was found. Then, it was found by a couple who happened to drive down and see it parked in a grove of trees.

They went to the funeral together. When they came home, Justin lay down on the couch and put a group of records on the phonograph. He lay there for several hours, his arm over his eyes, listening to the music, which was turned on loud. All afternoon he said nothing. Even at dinner he ate in silence, and when he looked at Caroine, his face had a blank expression, as though he didn't see her. It wasn't until they were in bed together that he spoke suddenly into the darkness.

"I remember we were once at a movie, I forget which one, I think an Ingmar Bergman, and Ariella said, 'I'm never going to make a suicide attempt.' At that time I thought she meant: 'I will never attempt suicide.' But I guess what she really meant was: 'I will never just attempt it. If I do it, it will be for keeps.'" He was silent a moment. "No, I'm not honest. I knew what she really meant. . . . I just didn't want to think about it."

"Do you feel . . . guilty somehow?" Caroline said, hoping that was all right to say.

"No, not guilty . . . but now she'll never find her way out of it." His voice broke.

Caroline stared at him. It frightened her to see him so upset.

"But you didn't love her anymore," she said, feeling cruel, but as though she had to reclaim him.

"In some way you always love someone," he said. "You never stop loving them."

Caroline's heart was pounding. "What do you mean?" she cried.

"It's part of you," he said. "It's part of your life. You don't just—It's there—always."

She felt as though everything was growing dark around her. "Was it because of me that she did it?" she said finally, because she couldn't not ask.

"Because of us, you mean?" he said. "No."

"Are you sure?" She felt she had to know. "Maybe it

bothered her, that you'd found someone and she hadn't."

"She had someone," he said dryly.

"Someone lasting," Caroline insisted, hating this, hating herself.

"She didn't think we had something lasting," he said. "She thought—well, I was using you. You know, she saw it as a cliché, you as the sweet adoring young thing that was readily available."

"Did she know we were going to live together and everything?" Caroline said, hating Ariella for that beyond anything.

"Yes, she was surprised. . . . But she still . . . You shouldn't feel guilty."

Caroline was silent a minute. "That's so awful," she said.

"What?"

"How could she think that about me? About us? That's so condescending. I wish she'd lived to see it wasn't true."

"Christ, Carrie, she's dead! Okay? What does it matter anymore?"

"All right," she said quickly, hurt.

"It's so complicated," he said. "She was jealous of my students, all of them. Not just you. Maggie. She hated Maggie! For being so good at science, the way her father had wanted her to be. She just didn't . . . Look, we were very happy once, you can see that, can't you? It went bad, but we were, Jesus, we were teenagers when we met, we didn't know anything. You don't have that again. You're not that . . . open again."

Caroline had wanted to think that what they had was better. She had a horror of his idealizing Ariella now that she had died, of idealizing their time together. "But you said she was irresponsible," she said.

"She was! She was a lot of bad things. She was a wreck in a lot of ways. But, damn it, we went through so much. . . . Vera. . . . She was as much a part of my life as . . . Noah. So accept it, okay?"

"I do," Caroline said, lying.

Justin reached over and took her hand.

"I want us to be happy," Caroline said, turning to him.

"I think we will be," Justin said.

"I want it to be definite though!" she cried. "I wish it could be definite."

He put his arm around her. "We'll be happy, Carrie."

"Why is everyone I know going crazy?" Maggie asked. She and Todd were in her room getting dressed. Her father and Nina had gotten married that morning; the reception, a party for their friends, was to be held in Nina's living room that afternoon. "I mean, first Daddy, then Caroline and Justin!"

"Not everyone thinks getting married is as crazy a thing to do as you do," Todd said, fastening his tie.

Maggie looked at him. Despite her aversion to ties and suits, she had to admit he looked very handsome. The suit was dark with pinstripes and made him look, she thought, like a sensitive gangster. "I wish we could just stay here and screw all afternoon," she said. "I hate parties."

"It'll just take a couple of hours," he assured her. He rumpled her hair. "Horny one."

"It's the weather," Maggie said. "I don't have the energy for anything else." Lately she had had a horrible sense of everything moving too fast, of her father and Caroline moving out of her life while she was left on the shore, waving. Then, in a few months, Cornell. What had happened to all the enthusiasm and excitement she had felt that weekend when they had gone up to meet Gordon Troupe? "Oh, I don't want to go to Cornell!" she said, pulling on the top to her pantsuit. She was wearing the same pantsuit of crinkly off-white Indian cotton that she had worn to graduation.

"You'll look at it differently in a few weeks," Todd said.

"I won't," Maggie said. She never liked it when anyone tried to make her feel less gloomy than she felt she deserved to be. "It's going to be terrible."

"Why should it be so terrible."

She frowned. "I'm afraid. . . . What if I do something crazy like leaping into bed with someone I don't even *like* out of sheer dumbness?"

He smiled. "What if *I* do?"

"*You* I'm not worried about."

"Why not?"

"You have a sense of values."

"Don't you?"

"I have a lot of strong opinions," Maggie said. "I don't know if that's the same thing."

"You have willpower," Todd reminded her.

"That's true," Maggie said, slightly consoled.

He was looking at her intently. "Anyway, if you do, don't tell me about it, okay?"

"That's the trouble," Maggie said. "I couldn't resist telling you about it. I think it's easier to resist doing it than resist telling you about it."

They had talked around this issue many times and she never felt they quite came to a meeting of minds about it. What she would have liked was if Todd had patted her on the head and said, in effect: "Go, my child, and have affairs with anyone you feel like, for whatever idiotic reason that enters your head. Sleep with tall men, short men, smart men, dumb men. Sow your wild oats. Get it out of your system" (He, of course, would be entitled to do the same). "Then in five or ten years, if we still prefer each other to anyone else, *then* let's sit down and talk about marriage or living together." Todd didn't look at it that way. He had nothing morally against sleeping with various people, but he saw the point of this as being part of a search for "the right person." If you were lucky enough to find that right person the first time out, you were that much ahead. You had saved yourself all that trouble.

Actually her motives seemed, even to her, somewhat frivolous. But even if you ate a perfectly cooked tender sirloin steak one night, was it so terrible to have a yen for lobster or shad roe the next? Todd didn't find this gastronomical analogy overwhelmingly convincing. He said that there was as much variety to be found in sleeping with the same person in different moods as with a horde of different people. He said variety, as such, was meaningless.

But Maggie felt there was another way to look at it. Face it, her life was going to be a worthy, puritanical, hardworking one. She had a superego the size of a tyrannosaurus! At eighty she would be one of those little old ladies who would be getting honorary degrees at small Midwestern colleges. No one would ever be able to say that she hadn't done her bit in contributing to society. So wasn't she entitled, at eighteen, to have a little dumb fun? It seemed only fair.

Nina's living room overlooked Riverside Park. In it fifty people roamed about, drinking champagne. Nina looked pretty in a low-cut dark-purple silk dress, a moonstone necklace glimmering on her soft skin. Her dark black-brown hair was parted in the middle and gathered into a bun, as always. Maggie had thought that the description "creamy," as applied to a woman's skin, was apocryphal, but she had to admit that Nina's skin, especially around her neck and shoulders, looked exactly the hue and texture of heavy cream.

Maggie's father had said no wedding gifts would be accepted other than small- or large-grain Iranian caviar. He was sitting on the piano bench, spooning caviar out of a glass bowl, looking beatific. "Why didn't someone tell me getting married was going to be like this?" he said. "I should have done it years ago."

Of Nina someone said, "She looks like the sister that got to Moscow."

"None of them got to Moscow," someone else said.

"Well, she looks like they *would* have looked if they'd made it."

Nina raised her hand. "I have an announcement to make," she said. "Now none of you will believe us if we say we're going to give up smoking . . . so I'll just say we promise never again to *say* we're going to give up smoking. If we do it, it will be discreetly and quietly."

"Hurrah!" someone shouted.

Someone asked Nina if she intended to make any changes in the Tarachow apartment. "Well, Ray's office, of course, I wouldn't touch," she said, "for the simple reason that he'd kill me if I did. . . . And Maggie's room, of course, we'll keep as it is. But the kitchen *is* like something out of the dark ages."

Maggie was glad to hear her room would be kept the same. Even if she no longer lived there, she hated the idea of it being made into a guest room. The party, now that she was here, didn't seem so bad to her. Slumped in a chair, she felt sleepy. Todd was standing next to Nina, talking to her and gazing occasionally at her breasts, which was hard to avoid doing due to the cut of her dress. Maggie just sat, eyes half closed, mentally undressing Todd and abandoning herself to erotic fantasies.

Todd came over to her. "Don't go to sleep, Maggie."

"I'm horribly drunk," she confessed.

"Are you?"

"Umm . . . champagne is so good, isn't it? Why were you gaping at Nina's breasts?"

"I wasn't gaping," he said. "I was gazing in quiet admiration."

"Humph!"

"Anyway, you're so covered up, there's nothing to gaze at or gape at."

"Come home and I'll give you something to gape at," she said.

"Well, we *have* stayed quite a while," he said, seeming to find this offer appealing.

"I'll go say good-bye to Nina," Maggie said.

She told Nina what a good time they had had.

"You know what it was that first attracted me to Ray?" Nina said. Her face was moist and glowing; she looked a bit high herself. "It was how he talked about you, Maggie. You know, my first husband just wouldn't even *think* of having children and hated it when the topic ever came up. And Raymond just took out all these photos of you and went on and on about how smart and wonderful you were. I think I fell in love with him right there!"

Maggie smiled. Todd put his arm around her. "We'll see you later," he said.

Outside it was over ninety degrees. "It's *crazy* to get married in weather like this," Maggie said. "Crazy!"

"June is traditional for weddings," Todd pointed out.

"It's traditional for crazy people. People are traditionally crazy in June."

At home the first thing Maggie did was turn the air conditioner on high cool and take off all her clothes.

"You know, it's amazing," Todd said. "No matter what you're wearing, you manage to get undressed in about three seconds."

Maggie flopped, naked, on the bed. "I thought I was going to pass out from horniness," she said. "I should never drink champagne."

"On the contrary. I think you should drink it all the time," he said, carefully hanging his jacket over the chair.

"Maybe when I'm with you. . . . Todd, if you fold up your tie, I'm going to kill you."

He approached her, finally naked. "O importunate, impetuous wench!"

"O importunate, impetuous wench yourself!" Maggie said, falling on him.

She had always liked air conditioners and had always

been amazed at people who said they willingly lived without them. Besides, for making love in New York when the temperature was over ninety, air conditioning was essential. Only in movies, she decided, did sweaty bodies slapping together have any real sensual appeal. Afterward she stretched and lay with her hands over her head, smiling. But then she thought of Caroline's news and frowned. Approach it from whatever angle she might, she still could not understand it. Her father and Nina—all right. After all, they had known each other thirteen years. But Justin and Caroline! That seemed like a final, gratuitous blow. Caroline she could excuse. For one thing, fond as you might be of Caroline, you couldn't deny that rationality was not exactly her strong point. And she was so head over heels in love with Justin that if he'd suggested they spend the rest of their life in a wicker cage, she'd have agreed. But Justin! He was almost thirty. He was a scientist! And, more than that, he'd just come out of a bad marriage. Wasn't there one single person in the whole world besides herself who used reason to govern his or her personal life? Here his wife had just killed herself. What better argument against marriage would anyone need than that? It was true, as Todd pointed out, that the two events had not followed each other in inexorable succession, but still they *had* both occurred, and it was certainly not irrational to say that if Ariella had never been married, she might still be alive. Why this haste on their part? Caroline wasn't pregnant; it made no sense.

Maggie rolled over on her stomach. "I wish I understood the thing with Caroline and Justin," she said. "I don't want to *approve* of it. I just want to *understand* it."

Todd had never found it so impossible to understand. "Look, he's twenty-eight, right?"

"Yes, but all the more reason. He should have some sense!"

"Sure, but at the same time he also probably has more

awareness of what he wants out of life. After all, he *was* married."

"Yeah, but look at his marriage! It was *awful!*"

"Evidently he feels that was due to the particular combination of him and his wife, not marriage itself."

"It just shows how self-destructive people are!" Maggie concluded. "They make one mistake and, instead of learning from it, they just go on making the *same* mistake all over again."

"You don't think second marriages ever succeed?"

"Oh, I suppose they do . . . sometimes," Maggie conceded.

"They seem to me to be very much in love," Todd said. "And they were planning to live together anyway. . . ."

"Precisely . . . so why wreck it by getting married?"

He laughed.

Maggie looked at him, at his soft, dark eyes. "You just think love solves everything," she accused him.

"I do not. Lots of people can be in love physically, but not have anything in common beyond that. I'm just saying if they do and if they're reasonably intelligent people and have thought it over, then I think their chances for happiness are pretty good."

Maggie sighed and closed her eyes. "I don't know," she said.

"Would you marry me, Maggie?" Todd said.

Startled, she opened her eyes.

"I don't mean now—I just mean could you ever entertain it as a possibility, say sometime in the future, even?"

"Todd, you shouldn't say that, really you shouldn't."

"Say what?"

"That you want to marry me."

"Why shouldn't I?"

"Because it's an insult. It shows you have contempt for me."

"To want you to be my wife?"

"It shows you just want someone to go around picking up your dirty socks."

He smiled ironically. "Somehow, knowing us, I think it would more likely be the other way around."

"You'd want to have children. You'd force me to."

"How would I force you? Would I sneak in at night and put little pinpricks in your diaphragm?"

"Seriously," Maggie said.

He became serious. "We wouldn't have to have children."

"But you want them. It wouldn't be fair."

"Well, marriage is compromising. If I felt it would make you miserable, then there wouldn't be any sense to it."

She looked at him suspiciously. "Deep down you'd be hoping I'd change my mind."

"Sure. . . . Is that so terrible?"

"Maybe I *would* change my mind," she said. That thought seemed even more terrible.

"Maggie, look, we're talking about something that might not take place for ten years. We won't be the same people then. Why decide now what we want to do *then*?"

"But that's the thing," Maggie said. "How can we even think about it when in ten years we'll be so different? Maybe we just have this fantastic physical attraction and once it goes away, we won't have anything to say to each other."

"We always *seem* to have plenty to say."

"That's true," she admitted gloomily.

"Anyway, why *should* it go away?" he said, running a hand down her spine.

"It just does," Maggie said. "When people get older, they aren't as interested in sex anymore, or not with the same person."

"Mom says that's hogwash. She says the first twenty

years are just practice—that's when it starts getting really good."

"Oh, your family!" It wasn't fair of his family, Maggie thought, to be the embodiment of everything she was sure was not possible. It just wasn't *fair*.

He was gazing at her, smiling. "I have a present for you."

"For me?" She was startled. "What did *I* do? *I* didn't get married."

He got up, went over and returned with a large flat white box which he presented to her. Maggie's heart sank. It couldn't be, he wouldn't have dared to do something as awful as getting her a ring. She thought of all the books she'd read in which packages which seemed large had been really stuffed with paper to conceal the fact that they contained small objects like rings. Please, she begged whoever ruled these things. Please don't let it be a ring.

It was something even more surprising than a ring. It was a nightgown. Maggie shook it out. It was a floor-length flame-colored chiffon nightgown with a low neck. "I never had a nightgown," she said, puzzled. She had always slept either nude or in pajamas.

"That's not to say you don't look better without anything on," Todd said, looking pleased. "I just saw this and it reminded me of you."

Maggie frowned. If any ultimate, final proof were needed that his opinion of her bore no passing connection to her opinion of herself, it was this nightgown. If she had been shown this nightgown and asked to list the first thousand people it reminded her of, it would never have occurred to her for a second to list herself.

"Try it on," Todd suggested.

She slipped it over her head.

"It looks great," he said. "I knew it would."

She went over and looked at herself in the floor-length mirror. "Jesus, I look like the cover of a Gothic novel,"

Maggie said, half in horror, half impressed despite herself. Somehow the way the nightgown was cut made her breasts look fuller. "It's beautiful," she had to admit.

"How come you never had a nightgown?" Todd said.

"I just never thought of it. . . . I always thought women who did had to be, you know, that Total Woman type, some kind of brainless idiot who would sit around spraying herself with perfume and waiting for her lover or husband to come home." She continued looking at the reflection of the two of them, him naked, her in her flame-colored gown. "I should get you white silk pajamas."

"Why that?"

"Don't you remember in *A Streetcar Named Desire* . . . what's-his-name, Brando, has this pair of white silk pajamas he wears on special occasions. You'd look nice in them."

He smiled sheepishly. "I don't know that I bear such an overwhelming resemblance to Brando," he said.

"Oh, you're better than him, any day," Maggie said. "He's just a blob." She sat down on the bed again. "Thank you for getting me the nightgown," she said slightly formally.

"You're welcome."

"Maybe deep down I always had a fantasy of wanting a nightgown like this, but I repressed it," she said. "Do you think that's possible?"

"I think it's possible."

"And you don't think it leads, irreversibly, to everything else?"

"In what way?"

"Well, that you start off saying what the heck, what's a sexy nightgown, and you end up ten years later with a passel of kids and a subscription to *The Ladies' Home Journal*."

"I wouldn't think there's any *necessary* connection," he assured her. He was gazing at her thoughtfully. "Maggie, there's one strange thing about you. . . . Maybe this is sort of a sensitive topic, but——"

"Only one?" she said trying to joke. "How come you didn't notice all the others?"

"You say you're a feminist," he said. "But you seem so defensive about women. I don't exactly understand it since your father is so supportive of your work and so on. Do you know what I mean?"

Maggie felt as though someone had taken a sharp knife and sliced her clean through the middle. "Yes," she said. "I know what you mean."

"It's as though deep down you don't think that highly of women, like you feel you have to go around convincing everyone else that they aren't so bad, but you never quite manage to convince yourself. . . . Why *is* that?"

She took a deep breath. She didn't look at him. "No, I know, he is——Daddy *is* supportive of my work, but I guess I've always felt he doesn't really think women are equal to men. I mean, when my mother was alive, there was always this thing of her going around whispering, 'Your father is working.' like it was this tremendous big deal, and his going around saying things like 'Anyone can cook.' It was like what *she* did well *anyone* could do. What *he* did well was special. . . . And all the generalizations he made always seemed to go to prove women aren't as fair as men, women aren't as rational. It was like he was saying maybe if you were terrific, if you spent every second of your life fighting, maybe then, if you were really lucky, you might be one of the exceptions."

"That's awful," Todd said.

"Well, but——" Maggie hated having somehow revealed her father in a negative light. "He didn't——"

"Didn't what?"

"He always says he doesn't want me to necessarily accept everything he thinks or feels. He's always saying: Rebel, spit in my face, reject my values." She laughed.

"But it's so damn hard to do that if someone tells you to. It's like smoking. He always said: Fine, smoke! So I never did."

"So deep down you're a conformist," Todd said, "not a rebel after all."

She made a wry face. "Maybe." It seemed to Maggie that was the most terrible thing that could be said of anyone. "Now you know my awful secret," she said with chagrin.

"Am I supposed to back away shrieking with horror and say I don't love you anymore?"

She nodded.

He let out a mock shriek. "Aaah!"

"But really, Todd, why *do* you—love me, I mean?" She felt that truly this was not a matter of begging for compliments. She really wanted to know and understand what seemed to her so absolutely incomprehensible. "I mean, what's *in* it for you? Why go through all this? What's the *point*?"

He looked right at her. "Maggie, if I say you're beautiful or sexy or smart, you'll give me an eight-hour argument on each point. If you love someone, you don't go around saying: "What's *in* it for me? You accept that there are certain mysteries to life and love is one of them."

"But how can you just accept that? That makes life so terrible—people just being shuttled back and forth utterly at the whim of their emotions!"

"I don't think it's so terrible. Think how much worse it would be if reason ruled everything."

"So you can just sit back and let yourself be carried away on a tide of emotion without even caring? Without being afraid?"

"Yes," he said.

"What if I—what if I said I didn't want us to ever see each other again?"

He thought a moment. "I'd be very, very sad for a long time, but after a while I hope I'd pull myself together and start looking for someone else."

Maggie started to cry.

Justin and Caroline got married at a small chapel at Yale, where he had gone to college. It was the last day of June and the temperature was ninety-seven degrees. Caroline was wearing the dress she had worn to graduation and Maggie had to admit that she looked incredibly beautiful. She had always thought it was a complete canard that women in love or women about to get married looked any different or better than they usually did, but Caroline's hair formed soft tendrils and curls around her face and her skin looked like a nine-month-old baby's after a bath. Justin, although he looked attractive enough in a seersucker suit, was, she thought, not exactly transformed. Maybe that was because men didn't look transformed or maybe because it was his second marriage.

It was cool in the chapel, but when they emerged into the heat everyone looked about to melt. Maggie felt her pantsuit sticking to her; her hair was soaking wet with perspiration. The wedding party was only about twenty people; after the ceremony they were going to gather at the home of a friend of Caroline's mother, a woman named Sylvia Disch. Sylvia Disch obviously had money. She lived on a hill surrounded by an acre of land. In the back of the house was a gigantic kidney-shaped pool. In spite of her disdain for wealth, Maggie had to admit that to have such a house and pool seemed like a very fine thing on this particular day. Everyone changed to shorts or bathing suits and drank champagne on the lawn.

Maggie wore her black bikini. She had decided if a sexy nightgown was all right, why not a bikini? She tried not to worry that this might be another step on the slow, tortuous path to Total Womanhood. She gave an ungainly leap into the pool and surfaced, shaking the water out of her face. If she ever had money, she decided, this would be the way to spend it. It reminded her of a Katharine Hepburn movie, lounging by the side of the pool drinking champagne.

Justin was sitting in the shade in a wicker chair. Maggie, a large orange beach towel over her shoulders, said, "This is a perfect wedding."

"It *is* nice, isn't it?" he said.

"It's the best wedding I've ever been to," she said, though, in fact, she had been to only two or three others. "It's the Platonic ideal of a wedding. I think from now on no one should ever get married, because you've attained the Platonic ideal. . . . Aren't you going swimming?"

"Maybe later. . . . I feel like sitting in the shade and being pensive."

That seemed a strange choice to Maggie. "How do you feel?" she said, suddenly curious.

"I feel good," he said.

"No, I mean, like, do you feel life is beginning anew and all of that? Is that how you feel?"

"In part," he said. "How do *you* feel, Maggie?"

"I feel terrific," she admitted.

"You look good."

"This bikini isn't really my fault," she said. "It's really Todd's, because he got me a nightgown and I figured why not a bikini as well?"

"There's nothing *wrong* with a bikini," Justin said, regarding it appreciatively.

"It's what it leads to," Maggie informed him.

"What does it lead to?"

"Oh, you know—becoming one of those women who sits in front of the mirror all day looking for gray hairs and crow's-feet and worrying if she should have her face lifted."

"I can't quite imagine you as that type."

"Well, I better not be." Maggie took another glass of champagne. "Is it okay to swim if you're drunk?"

"I would think so."

"I was just afraid I might sink, but not even notice."

"If you don't seem to be surfacing in half an hour, I'll jump in after you," he promised.

When she came out, she decided it was getting cooler and went upstairs to change into slacks and a sleeveless shirt. She was glad she didn't have to get into her sticky pantsuit again. In the living room wonderful food was being laid out. There were several gigantic boned sea bass with pitchers of hollandaise sauce conveniently placed nearby. Maggie poured so much hollandaise over the fish that all that could be seen on her plate was a yellow pool of sauce.

"This is fish?" Caroline's father's girl friend, Danielle, asked her.

"Oui, poisson," Maggie said, wondering if it should have been *"le poisson."* She wanted to speak French, and she was drunk enough not to care about her grammar. Over in the corner she saw Caroline's father talking to Sylvia Disch. Caroline's father was a big disappointment to Maggie. She had always imagined him as a combination of André Malraux and Jean-Paul Belmondo, a man with hooded dark eyes who would speak with much gesticulation and cries of *"Alors!"* and *"Formidable!"* Of course, since he was American, there was no real reason he should have been like that, but she had assumed that years of living in France would have rubbed off on him. Instead, he had turned out to be a not-very-tall, stoop-shouldered man with thinning hair, congenial enough, but not especially sexy. About Danielle Maggie felt more or less the same. She had imagined her as Jeanne Moreau-like, with pouty lips and a world-weary expression, as though she had lived through thousands of fantastically complicated sexual experiences. Instead, Danielle was thin

205

with dark-red hair tied back severely from her face and a very soft, tentative voice; she seemed shy. Maggie tried to launch into a conversation in French, but Danielle looked at her with her eyebrows up and kept saying, *"Pardon?"* about every three seconds. Finally Maggie gave up.

She saw Caroline's mother near the kitchen. "Did you go for a swim?" she said. "It's wonderful."

"Oh, I don't really swim," Caroline's mother said. "It *is* a nice pool, though."

"Where does she get all this money?" Maggie said.

Caroline's mother lowered her voice. "It was her first husband," she said. "I believe he did something with stocks."

Maggie smiled. "I feel so guilty about that day we were talking about Carrie and I knew about Justin, but I couldn't admit to you I did."

"I forgive you, Maggie. . . . You were right to keep a secret."

"It was hard, it really was." Maggie glanced around. "I like Malcolm," she said.

Caroline's mother smiled quietly. "I saw you talking to him. . . . Crazy luck, I guess. I suppose it shows it can happen. I hope with Carrie—" She broke off.

"Why aren't they just going to live together?" Maggie said. She felt only Caroline's mother would understand how she felt about this. "I mean, why get married?"

"Search me. . . . Carrie says it's for Noah. I think it'll be okay, Maggie."

"Do you really?"

"What can I say? I hope . . . You like Justin, don't you?"

"Sure, but it's not just Justin as a person. . . . It's—"

"—his being older," Caroline's mother finished. "If he stops her from going on with her art, I'll go over and throttle him. What more can I say?"

"I don't think he'll do that," Maggie said. "He better not."

"What I dread is," Caroline's mother said, "how being happy can *lull* you. It's like a drug. Carrie's so talented; I hope—"

"I know!" Maggie exploded. "Damn it! We should have stopped them."

Caroline's mother smiled. "We're being—you know, we're overdoing it."

"People always tell me that," Maggie said, feeling calmer.

Todd had just appeared from outside. He had a towel draped over his shoulders. He came over to Maggie.

"Go get some fish," Maggie advised him, "and smother it in hollandaise sauce."

He did so. When he returned, Caroline's mother had moved off. "Isn't the pool wonderful?" Maggie said. "I've decided I want to be rich when I grow up, and don't say that's an interesting discrepancy with my socialist convictions."

"It is a great pool," he agreed.

"Don't you think if you earn money honestly it's okay?" she asked. "I mean, not by grinding down the poor, but just by doing whatever you would have done anyway?"

"This is good fish," Todd said.

"Come on, argue!"

"I've had too much champagne."

"Me too. . . . You know what we should do?"

"What?" He looked uneasy at the gleam in her eye.

"We should take a swim in the nude."

"Now?"

"Sure, everyone's inside. . . . Let's! Come on!"

"Maggie, don't be ridiculous. Someone could come out at any minute."

"Then let's get up in the middle of the night and do it.

It'll be great! In the moonlight and everything. Will you?"

He hesitated. "Sure."

"Are you afraid I'm getting too drunk?"

"How many glasses have you had?"

"I'm not sure. . . . But what's good, I think, is that when you're drunk from champagne you don't get surly or sick, you just feel very light and peaceful."

Caroline had changed into a plain white skirt and off-the-shoulder blouse. She still looked beautiful.

"You look amazing," Maggie said. "It's weird."

"Why is it so weird?" Caroline said.

"I always thought it wasn't true that people in love looked any different."

At the mention of being in love, Caroline blushed and looked even prettier.

"Carrie, I was so good all year," Maggie said. "I never told anyone except my father."

"You weren't supposed to tell even him," Caroline reminded her.

"Oh well, he doesn't count. He never tells secrets. But I was so good with your mother and with everyone at school."

"Thank God no one found out," Caroline said.

"Well, now it won't matter. . . . Are you going to take a regular honeymoon and all that?"

"I don't think so. We've rented this house in Vermont for the summer. Why don't you and Todd come up and visit us?"

"Okay," Maggie said. She looked around. Noah was playing outside with another child. "Is Noah coming too?"

"He'll be with us one month and with his grandparents one month."

"Which month will he be with you?" Maggie asked cautiously.

Caroline laughed. "He's so nice, Maggie! Really."

Maggie frowned. "Yeah, he seems pretty good. . . . But still. I guess I do have this prejudice against little boys," she admitted. "They always seem to be going around shouting and knocking things down."

"Noah's not like that," Caroline said. "He's almost the exact opposite."

It was growing dark and cool. Several people wandered out onto the lawn. There was even some talk of playing croquet, but it never came to anything. Maggie and Todd were staying at Sylvia Disch's house, but most of the other guests were driving home to New York. They began departing.

"I gather you're Caroline's best friend," Sylvia Disch said to Maggie.

"Yes, well, we met at Whitman," Maggie said. She was looking at the pool and thinking how nice the midnight swim would be.

"She's so lucky to have found Justin."

"In what way?" Maggie countered.

"There just aren't that many decent men around anymore."

"Aren't there?" Maggie said.

"Not really. I often wish I could talk myself into being a lesbian—there'd be so much better pickings."

"I guess that's not really possible," Maggie said.

"Of course, your young man seems very nice too. I haven't had a chance to talk to him that much."

"He *is* very nice," Maggie said.

"No special plans yet?" Sylvia Disch said with a smile.

Maggie felt too benignly drunk to get enraged. "For getting married?"

"Umm."

"Maybe in ten or fifteen years," Maggie said.

"That seems a long way off," Sylvia Disch said.

"Well, time passes quickly," Maggie said vaguely.

"Have you tried the cake?" Sylvia asked her.

"No, it looks wonderful. I think I'm going to have a strawberry shortcake when I get married too."

"Those wedding things are usually so inedible."

Maggie took her cake out on the lawn and sat crosslegged, eating it. Everyone was inside. Fireflies were coming out, glowing and vanishing into the darkness. She felt extraordinarily peaceful and contented. It had all happened, her father getting married, and Caroline and Justin, and she didn't feel bereft. She felt slightly melancholy, but in a genial, calm way. She looked inside at Todd standing talking to Caroline. Inadvertently the thought passed through her mind for the hundredth time: Why didn't he pick someone like that? Life could be so peaceful for him. "It would be like eating poached eggs every day," he had said when she had proposed this. Still . . . Caroline had her head tilted to one side in a characteristic posture. She looked so glowing and soft. He's crazy, Maggie finally concluded, but even this, in her present mood, she accepted as being his right. Then she noticed that Justin was sitting in a chair under a tree about ten feet from her. "Were you out here all the time?" she said. "I didn't see you."

"I didn't want to disturb you," he said. "You looked so intent. What were you thinking about?"

"Life," she said, "and people being crazy."

Justin smiled.

Suddenly Maggie went over to where he was sitting. "Justin, listen, there's something terribly important I have to say to you," she said. She knew she was drunk, but it seemed to her that being drunk had given her a unique clarity of vision.

"What is it?" he asked.

"Don't ever have affairs," she said. "Ever! I mean, Carrie just isn't suited to open marriage and all that kind of thing. She's much too sensitive, and it would wreck her whole life!"

"I'm not intending to," he said.

"Of course you're not *now*! You just got married! No, I mean ever, even in, like, a hundred years, even if you're separated for several weeks or several months or if you meet some fantastically sexy, gorgeous person, just don't *ever* do it. . . . Promise me."

Justin smiled. "Maggie."

"Promise me, Justin. Seriously. It's important."

"I promise," he said.

She sat back and sighed. "Why did you get married?" she burst out suddenly. "I don't understand it!"

"I thought you said our wedding was the Platonic ideal," he said.

"If you believe in them," she said.

"I do," he said, seeming uncomfortable.

"But why in such a rush?" she went on. "You were going to live together for a while."

"I know." He was silent. "Carrie seemed to want it so much," he said. "I agree with you. Waiting might have been better."

Maggie stared at him, dumbfounded. It had been Carrie! How much easier it had been to cast Justin as the villain. "Oh," she said. "I didn't know."

"I think it will work," he added hastily.

"You don't think it matters that you're older?"

"Matters?"

"I mean, I just have this horror that you'll use it somehow, like 'I know everything and you know nothing.' You'll, like, stunt her growth."

"Maggie, I think this may be the end of a beautiful friendship."

"Justin, I'm not insulting you!"

"You're not?"

"No, I'm just worried, that's all. . . . I mean, it happens all the time."

"What happens?"

"Men trampling women underfoot, for one reason or another."

"I hate you when you're like this," he said impatiently. "It's all clichés. Men are all this way, women are all this way. . . ."

Maggie sighed, seeing his point, but not quite willing to give way. "But listen," she said. "It's more than just—it's not just *not* doing bad things, it's . . . I mean, Carrie is so . . . vulnerable in a way. You have to encourage her. You have to make her stronger and more independent."

"I know," he said. "I want her to be."

Maggie sat back. "Okay," she said, satisfied. Then abruptly she got up and turned a cartwheel.

"You turn a good cartwheel, Margaret," Justin observed.

"I turn a perfect cartwheel," she corrected him and turned several more. When she stood up again, he was gone. Todd was standing watching her. "Aren't I good?" she said.

"You are good, Maggie," Todd said. "You're the best."

"*You're* the best," she said, hugging him. "Oh, I wish it was midnight! Why don't these dopey people go to sleep?"

It was past one before the house completely quieted down. They crept downstairs. Maggie dove into the cool, quiet water, and swam peacefully. It was just as she had imagined: the water, the moonlight, the delicious feeling of being naked. This has been a perfect day, she concluded.

Afterward she convinced Todd to make love to her behind one set of hedges so that, if someone else had an idea about a midnight swim, they would not be observed. The lovemaking was perfect too, Maggie thought: the soft, wet grass, the smell of flowers, the starlit sky overhead, their cool bodies fitting together so effortlessly.

In the morning, seeing Maggie sneeze over her English

muffin, Todd looked at her and smiled a private smile. But she just sat up straighter and poured herself more coffee. She did end up getting a bad cold, but she never regretted a moment of it.

11

Maggie was wearing a dress. She unwound her long body from the small car and stood in front of Justin and Caroine. Todd got out of the other side.

"Maggie, you look fantastic!" Justin said, almost in amazement.

It wasn't just the dress, attractive though it was—peasant style and very casual. It was the fact that Maggie was wearing sandals with heels and wraparound sunglasses, had a deep tan, and looked—was it possible that one would say Maggie looked glamorous, Caroline wondered? Maggie waved a hand in front of both their faces as though to pull them out of a trance. "Okay, folks, enough is enough," she said. "I mean, I know I usually look like a sob, but still!" She pointed at Todd. "*He* made me get the dress. It's all his fault."

"I think Todd ought to have complete control over your wardrobe," Justin said as they all walked toward the house.

"Remember when you never wore anything but overalls!" Caroline said.

"The good old days," Maggie said. She looked around. "It's beautiful here."

"Oh, it's been wonderful," Caroline said. "We've had such a terrific summer." She wanted very much to get Maggie alone; she had found out two weeks earlier, in mid-August, that she was pregnant, and she felt compelled to tell Maggie. Maggie would surely make some caustic remark, but after that, Caroline hoped, she would come around. Maggie always came around in the end.

"Didn't Noah mind?" Todd asked. "Your being so isolated?"

"No, he's very self-sufficient," Justin said. "And then he and Carrie would go off on these long, mysterious walks."

"They weren't mysterious!" Caroline protested. "Just to the cemetery."

There was nothing morbid that led them in that direction; it was simply the nicest of the walks. The cemetery was quiet and shady. It was situated on a hill overlooking a valley. Justin felt worried that Noah seemed to have had so little overt reaction to Ariella's death. He never referred to her at all, and seemed to have completely accepted Caroline as his mother, although he always called her Carrie, as he had before. Caroline felt it was all right that he not talk about it if he didn't want to; that was his right. Only once, one of the first times when they had gone to the cemetery, he had said, "Mommy's there." She had thought at first he meant in that particular cemetery. "If you die, you make the plants grow," he had added with childlike lack of connection. Caroline had never liked the explanation, which she knew was offered to some children; she had been told it when her grandmother had died. It didn't seem to her either honest or satisfying. "Well, it's more—" she began, but he had interrupted her. "Grandma says you don't really die if people still remember you," he said, as though uncertain. "I think that's so," Caroline said. The conversation had ended there. Hand in hand they had walked home. Still, she felt, as she always did with Noah, as though more had been said between them than just the words. She hadn't told Justin about the conversation, though; she was afraid he would worry.

Justin took Maggie and Todd on a walk around the property while Caroline took the roast chicken out of the oven to cool. It was so hot, she had decided cold chicken would be better. This summer was the first time she had ever felt she could live perfectly easily outside the city.

She liked the silence and the long, still afternoons. Often Justin would lie reading in a hammock and she would walk by herself, now that Noah was with his grandparents, and these walks never seemed long enough. The entire two months she had seen no passersby; it was twenty miles to the nearest town. They had left home only once, to visit Vera.

When Justin, Todd, and Maggie returned, Caroline said, "Did you see the tennis court?"

"No, where is it?" Todd asked.

They all walked around to the other side of the house. "I really feel like I'm living out my fantasies of being rich," Justin said. "I've always dreamed of having a house with its own tennis court. It's made of asphalt so you don't have to do anything to keep it up, just sweep the leaves off. Did you bring your rackets, by any chance?"

They shook their heads.

"It doesn't matter; we have a couple of extra ones. . . . Do you feel like playing?"

"Sure," Maggie said. "That would be fun."

They played two sets of doubles. It was growing cooler now at three, but the heat was still intense. Caroline was not bad at tennis. She knew the rules and played with good form, gracefully, but she was never especially interested. She forgot the score, even when it was set point. At times this lackadaisicalness was to her advantage, because even at crucial points, not knowing the score, she played with equal calm. On the other hand, it also meant that at crucial points she would decide: Why bother running after the ball? and it would turn out they had lost the set.

At the start of the second set—they had lost the first—Justin said, "Honey, please play net this set."

Caroline hated playing net. She hated having the ball whiz past her or at her. "I play better from the back," she said.

"But if you play back, it's not real doubles," he said.

"They're coming to the net, so we're giving them an unfair advantage."

"I'll miss it, though," she said.

"I don't care. Just stand there for my serve. Duck if you want."

With some resentment Caroline moved to the net. She stood as far back as she could and still have it be considered that she was playing net, unlike Maggie, who was practically leaning over to the other side. Maggie rushed to the net on every single occasion, and it alarmed Caroline to see her charging forward like an enraged rhinoceros, racket held high. The fact that Maggie missed as often as she made a point seemed irrelevant. It still made her nervous. Actually, they were fairly well matched due to the defects of each person's game. Justin ran around his backhand, Todd had an erratic serve, Maggie played net too often and not that well, and Caroline was methodical, but absolutely lacked an ability to put the ball away. The only way she ever made a point was by someone else's error. Still, despite herself, Caroline was impressed by Maggie's ferocity. She wondered how it was possible to care that much who won.

Caroline and Justin won the second set, evening the score.

"How about a third?" Justin said.

"Sure," Maggie said eagerly.

"I'm game," Todd said.

They all looked at Caroline. "I'm a little tired," she confessed.

"Oh, well, yes, maybe you better not overdo," Justin said quickly. Caroline knew he was thinking of her being pregnant. In fact, that was not why she felt like stopping, but she was glad to take it as an excuse. He looked at Todd. "How about some singles?"

"I don't know," Todd said. "I'd just as soon call it a day, frankly.

"I'll play you singles," Maggie said.

"Okay, great."

Just a week earlier Justin had been saying how playing singles in the broiling sun made no sense and was actually dangerous. True, the sun was lower now—it was half past four—but still Caroline wondered why he would bother. "Do you think you should?" she asked anxiously.

"Oh, sure, an extra set or two can't hurt," he said.

Caroline sat down under a tree with Todd. She felt a certain resentment at both Maggie and Justin. They seemed to her crazy, racing around in this broiling weather. Where was Justin's sense? "I never see the point of games," she confessed to Todd.

"I know what you mean," he said. "I like tennis, though, up to a point. Maggie and I have been playing a lot this summer, in the park. It's not like this, though. This is really beautiful."

"We've had such a wonderful summer," Caroline said. She was glad now that they had had no official honeymoon, just this longer vacation. "I wish we didn't have to go back."

"Wouldn't you miss the city after a while?" he said. "I think I might."

"I don't think so," Caroline said.

"How are you finding being a stepmother?"

Todd was the only person who had thought to ask her that. "I like it," she said. "I mean, I knew him so well before . . . but I don't know."

"What?"

With his soft, sympathetic eyes fixed on her, Caroline wanted so much to tell him she was expecting a baby. But she felt it would be disloyal not to tell Maggie first. In fact, she was worried about how Noah would react to the new baby, but she was even more worried about Justin. Justin, though he tried hard to simulate delight on her account, had not seemed happy about it, much to her great disappointment. Finally, when she had pressed him, he had said he thought it was too soon, that it would interfere with her studies, that he was not sure he was ready for it himself. "Should I have an abortion?" she had asked, frightened, furious, hoping he would suddenly reverse himself. But he had just said, "Only if you want, Carrie." But she didn't want! She wanted the baby! She hadn't even told her mother, knowing how disapproving she would be. For a week or two she had toyed with the idea of abortion, and then Justin seemed to come around and to begin looking forward, making plans, and she had allowed herself to put the earlier confrontation between them out of her mind.

It seemed to Caroline that their lovemaking, which was always so wonderful anyway, was even more special after she was pregnant. The fact that between them, when they made love, was the baby, waiting, growing, seemed such a magical thing, the three of them locked in this embrace. Of course later, no doubt, it would be difficult, when she got large, but now it was like a special secret.

"Do you ever think of having other children?" Todd said quietly.

Caroline wondered how he could be reading her mind. "Well . . . yes," she said softly. "I do."

"My sister would like a third, but she feels it just isn't right, the idea of having more than two."

"She could adopt."

"They may. But she really loved the whole thing of being pregnant and giving birth. I guess it's hard to give that up just for ideological reasons."

"Maggie said she had her babies at home."

"Just the second one. . . . Yes, Mom feels she makes too much of a thing of that. She thinks it's dangerous, but Lindsay says it isn't, if you have the right equipment."

Looking at him, Caroline wondered if he and Maggie would ever get married or have children. She would never have dared bring up either subject to Maggie, who went off like a firecracker at the word "marriage" or "child." She couldn't, no matter what, imagine Maggie pregnant. It was almost easier to imagine Todd pregnant than Maggie.

Justin and Maggie were walking off the court. By Maggie's gloomy expression, Caroline assumed Justin had won; she was right.

"It was close," he said cheerfully. "We had to go to a tiebreaker."

"The light is weird at this time of day," Maggie said grumpily.

"It *is* bad," Justin said. His face was bright red, the sweat streaming down his neck and forehead. "The perfect time to play is seven in the morning. I did that a couple of weeks ago with a friend who came up. It's cool and perfect."

"Let's do it, then," Maggie said. "I'll get up at seven. I want a challenge match."

"Will you? Terrific!"

Caroline smiled. "Seven is crazy," she said. "I never could do it."

"It's beautiful," Justin said. "I love the early morning."

"I love it too," Todd said. "I guess I just love sleeping late more."

They went back to the house and showered, though by now Caroline no longer felt sweaty at all. Justin started getting in the shower with her, but she said he should wait. First, she really didn't like showering with him because it always turned into a prelude to lovemaking and she thought showers should be simply for getting clean. Also, she felt they wouldn't have time since Maggie and Todd were there.

She was sitting on the edge of the bed, staring pensively out the window when Justin came out of the shower.

"Sure you haven't changed your mind?" he said, sitting beside her.

She saw he had an erection and thought maybe it would be nice, but then said, "They'll wonder what happened to us."

"They may be doing the same thing," Justin pointed out.

"Why don't we wait until later?" she said.

Justin began getting dressed.

"Why did you play so long?" Caroline said. "You said you weren't going to anymore."

"Oh, we just played one set."

"Is Maggie good?"

"She is. . . . She's better at singles. I mean, I think I'm somewhat better, but she's pretty good. . . . I can't get over how she looks!"

"I know," Caroline said, suddenly jealous despite herself. "If I'd seen a photo of her a year ago, looking like that, I'd have fainted."

"I think they're very good together."

"He's so nice," Caroline said, thinking of their conversation while Maggie and Justin had played. "In some ways, it's funny, I find him easier to talk to than Maggie. He's not so dogmatic."

"No one's as dogmatic as Maggie," Justin said. "But even there, she seems a little . . . like the sharp edges have been worn down a bit."

Caroline hoped so, since she planned to tell Maggie about being pregnant that evening. "I hope she won't . . . say something awful about my being pregnant."

Justin frowned. "I don't think she will."

"Well, she can be funny about some things," Caroline said.

She went into the kitchen to get out the chicken. Todd was standing there, drinking some orange juice. "Can I help you set the table?" he asked.

"I thought we might eat outside," Caroline suggested. "There are some bugs, but it's not too bad."

"I'd like that," he said. He took the paper plates she handed him and brought them out to the long wooden table. When he came in, she gave him a tray of glasses. "Where's Maggie?" she asked.

"She's lying down."

Caroline felt concerned. "Is she okay?"

"Yes, she's just a little . . . tired." But his face expressed something which he didn't say.

"Has she had a tiring summer?" Caroline asked, not wanting to pry.

"Yes, in a way." He took the glasses outside. Caroline went outside with him and sat down under a tree. "This is such a nice time of day," she said. "It's my favorite."

"Carrie?"

"Yes?"

"I'd like to draw a picture of you. . . . Would you mind?"

"Now?"

"Yes. . . . I brought some paper and pencils with me." He went and got them. Carrie sat self-consciously, her arms around her knees.

"Should I look at you," she said, "or what?"

She knew she looked pretty and that Todd was gazing at her with more than artistic admiration; it pleased her. Then, remembering she was pregnant, she felt guilty. Suddenly she felt a pang of regret for having given this up, just the silly thing of dating boys and feeling they were attracted to her and she to them and that it needn't have any special implications. Isolated from the "real world" all summer, she had thought of none of this, but Maggie and Todd had brought with them, innocently, all the other possibilities, the turns her own life might have taken. It had shattered the surface of what had seemed to her a smooth pond.

"Just do whatever seems natural." He looked at her intently and she saw his hand moving with the pencil.

"Do you draw Maggie, ever?" she asked. "I used to."

"Yes, I have a lot of drawings of her. . . . She doesn't like to pose, though." He smiled. "She doesn't like to sit still. . . . It's hard to catch her face, too. It's so expressive when she's talking that when she's not you lose something. There's one I thought caught something."

"What I always liked about drawing people," Caroline said, "was it gives you an excuse to stare at them."

"Exactly." He turned the page.

While he was drawing, Justin came out. He looked over Todd's shoulder. "That's marvelous!" he said with some surprise. "Could we . . . buy it from you?"

"Oh, I'll leave it," Todd said casually. "I don't do this for money."

"You should, though. . . . Carrie, did you see?"

She shook her head. "Can I move now?"

"Sure, I'm finished."

Caroline walked over to look at the two sketches he had made. One was just of her face and shoulders; the other showed her entire body and the tree. I should draw again, she thought suddenly, remembering an idea she'd had for a children's book for which, earlier in the summer, she'd done some preliminary sketches.

"Where's Maggie?" Justin asked.

"She's lying down."

"I hope she didn't overdo," he said. "Maybe we shouldn't have played that extra set."

At that moment Maggie came out. "Nonsense! And don't try to get out of tomorrow morning!"

"I won't—but are you sure—?"

"Positive. . . . I just didn't sleep that well last night. Now I'm fine."

"Todd made some drawings of me," Caroline said, showing them to Maggie.

Maggie looked at them, smiling. "Yes, those are nice. . . . I like the one of you under the tree."

"It's a great tree," Caroline said.

"It looks very solid, as though it were protecting you."

They ate outside. When the meal began, the light was already fading. As it progressed, it became so dark Justin brought out some lanterns. "Should I open more wine?" he said after they had finished one bottle of soave.

"I think one is enough," Caroline said. "Maybe we should have coffee."

He and Todd got up to clear, leaving Maggie and Caroline together. The night was completely silent around them except for the sound of frogs and night creatures. Into the silence Caroline said, "Maggie . . . I'm going to have a baby."

Maggie's face was illuminated softly by the lantern. Her large eyes widened. "How come?" she said.

Caroline smiled "Because I want to," she said. "And Justin does too."

"When is it due?"

"April. . . . I'm not sure what I'll do about school. I'll finish the fall term out anyway."

"Won't you go back?" Maggie sounded horrified.

"Well, I might take a year off, just the first year."

"Why?"

Caroline swallowed. Telling Maggie was turning out to be even worse than she had feared. "Well, I think . . . I'd hate to leave the baby with a baby-sitter."

"Why would you?" Maggie was sounding more than slightly belligerent.

"I just think . . . Well, maybe it's partly selfish. I'd like the experience of being with him—or her."

"That's *all* you're going to do—sit home with the baby for a whole year?" Maggie sounded flabbergasted.

"I think there's probably quite a lot to do," Caroline said hesitantly.

"No, there isn't!" Maggie said. "All they do is eat and sleep. That's what Todd's sister says."

"Jesus, with unemployment what it is, you could get millions of sitters," Maggie said. "I've heard there are people with doctorates in child psychology looking for jobs as baby nurses."

"It's not that," Caroline said, wishing she could express herself better. "It's just that I really would rather be at home for the first year."

"You might never go back, though," Maggie said.

"No, I will eventually," Caroline said stubbornly. She hated the way Maggie seemed to assume her life would go down the drain so rapidly. It seemed condescending.

"Carrie, listen, why now? Why have a baby now? What's the point of it?" She sounded urgent and leaned forward, her eyes bright.

"I want one," Caroline said.

"But *why* want one now? Why not wait a few years till you know where you're going, till things are settled with you and Justin?"

"I feel like they *are* settled," Caroline said. She felt terrible at the memory of Justin's not wanting the baby at first either.

"Is it that you're against abortion?"

"No! . . . I was so happy when I found out," she said, almost inaudibly.

Maggie was silent, obviously at a loss for words.

"Remember how you used to say about my mother how you couldn't understand how she could be celibate, how if you had a body, you felt you would want to know about it, what it could feel?"

"Umm," Maggie finished off her wine.

"Well, I feel that way partly about getting pregnant. . . . Don't you *ever* feel you'd want to?" She tried to shift from a defensive to an offensive position.

"I don't know," Maggie hedged.

"Doesn't Todd want children?"

"Carrie, we're not even married!"

"Oh, I didn't mean now," Caroline said quickly. "I just meant . . . I just wondered if it was something you ever thought about."

"I think about it sometimes," Maggie admitted, her voice a little calmer.

"But you never feel tempted?"

"Not especially. . . . Carrie, listen. I'm sorry. It might not be so bad. It better be a girl, though!"

"A boy wouldn't be so bad," Caroline said.

"Yes, it would! Have a girl!"

"I'd like a girl," Caroline admitted.

"What names have you thought of?"

"Well, for girls there are so many nice one—Vanessa, Agnes . . ."

"Agnes!" Maggie let out a shriek. "You can't call her Agnes "

"I like Agnes," Caroline said.

"You'll wreck her life," Maggie said. "You're dooming her. . . . Pick Vanessa."

"When I was in third grade there was a Vanessa and everyone called her the Loch Ness Monster."

Justin and Todd came out with coffee and a pie. "What Loch Ness Monster?" Todd said.

"Carrie's having a baby," Maggie said, looking up at him.

"That's wonderful," he said.

"She wants to call it Agnes!"

"I like Anne," Justin said.

Maggie frowned. "That's too plain. Anyway, it doesn't have a nickname. Everyone should have a nickname."

"I don't," Justin said

"I don't," Todd said.

"Well, maybe with men it doesn't matter," Maggie said.

"Now I want you to pay attention to this pie," Justin

said. "It's a Prager specialty. I made it out of blackberries, apples, and plums."

They looked at him uneasily.

"I've been trying mixing different fruits together," he explained, cutting into it. "It's good."

"Do you cook usually?" Maggie said.

"Sometimes, why? . . . I know! This is the test of am I a liberated husband, right?"

"You knew we were coming," Maggie said, "so you rushed into the kitchen and said, 'I've got to make something. How about a pie?' "

"And the minute you leave, I'll chain Caroline to the stove?"

"Exactly," Maggie said.

"Margaret, after all these years, how can you think so ill of me?"

"I don't think ill of you," Maggie said. "I'm just checking up."

"I even take her breakfast in bed," Justin said. "How about that?"

"Is that because she's pregnant?" Maggie said.

"Well, partly," Justin admitted.

"Then that's sexist," Maggie fired back.

"I think I did it even before," Justin said. "Didn't I?" He looked at Caroline.

"A few times," she said, smiling.

"Do you really think it's good to have a baby?" Maggie said.

Caroline felt almost sick with tension, waiting for Justin's reply.

"Good in what sense?" Justin said hesitantly.

"Wise," Maggie said. "For the good of all."

"Yes, I do. We both love children. . . . And I've never liked the idea of Noah being an only child."

"I'm an only child," Maggie said. "I never minded."

"You said you did sometimes," Todd said.

Maggie looked at him angrily, as though he had betrayed some kind of secret. "Well, everyone minds anything sometimes!" she said. "People who have brothers and sisters mind that."

"I didn't like being an only child," Caroline said. They all looked at her. "I guess . . . well, it was lonely so much of the time."

"But that was partly because you didn't have both parents as well," Justin said. "No, but I agree. Sure, I fought a lot with my brothers, but it was good being part of a big family. I wish that weren't considered such a bad thing nowadays."

"How many of you were there?" Maggie asked.

"Four . . . four children, that is."

"But how about your mother?" Maggie said. "What did she do with her life?"

"My mother is very happy," Justin said. "She had her garden and her—"

"That's all bullshit!" Maggie said. "I don't believe a word of it."

"Why can't someone like tending a garden?" Justin asked, curious.

"They can . . . but not as a life!"

He put his hand on her arm. "Maggie, calm down."

"I won't," Maggie said. "Why should I?"

"Why should you care about my mother?"

"I don't," Maggie said, "but I care about Carrie."

Caroline felt as though she weren't there, as though she and Todd were silent onlookers in this battle.

"What are you afraid of?" Justin said.

"I'm afraid she's going to drop out of college, never go back, have baby after baby—"

"We couldn't even afford to have baby after baby," Justin said.

"She'll lose all sense of herself, of being able to accomplish anything, do anything, she'll start drinking, her life will be shattered . . . like your wife's."

There was a long silence. Maggie seemed to sense she had gone too far. "I'm sorry," she said.

"Maggie, you are incredibly intolerant," Justin said, his mouth set. "You have to allow other people the right to live a life different from the one you want to live."

Maggie sat back. "Okay," she said.

"Okay what?"

"Okay, I have to—so I will."

"And, if you ask me, you're in danger of narrowing your own life down to the point where it will be meaningless. So think of that!"

"I *have* thought of it," Maggie said.

Caroline felt very nervous. She had wanted Justin to take Maggie on, as it were, but in the last few minutes the level of tension had risen unbearably. "Um . . . would you like some more pie?" she asked Todd.

"Thanks, I would," he said. He put his hand on Maggie's shoulder.

"Look, have babies," Maggie said. "Have them if you want them."

"Well, we weren't waiting for your permission," Justin said.

"Will you stay in the same apartment?" Todd asked.

"For a year or two," Justin said. "Maybe after that we'll look for another place."

"My sister likes the Columbia area," Todd offered, as though to make up for Maggie's rudeness. "But it is pretty far uptown."

"I like that area too," Justin said. His voice was flat and distant, as though his mind were still on the blowup with Maggie, who was just sitting, staring into space.

"Justin's apartment—I mean, our apartment," Caroline corrected herself, "is rent controlled, so we get a pretty good deal on rent. If we moved—"

"Yes, well, I guess that is something to think of," Todd said.

"Does your sister have a girl and a boy?"

"Yes. . . . They share a room. There are just two bedrooms, but they talk of moving a lot."

"Of course if it's a girl and a boy, it's more necessary for them to have different rooms," Caroline said. "Maybe if our baby is a boy, we won't have to move."

"Why should that matter?" Maggie said, but also in a distant voice, as though she were protesting just by reflex action. "I would think it would be a matter of privacy."

Justin stood up. It was as though he couldn't stand to get into one more argument with Maggie over anything. "Let's turn in," he said abruptly.

But when they were in their bedroom, he suddenly said, "I'm going for a walk. Do you want to come?"

"Okay," Caroline said, buttoning up her blouse again.

It was dark and cool out. Caroline was glad she had brought her sweater. Justin strode along, as though he were going somewhere in a hurry. He did not speak. When they came to a clearing, he stopped. "Damn it, she is impossible! Absolutely impossible."

"Well, that's just the way she is," Caroline said lamely.

"I don't care. When is she going to grow up?"

"She's just . . . trying to be honest," Caroline said. "She doesn't like to pretend."

"How can she say things like that?"

"You mean—about Ariella?"

"No! About you! You're her best friend! Doesn't she have a single ounce of sensitivity to other people's feelings?"

"Really, she's thinking of me," Caroline said, trying to defend Maggie. The jealousy she had felt for Maggie earlier had dissolved in Justin's attack on her. "She wants me to be happy."

She wanted to explain it to him because to her it

seemed so crystal clear. Since she had been married, since she had begun to love Justin, it seemed to Caroline she saw Maggie differently from before. She no longer put her on a pedestal, but on the other hand Maggie's fierceness, her defensiveness, seemed so transparent to her. It seemed to her she could see through to the fears and uncertainties that lay beneath it. Maggie no longer seemed so strong to her. In a funny way she felt that she was stronger, and this made her less angry at everything Maggie had said. She took his hand. "Thank you . . . for taking my side about the baby."

"Your side?"

"I mean, making it seem like you want it too."

He sighed. "I do want it, darling. It's complicated. It was that it seemed so soon . . . but I think I've come to terms with it."

"I could still get an abortion," she offered, knowing he would say, as he did, "No, of course not. We'll work it out." he looked up. "Look at the sky," he said.

They had had many nights like these: cool, perfectly clear, with every star visible, the air smelling of pine. "I wish we didn't have to go back to the city," she said.

"It's been wonderful," he agreed.

They stood there for several moments looking at the sky, and Caroline felt a mood of peacefulness return. They walked back slowly, hand in hand.

Back in the bedroom Caroline got undressed. For a long time she had always worn a nightgown at night, even when she knew they were going to make love. It had seemed forward to her to simply take all her clothes off. But now she did just that and lay contemplatively on the bed, watching Justin undress.

Usually when she watched him, she thought how wonderful his body was and how lucky she was to have him as her husband, as someone to make love to her. But now she found herself thinking, not with bitterness or excite-

231

ment but with a strange detachment: Other men must look nice too. I wonder what it would be like. She caught a glimpse of herself lying on the bed, naked, her blond hair loose, and she thought how conventional the whole thing was, their romance which had seemed so unusual and daring. Now, in her present mood, it all seemed calculating. She had wanted him, she had bought a pretty bathrobe, she had clung to him and made him feel she could not survive without him. She had wanted all those "grown-up" things—a home, a child, a husband, and now she had them, and part of her wanted them to vanish in a cloud of smoke.

"You have a strange expression," he said, coming, naked, toward her and getting into bed beside her. He clicked off the light.

"I should have had the loop, I guess," she said reflectively. "The diaphragm is such a mess."

"You can switch."

She laughed. "Now?"

"After the baby is born."

After a second she said, "Do I even like babies, Juston?"

"Sure you do. You're great with them."

"I don't know. . . . I feel like I'm digging my own grave."

"It's not too late to—"

"No, I don't know. That seems. . . . No, it'll be good. Don't you think? I'll show Maggie. I won't let it interfere with anything. . . . Maybe I'll be more famous than she is someday." Caroline laughed. "I bet that would surprise her."

Justin laughed. "I bet it would."

She put her arm over his back. "Should we fuck? Do you want to?"

"You don't usually use that word."

"Well, I might as well. . . . The others are so—I

mean, that's what it is." She found she wanted him, despite her earlier thoughts. And as they rocked together, she pretended they weren't married at all, but were back in his apartment and she was worried that someone, her mother, someone at school, might find out and then terrible things would happen.

12

Maggie had thought she would fall asleep immediately, after the amount of physical exercise she'd had during the day, the wine, and even the emotional exhaustion she felt from her run-in with Justin. But after lying in bed half an hour, she was still awake. She got up and sat on the windowsill, looking out at the moonlit lawn.

"Can't you sleep?" Todd said. His voice sounded sleepy, as though he had been dozing.

"No," Maggie said. She continued staring out at the lawn. "God, I was awful tonight," she said.

"Well . . ." Todd said.

"Why am I like that?" she appealed to him. "Why do I say things like that?"

"You want to be honest."

"That's no excuse. . . . To be so cruel! I don't know." She sighed. "I was going to tell Carrie about the abortion, but I know now she'd think everything I said was because of that."

Maggie had had an abortion in July, four weeks earlier, long enough ago so that she no longer thought about it often. The only effect it had had, she thought, was to make her decide to switch to an IUD. For years she had gone around saying that the legalization of abortion was the greatest legal decision in human history, that every teenage girl should be forced to have an abortion to prove to her that she was able to have control over her body. Despite that, and despite the fact that it had not hurt, it had taken more out of her than she expected. Todd had been completely sympathetic, had never uttered a word about any possibility other than abortion, had gone with her and waited while she had had it done. Afterward, coming out, she had seen him sitting there, *The New York Times* and a paperback book on his knees, staring into space with a complicated expression which she had been too wrought up to even want to analyze. That night, when she had, to her own amazement, begun to weep, he had held her in his arms and tried to comfort her, stroking her hair, kissing her, being tender rather than passionate, a friend rather than a lover, and she had appreciated that in a way for which she had no words.

"Why do you mind so about their having a child?" Todd asked.

"No, it's not the child I mind," Maggie said. "It's that, but—he isn't thinking of her. It's just selfish."

"Don't you feel she wants it too?"

"Oh, Carrie would want anything. If she loved someone and they told her to sit on a mountaintop for six months in the snow, she'd do it."

"Do you think it's just that? That she wants it because Justin does? I had the feeling it was more the other way around. That he might have waited, but that she convinced him."

"Yes, but it's such a dodge!" Maggie said. "She doesn't know what to do with her life so she's having a baby! That's the oldest dodge in the world."

"I see Caroline differently," Todd said. "I think she has a certain sense of what she wants out of life, and in a rather inward, calm way she knows exactly what she's doing."

"She doesn't!" Maggie protested. "What does she know about babies?"

"She's done a lot of baby-sitting, you said."

"Yes, but it's different with your own. She'll be getting up at night, she'll be exhausted. They aren't even going to have a baby-sitter or a nurse or *anything*."

"Justin will help."

"Oh, come on," Maggie said impatiently.

"Don't you think he will? He doesn't strike me as such an arch male chauvinist. I thought you liked Justin."

"Oh, I do," Maggie said. "But—oh, sure, he'll help. But he'll be teaching. He'll have other things to do. . . . It's just a classic sexist setup. The fact that he's older, everything!"

"I don't think you give Caroline enough credit," Todd said.

"Really?" Maggie looked dubious. "Do you think he really made that pie?"

Todd laughed. "Who do you think made it?"

"I don't know. . . . Maybe they bought it at a store."

"Maggie, come back to bed."

She did. "Why did I say that about his wife? That was the most awful of all."

"It *was* pretty awful," Todd agreed.

"I know he wasn't responsible for her death," Maggie said. After a moment she added, "But maybe in a certain way he was."

"Maggie, come on."

"No, I don't mean directly . . . but, well, there she was, floundering, desperate, and he just turned away. He left her to sink."

"I thought she left him."

"Yes, but . . . she left because she saw that as a married couple, as part of a marrried couple, she was doomed. She saw that."

"But she was doomed anyway."

"Do you think she was really doomed?" Maggie said urgently.

"I never met her."

"I know. . . . But from what I've told you."

"She sounds like an unhappy person who never quite found what she wanted in life."

"But why didn't she?" Maggie wanted to know.

"I don't know, Maggie." He sighed. "Why does it matter so much?"

She lay back again. "I don't know. . . . Except I guess I feel life let her down. It didn't give her what she wanted."

"Maybe she wanted more than was humanly possible."

"Umm." She lay her head on his chest. "Do *I* want more than is humanly possible?" she said.

"No," he said.

She didn't know if she accepted that, but she wanted to. Maggie woke up at six and lay in bed, quietly anticipating the tennis match with Justin. She wondered if he would come to the court, despite the argument. It seemed to Maggie crucial that she beat Justin. Basically she was not athletic. If she didn't play any sport for months, she never missed it. But whenever she was thrown into a situation where it was possible to win and possible to lose, a tremendous, overwhelming desire to win overcame her. Doubles she never cared about. But if it was she against one other person, this demon possessed her and now, after the argument, it seemed doubly important. It was as though if she won, she would force him to admit she was right.

Justin was at the court in white shorts and a green shirt. The air was cool and fresh, the sun barely risen. "Did you sleep well?" he said, but formally, as though they had met for the first time the day before.

"Yes, quite well," Maggie said, equally coolly. Something about the scene reminded her of a scene from *Eugene Onegin*, where the hero and his best friend meet early in the morning for a duel to the death. Only there was no snow.

She served first. It seemed to her she was playing about ten times better than she had played the day before, in fact she felt she had never played better in her life. Her first serve was going in consistently, her lobs just grazed the back line, her short shot dropped deftly and precisely over the net. The trouble was Justin too was playing about ten times better than *he* had played the day before. Every shot she got back, he got back. Each game seemed to go on for an eternity. Maggie felt that she was willing to literally die on the court in an attempt to win. When he was ahead five-four, he said, "Maggie, do you mind if I take off my shirt?"

"No, go ahead," she said. These were almost the only words they had exchanged in the set, other than checking in the score.

But once he took his shirt off, she wished he had not. She began being aware of his body and she minded this, not in and of itself, but because she was afraid it would distract her and make her lose. Whenever she and Todd had played together in the park over the summer, they had always gone back afterward and made love. She had come to think of tennis almost as a kind of foreplay to making love and now, seeing Justin tanned and in good shape, wearing only shorts, bothered her. Damn it, why couldn't she take off *her* shirt and even it. It wasn't fair. In a last, insane effort Maggie played as she knew she would never play again in her life. She won 7–5. The one set had taken an hour and a half. When they walked off the court, she could hardly speak, she was so out of breath. She felt slightly dizzy. Her T-shirt was wringing wet and clung to her body.

"That was good," Justin said. His voice sounded calmer, as though something had gone out of him too.

Maggie laughed. It suddenly seemed foolish to have wanted to win so desperately.

"You're a vehement opponent," he said, smiling.

"I thought I was going to pass out during that last game. I must have served twenty times!"

"Maggie, there's a brook right down the path here. Do you feel like going in for a quick swim?"

She pointed to her T-shirt and cut-off blue-jean shorts. "I'm not wearing a suit."

"Well, you can go back and change . . . or just jump in as you are."

Maggie decided that jumping in as she was sounded the best.

The brook was completely in the shade, overhung with trees.

"Look out, the water's freezing," Justin said. "Once you get used to it, it's great, though."

Maggie took off her socks, sneakers, and watch and plunged in. She came up with a gasp. "Yow! It's icy!" she yelled. She dove in and out like a dolphin, letting the current carry her downstream, then swimming up again. Justin went in more slowly, splashing his body first. When she climbed out, Maggie felt better. She recalled movies in which hysterical people had been slapped to bring them back to sanity, and she felt as though the cold water had had that effect on her. The anger, the fierceness of wanting to win, seemed to have left her so totally that it might have been something she had felt ten years earlier.

They sat in the sun, drying off. "It was nice getting up so early," Maggie said. "I've always been a morning person, anyway. I like the way it's so quiet then."

"I do too," he agreed. They sat in contented silence.

"I'm sorry about last night," Maggie said.

"That's okay."

"It's just . . . I'm afraid—it seems so soon, too soon—"

"It *is* too soon," he said, so flatly Maggie stared at him. Before she could say anything, he added, "I didn't want her to have it. I still don't."

"But then why did you let her get pregnant?" Maggie said.

"Maggie, come on!"

"You know what I mean."

"I know that when we made love I assumed she was wearing her diaphragm and that she either wasn't or had it in wrong. When she told me she was pregnant, she had a kind of shy pleased expression on her face. What could I say?"

Maggie could imagine this so clearly, Caroline's expression. "And what *did* you say?"

"I said I thought it was too soon. I suggested the possibility of an abortion. She looked crushed."

"Yeah," Maggie could picture that too. "Okay," she said after a second. "I'm sorry." Somehow she had preferred the idea that Jusin was the villain.

"You know, Maggie," Justin said, "it's sweet in some way, your concern for Caroline and her welfare, and I share it, ironically . . . but, damn it, *I* have a life too! I'm twenty-nine, not eighty! How about me? Think of that once in a while. I'd have liked some time with the two of us together, getting to know each other better. This whole year was a mess, with Ariella and then sneaking around behind Carrie's mother's back. It wasn't a real preview of what our life together could be. We needed time together. Now we won't have it. We married too fast."

"You shouldn't have. Why do you let her bully you into these things if you feel that way?"

"Because Caroline . . . I don't know." He smiled wryly. "You know, girls seduce men too, Maggie, not just the other way around. They look at you with big soft blue eyes."

"Oh, cut it out! And you're putty in their hands?"

"Listen, you're trying to look at this from my point of view now, right? Okay, I was in the middle of the worst fucking year of my life, my wife off screwing with everyone in sight, coming home with long reports on this one and that one and raving on about open marriage. I felt like shit, okay? I wasn't looking for anyone, far from it. I didn't have the heart. I was just lying there, stunned. So along comes Carrie, adoring. Okay, it's a cliché, but adoring, looking as though I could never ever do any wrong, as though I were the greatest lover the world had ever seen. So stronger men have faced that down, but I wasn't one of them. I needed her, maybe not in the most noble of ways. I fell into it—and fell in love with her too."

Maggie was listening to this with a mixture of sympathy and surprise. "What if she hadn't had big blue eyes?" she said drily.

He smiled. "Maybe I wouldn't be here. Maybe if we'd had a baby-sitter with little beady eyes and a lousy figure who didn't have a soft, low, voice and who wasn't terrific with children, I wouldn't be here."

"Was it the non-Jewish thing too?" Maggie said.

"Maybe. It's always everything!"

"Yeah." Maggie smiled. "Okay, I see it differently now, but still I—"

"I think we'll make it together," he said. "Carrie isn't the marshmallow you see her as."

"I don't—"

"You do, in a way. I don't blame you completely. She encourages it. That's her 'game.' With me too. She's so good at it. I'd like to shove her away from that."

"But wouldn't you miss it?"

"I don't think so. . . . I don't relish the Pygmalion thing. And it's phony. There's a lot of stuff bottled up there which has to come out, and when it does, Carrie won't be so sweet or so soft-spoken and maybe we'll both miss it, but I think what'll be there will be better." He was gazing at her reflectively. "Are *you* happy, Maggie?"

"Me?"

"Is that such a strange question?"

She smiled ironically. "I guess I'm happy . . . to the extent someone like me is capable of being happy."

"You and Todd seem to get along so well together."

"Yes," Maggie agreed. She stared off at the brook. "I guess I'm afraid that when I go to Cornell—"

"Afraid of what?"

"That I'll be unfaithful to him."

"Why should you do that?"

"Well, there's the defensible reason and the indefensible reason," Maggie said. "The defensible reason is that I really think eighteen is too young to settle down with one person, inside marriage or outside. I think one should try other people, just to know, to make sure one has made the right choice, sexually, in every way."

"What's the indefensible reason?"

She smiled. "The indefensible reason is that I think partly I want to do something so unforgiveable that he'll finally say: 'Okay, I've had it. This is enough.' "

"Is having someone love you so threatening?"

"I guess it must be."

"Look, life creates enough difficulties for most people. . . . You don't need to go out and create them."

"No, it's true," Maggie said. "Sometimes I do feel guilty, as though—well—I'd been given so much and I want to somehow . . . handicap myself."

"Don't—it's not necessary."

"You don't think so?"

"I know it's not."

She was staring at him, aware of him physically again as she had been during the tennis. "The thing I feel worst about, about last night, was what I said about your first wife. . . . I really am sorry. I didn't mean to imply that you'd been responsible for her suicide."

He looked at her. "You know, I loved Ariella. . . . I had stopped being in love with her when it happened, but still I don't think you can imagine what it's like to have something like that happen to someone you've been so close to for so many years. It's—"

"Well, my mother," Maggie said after a moment. "She died when I was nine."

"That's right . . . but it's not quite the same."

At that moment, for no reason Maggie could fathom, she began feeling attracted to Justin. Partly it was that the taboo of his being a teacher had been lifted, to be replaces, it was true, by the taboo of his being married to her best friend, but that latter taboo didn't seem as forceful. She knew she wouldn't have wanted to be married to Justin and she wasn't even sure she would really, under other circumstances, have wanted to have an affair with him. But it suddenly seemed absolutely crucial to her, as crucial as it had been for her to win the tennis match earlier, to have him give some indication over this weekend that he wanted her. Nothing overt—just a look, something.

"Why are you staring at me that way?" Justin asked.

"What way am I staring at you?"

"Like you're hatching some plot in your little head."

Maggie laughed. She got up. "I'm starving," she said. "Let's go back for breakfast."

All afternoon Maggie lay around in the hammock in her black bikini talking about science with Justin. With Todd she always felt that although he understood the general principles of what she was interested in, he was not really interested. It was a pleasure to exchange ideas once again with someone who really cared. She was hardly aware of Caroline, who moved silently to and fro, carrying drinks in and out, not speaking very much. Caroline had become, for Maggie, a bit player, not worth talking to and, although she sensed Caroline was hurt by her paying exclusive attention to Justin, she felt powerless to act otherwise. Todd had gone off to do some sketching of the landscape.

She closed her eyes and lay languidly in the hammock, feeling the sun on her face.

"You can't get more tan than that, can you?" Justin said. "You look so dark."

"I don't do it to change color so much—more just for the feeling." She was pushing the hammock back and forth with her toe. "I remember how at the beginning of this year Carrie and I used to sit around talking about sex and I'd say how awful I thought it was going to be. . . . I was really pleasantly surprised."

"Why did you think it would be so awful?"

"Oh, I don't know—it just sounded so—"

"You were afraid of being dominated."

"Partly."

"But you're not anymore?"

She shook her head. Then she looked around. "Where's Carrie?"

"She went into town to get some groceries," Justin said. He looked around. "I guess Todd is still sketching."

"He loses all sense of time when he goes sketching," Maggie said. "He doesn't even wear a watch."

It was then that the look she had been waiting for passed between them. It was a look which said: We're alone and anything we want to have happen can happen. It also said: We both love Carrie and nothing will happen. That look satisfied Maggie. She felt relieved to have it over. She got out of the hammock. "I think I'll go change," she said.

She took off her bikini and changed into shorts and a shirt. When she emerged, Caroline had returned from the store. Once again she began talking to Justin, but this time it was, for her anyway, a tension-free conversation. Caroline came over and sat beside them on the grass, listening.

"Have you heard about this work they've been doing at

the Museum of Natural History on the sex life of cats?" Justin said.

"Who is Katz?" Caroline asked in her mild voice.

"Cats!" Maggie yelled. "Cats!" And then she and Justin looked at each other and simultaneously burst out laughing. Each time one of them tried to stop, the other would start up again. Caroline sat watching them with a hurt, puzzled expression on her face. "I thought it was a person," she said stiffly. She walked away.

"Oh, God," Maggie sighed, calming down. "It really wasn't so funny," she said.

Todd came back with his sketchbook. "It's so beautiful around here," he said, joining Maggie and Justin on the lawn.

"You know what we should do?" Justin said. "We should both buy a lot of land up here and build houses about a mile or so apart. That way we could visit each other, but still have a lot of space."

"Where do we get the money?" Maggie wanted to know.

"Good question. . . . I'm just fantasizing."

"I've heard that land isn't very expensive up here," Todd said.

"Still," Maggie said.

"There's a big garden out in back," Justin said. "We haven't done much with it, but there are tomatoes, beans . . ."

"Just like your mother," Maggie said.

"Margaret."

"What?"

"You would like my mother."

"I'm sure I would."

"She's a crusty, vehement, sharp-tongued old lady, just like you'll be at sixty."

"Does she ride a motorcycle?" Maggie asked.

He looked startled. "No . . . why?"

"I just think when I'm sixty, I want to ride a motor-cycle."

"Not till then?"

"Maybe starting at seventy."

Justin got up and went inside the house.

"How do you feel?" Todd asked.

"Okay," Maggie said. "I still feel a little played out from the tennis, but in a good way."

"We could take a nap," he suggested.

"Let's," Maggie agreed. They turned the fan of the air conditioner on so they could make love without worrying about Justin and Caroline, whose bedroom was across the hall.

"You look like a Polynesian maiden," Todd said when Maggie was naked. Looking down, she saw how dark her skin looked against the white sheet. "We should have a platter of ripe mangoes and melons for you to nibble on," he added.

"I'll find something to nibble on," Maggie said. They lay together a long time, caressing each other, almost too lazy to move beyond that. Even when they made love, it was slow and languid, as though they really were lying on some white beach with flower-scented air around them. Afterward Maggie fell sound asleep. When she woke up, she saw it was five. Todd wasn't in the room. She showered and dressed.

She found him in the living room, reading. Justin was standing nearby.

"Maggie," Todd said. "Listen . . . something's come up. It's Caroline."

"She's bleeding," Justin said.

Maggie frowned. "Since when?"

"Since this afternoon. It seems to have stopped now, but she's lying down."

"Do you think she's having a miscarriage?"

"I don't know," Justin said. "The trouble is, she *is* in

246

that time when it's most likely. I guess we'll just have to wait and see."

"Did you call the doctor?"

"I've been trying to get him, but he seems to be out. It's always hard to get hold of them on weekends."

During the evening Justin, Maggie, and Todd sat in the living room reading and listening to music. Caroline had gone to sleep early. Justin kept yawning. "That tennis really did me in," he said.

"I had a long nap," Maggie said, "so I don't feel tired." Under other circumstances, she might have suggested they play again the next morning, but she knew neither of them would be in the mood. Also, she hesitated to spoil her unequivocal victory.

"I could call my sister," Todd said suddenly. It was understood that they were all thinking of Caroline, even though they occasionally reverted to other topics. "Her husband's a gynecologist."

"Maybe in the morning," Justin said. "I'm not sure what they would say to do except rest."

"Sometimes women have to rest the whole nine months," Maggie said.

"I wish Carrie hadn't played tennis with us yesterday," Justin said. "Maybe that wasn't such a good idea."

"Lindsay played up through her eighth month," Todd said.

"Yes, but I think, well, after the fourth month it's pretty safe, but in the early weeks . . . Though we did ask the doctor and he said tennis was okay."

"She didn't play that hard," Maggie pointed out. "It's funny how all these things which are supposed to be so simple like getting pregnant turn out to be so complicated."

"They're not really," Todd said. "Mainly they're pretty simple."

"I don't know," she said. "It seems like something almost always happens."

At midnight Todd said he wanted to go to sleep. Maggie felt wide awake. "Is it okay if I stay up another half hour?"

"Sure, stay up as long as you want."

Justin went in to bed also. Maggie didn't mind being the only one in the house who was awake. She turned off the phonograph and sat reading. At quarter to one Justin came out of the bedroom. He was wearing pajamas and a robe. "I just can't fall asleep," he said. "I guess I'm too keyed up." He sat down beside her on the couch.

"I had an abortion last month," Maggie said, almost wanting to offer up something equivalent to Caroline's possible miscarriage.

"That must be somewhat grueling psychologically."

"It was," Maggie admitted. "I didn't expect it to be."

"I would have thought you were too organized to get pregnant by mistake," Justin said. "Or wasn't it a mistake?"

Maggie's eyes opened wide. "Of course it was a mistake. . . . What do you mean?"

"Well, this is different, but we knew a couple who were married for years and the wife really didn't want to have a baby, but she got pregnant and had an abortion and she said it made her feel good to know she could get pregnant if she ever wanted to."

"What does that have to do with me?" Maggie said belligerently.

"Maggie, don't get excited. I just meant. . . . Well, forget it."

"Tell me what you mean," she insisted.

"I meant that even you might have some deep-seated desire to get pregnant . . . despite all your convictions, theories, etc."

"If I do, I should be shot," Maggie retorted fiercely.

He laughed. "You're so severe with yourself. . . . Why would that be such an unspeakable crime?"

"Because that's how women wreck their lives!" Maggie cried. "They get pregnant to put off accomplishing anything and that's the end, the end of *everything* for them. Besides, I'd make such a terrible mother—it wouldn't be fair."

"You wouldn't."

"How do you know? Look at what I'm like! I'm selfish, I'm crazy, I go off the deep end every three seconds."

Justin smiled. "That's an impressive list."

"Justin, I mean it. . . . I'm not just saying this. It's true. All of it."

"You're a terrible person, Maggie," he said affectionately. He leaned over and kissed her.

Maggie was gazing at him reflectively. "I guess, despite everything you've said, I envy Carrie. Not just for having you, but for having some kind of security, a home, a baby, even though I know it's all based on shaky things."

"She envies you for what she sees as your freedom, so you're even."

"You don't think it's really freedom?"

"I think"—he faltered—"everything is based on shaky things." He stood up and yawned. "I'm going to bed."

She smiled. "I guess I better too."

In the morning they ate together, the three of them, but it was a silent meal. Justin took Caroline breakfast on a tray. Maggie went in to see her. Caroline was half sitting up in bed, leaning back against some pillows. She looked pale and fragile in her pale-blue nightgown. A stab of guilt hit Maggie. "How do you feel?" she asked softly.

"I'm okay," Caroline said. "I guess mostly I'm scared."

Maggie swallowed. "Lots of people bleed, though," she said. "Remember that book we read in school that said some women even bleed till their ninth month?"

"I remember," Caroline said. "but I'm still worried."

Maggie didn't know what to say. "You'll be okay, Carrie."

"I hope so." She still looked worried. Maggie saw she had hardly eaten what was on the tray.

After breakfast Maggie and Todd took a walk outside. Maggie showed him the brook and they sat beside it. She thought of the day before and her talk with Justin.

"I hope she doesn't lose the baby," Maggie said, "despite everything I said."

Todd was silent. "I hope not too," he said finally.

"I feel so guilty," Maggie said. "I'm afraid if she loses it, it'll be my fault."

"In what way?"

"I was so terrible— Those awful things I said the night before last. I was so critical and cold."

"That doesn't cause a miscarriage."

"No, but psychological things do make a difference. And Carrie is so sensitive. . . . Why did I *do* that? What's wrong with me?"

"Listen to me," he said. "You're not God. If Carrie has a miscarriage, she'll have one. But it won't have anything to do with anything you said or didn't say or did or didn't do."

"Do you know that for a fact?" Maggie said.

"Yes."

They returned to the house and found Justin in the kitchen, making toast.

"How is she?" Maggie said.

"Pretty good. . . . She's still bleeding a little. That damn doctor! You'd think he'd at least try to call back."

Todd said, "Should I call my brother-in-law?"

"Thanks, but . . . I really think someone has to come and look at her."

"You know," Todd said, "maybe it would be better if we headed back to New York before lunch. I just think—"

"It might be better," Justin agreed. "I'm sorry. I mean, it was really great that you came up."

"We had a good time," Maggie said miserably.

"We'll see you in the city anyway," Justin said. "We'll be back next week."

They packed and took their luggage out to the car. Justin stood waving as Todd drove down the country road; then he disappeared from sight. Maggie sat back and stared out at the leafy green landscape. The security she had seen in Caroline's life seemed as illusory as the freedom of her own, and yet for the first time it didn't seem to matter.

"Tell me when you get tired," she said. "I can take over then."

"I will."

"When do you think we'll get there?"

"Who cares? We'll have a good trip," Todd said.

"Okay," Maggie said. She hoped he was right.

A NOTE ABOUT THE AUTHOR

Norma Klein grew up in New York City and received a B.A. from Barnard College and an M.A. in Slavic languages from Columbia in 1963. At that time she decided to devote herself full time to writing and has done so since.

Ms. Klein's many novels include *It's OK If You Don't Love Me*, *Love Is One of the Choices*, and *French Postcards*. She lives in New York City with her husband and two daughters.